Warwickshire County Council

WEL 8/17			

This item is to be returned or renewed before the latest date above. It may be borrowed for a further period if not in demand. **To renew your books:**

- **Phone the 24/7 Renewal Line 01926 499273 or**
- **Visit www.warwickshire.gov.uk/libraries**

Discover • Imagine • Learn • *with libraries*

Warwickshire County Council

Working for Warwickshire

SOOT

Andrew Martin

corsair

CORSAIR

First published in Great Britain in 2017 by Corsair

1 3 5 7 9 10 8 6 4 2

A CIP catalogue record for this book
is available from the British Library.

ISBN: 978-1-4721-5243-5

Typeset in Caslon by M Rules
Printed and bound in Great Britain by
Clays Ltd, St Ives plc

Papers used by Corsair are from well-managed forests
and other responsible sources.

MIX
Paper from
responsible sources
FSC® C104740

Corsair
An imprint of
Little, Brown Book Group
Carmelite House
50 Victoria Embankment
London EC4Y 0DZ

An Hachette UK Company
www.hachette.co.uk

www.littlebrown.co.uk

For Lisa, who bought me a silhouette.

Letter from Mr Erskine, Attorney-at-Law, to Mr Ralph Taylor, Chief Magistrate of York.

Precentor's Court, York, Wednesday January 16th, 1799.

My Dear Taylor,

You will find herewith a narrative of the events following the murder of Mr Matthew Harvey, the painter of shades, or silhouettes as they are sometimes called (after a certain French minister, a somewhat shadowy and insubstantial personage no doubt).

The greater part of the relation is made up of transcriptions from the diary of Mr Fletcher Rigge, in which he described the commission he undertook on behalf of Captain Harvey, son of the murdered man. You will discover in Mr Rigge's writing some disobliging remarks about the judicial system of the city. You may find these painful to read or possibly — as you have suggested to me, with your customary good nature — instructive, as reflecting the views of the more intelligent sort of York citizen, for Rigge was undoubtedly among their number, whatever else we may say about him.

Also presented are transcripts from another diary, that of the young woman called Esther (her surname has not yet come to light), mistress to the Captain. These are bawdy and occasionally obscene. Some of young Rigge's writings show a similar tendency, which he apparently reprehended, if his frequent crossings out are anything to go by. I have asked my clerk, Mr Bright, to decipher these passages – at which he is remarkably adept – and to transcribe them in a clear hand.

For the rest, it is a matter of letters, and transcriptions of the examinations conducted by myself or – more often – Mr Bright, who remained forbearing in the face of the great unreasonableness of some of his subjects. As to dates, I have included these where they seem of assistance. (Where information was obtained after the principal events I have left them off, as being anterior to the main story.) Where the documents demand further amplification, I have deployed prefatory notes or postscripts written by myself or by Mr Bright.

As we have discussed, Mr Bright and I were destined to become actors in the story ourselves. We were involved in the question of the house, Aden Park, and the disposal of the estate at Adenwold. Only when we discovered Rigge's diary – in circumstances disclosed at the end of this documentation – did we begin to appreciate the fuller picture.

I preface the bundle with two items from the public record. The first is an account of the murder of Matthew Harvey, as given in the York Courant, with all the extreme brevity that illustrious journal reserves for the most interesting events. The second is the entry for Mr Rigge in the Castle Journal, made when he was admitted, a prisoner for debt, in September of last year. But before we come to those, I ought to give a brief description of our young protagonist.

I believe that Fletcher Rigge was twenty-one or twenty-two at the time of these events. In looks, he was a slender, rather graceful young man, with an habitual expression varying between wistful and downright forlorn. His lowness of spirts — offset by a mordant wit and a prideful obstinacy — can be readily understood. His mother had died when he was at an early age; his father was esteemed for a man of honour, but came to be in the grip of a mania for cards and dice. This poor fellow ended by forfeiting his estate — which had fetched about three thousand a year — and then his own life, by a self-inflected gunshot wound. Yet Rigge idolised his father, whom he took to be the best sort of old-fashioned country gentleman.

You see, my dear Taylor, our young man was afflicted with rural romanticism. He was anti-modernity in farming, and against enclosures especially since they are invariably accompanied by the destruction of the common lands, and the creation of a labouring class where once had been — to his mind — a happy peasantry. The prejudice is well expressed (I am told) in Goldsmith's poem, The Deserted Village:

> *'Ill fares the land, to hastening ills a prey,*
> *Where wealth accumulates, and men decay . . .'*

Rigge's father had kept up the rights of common, and the cost of doing so had driven him to the gaming tables. In the brief interlude during which he controlled the estate, Rigge tried to perpetuate this Merrie England but the expense of repairing some of the labourers' cottages quickly sunk him, and he was removed to the York Castle, a prisoner for a sizeable debt.

At the outset of our tale he had been incarcerated for three months, with no prospect of release, for he refused to seek any charitable assistance. Not that any such offer was likely, for he had no surviving family, and the sum he owed would have daunted all but the wealthiest of benefactors.

In Rigge's character, capability and ambition (to reclaim his estate, and to marry a certain pretty young woman) contended with fatalism. There were further paradoxes besides. While Rigge professed to disdain the vanities of York society, few members of 'the dandy set' were as carefully attired as he, or acquitted themselves so well at a country dance. And Rigge was acute in his observation of his fellows – which is surely a metropolitan sort of skill, and one that had been noted by the initiator of his adventures, namely Captain Harvey.

Rigge had another talent – for writing – which he disparaged as nothing more than a means of passing away the time. In the Castle, he began keeping a journal, and perhaps he sought to understand himself by his writings, I cannot say. What is certain is that his diary kept pace with the frenetic drama in which he found himself embroiled, one of the strangest – I daresay, my dear Taylor – to have unfolded within the walls of this ancient and noble city of ours.

From the *York Courant*, Tuesday August 28th, 1798.

On Friday last, Matthew Harvey, an artist, was found dead, presumed to have been murdered, having been discovered amid a scene suggestive of violent attack, at his house in Coney Street. An inquest is to be held.

York Castle, Gaoler's Journal, Volume 6.

Prisoner: Fletcher Rigge
Prisoner became bankrupt: 1798.
Date of admission: September 15th.
His debts: £150.
His effects: £7 approx.
Notes: A young gentleman, a debtor of the first class,
chargeable at three shillings a week for his commons at table.
Fines, Solitary Confinements, Whippings: None as of
November 1st.

Diary of Fletcher Rigge,
Friday November 16th, 1798.

I write this at nine o'clock at night.

At nine o'clock this *forenoon* I was standing at the
window of the Day Room, and looking out. I had left
off reading at the long table, and was contemplating
the Castle Green, which was just then *white*, being
snow-covered. Some of my fellow debtors huddled in the
far end of the room, where a very small quantity of coals
burned in the very large hearth.

As I watched the snow coming down slantwise, I listened to the new machine that powers the Castle Mills, which contraption I hate. It beats like a broken windmill, keeping not only the debtors but also the felons awake in the prison-mansion that has been my home these past three months. I was calling to mind the contrasting silence of Aden Park after a fall of snow, when it would become a sort of sleeping fairyland. I recollected the sight of a man riding a white horse over those white fields: a farming gentleman from Pickering, coming to game with my father. Their acquaintance marked the start of my season of difficulty, although I did not know it at the time.

Some few seconds after the ninth chime of the prison bell, I heard the Day Room door opening behind me. Under-gaoler Derek Hill entered and declared his presence by a loud fart, which unseemly retort I affected not to hear.

'Morning, Mr Rigge,' said the under-gaoler.

'Good morning to you, Hill,' I said, turning half about. I could see my own breath as I spoke.

The under-gaoler was clutching a document of some kind. 'This weather en't right,' he said. 'They reckon summat's amiss with the moon. They say it stands in the wrong relation to the sun.'

'What sun?' I sighed, contemplating the medieval ruins, the collapsed Castle on the far side of the Green, which gives the prison compound its unwontedly romantic name.

'Or it may be a retrocession of the lunar nodes,' suggested Hill.

'Very likely,' I said. 'Is Lund awake?'

'He en't.'

'Good.'

Having taken his very brief trial, Edwin Lund, sheep stealer, had been elevated from the lower grates to the condemned cell, situated in the debtors' quarters. As he awaited his fate, he had requested to be read to, and I had carried through to him a selection of literature – so-called – from the debtors' library. Rather than some tale of witches or a two-headed calf, the poor fellow had selected a catchpenny work called *A York Calendar*. The thing had been slung together by 'A Citizen of York' and I am heartily ashamed to say that I was the Yorkist in question, the volume being one of my productions for bookseller Skelton. I forbore to mention my involvement to Lund, who in any case had paid attention to my readings for little more than five minutes, after which he would begin to speak in his rapid, stuttering voice, of his favourite – and only – subject, viz. *sheep*.

The execution of Lund was fixed for midday, but Hill did not want to speak about that. He was smiling strangely at me; he held a document, which I first thought was a page from the *York Courant*. Hill would often bring me the *Courant*. 'Now if I was in your sort of pickle,' he'd say, 'I'd give this fellow a go,' and he would indicate a paragraph detailing the bequest of some eminent citizen to a school or hospital. I believe he did this mainly so I would buy another quire of black-edged letter paper off him, but I would petition these self-declared philanthropists, never seeking charity but offering my labour in return for the discharge of my debt. There had never been any reply, but here perhaps was the first.

The paper that Hill passed over was a letter, on goodish paper, yet smudged with soot. It had been addressed to 'The Keeper of His Majesty's Castle of York, or his Lawful Deputy.' It was signed by a Captain ... somebody-or-other.

'Your benefactor has appeared,' said Hill.

I told him I had not written to any captains.

'Nonetheless, you are to be set at liberty with immediate effect.'

'But ... There must be some condition,' I said.

'You're right,' said Hill, grinning so as to display his teeth, of which he had approximately four, 'there is.'

I returned to the letter. It was all rather jumbled, and I sought amplification from Hill. It appeared this Captain had proposed an arrangement that had been agreed to, as of yesterday's date, by all the concerned parties, viz. my creditor Mr Burnage (the above-mentioned gamester from Pickering), and the Deputy Sheriff of York who had despatched the bailiff to execute Burnage's writ.

The proposal was bizarre indeed. The mysterious Captain had offered, and Burnage had accepted, seventy-five pounds, being half the sum I owe him. In consideration of this, Burnage had consented to my release for one calendar month, in which time I would perform a service – unspecified in the letter – for the said Captain. If the service were performed satisfactorily, and within the month, Harvey would remit to Burnage the balance of the debt, and I would be free from the shadow of the Castle. If the task were performed unsatisfactorily, or not completed within the month, I would be delivered back into custody. I would be required to engage my word that I would not abscond during the performance of the commission. If I should do so, not only would I be pursued as a common criminal, but an additional seventy-five pounds that the Captain had put in bond for my bail would be forfeit, and since the Captain would be coming after me for that, there would then be *two* plaintiffs against me, and I would be liable for a total debt no smaller than the one I presently owe.

'Take a peep at the address,' said Hill.

I read, 'First Water Lane' – an odd place for kindness to come from, being about the most tumbledown and dangerous thoroughfare in the city. The watchmen only ever go along there in their patrols, never singly; but I recalled that a couple of larger houses kept company with the shambling hovels.

'You'd better say how inexpressibly thankful you are,' said Hill, 'and you'll be able to do it in person, since he requests a conference with you tomorrow.'

'But who exactly is he?' I said. 'I can't make out his name.'

'Harvey – Robin Harvey – son of the shade painter. Him as was killed.'

I nodded, recollecting. The murder of Matthew Harvey, painter of shades, had been much discussed in the city. It had occurred in the week of the August race meeting. Harvey had been pierced in the stomach by a pair of the 'special scissors' he used for cutting out the cheaper sort of shade. It was presumed that one of his sitters had done it, since Harvey received them alone, in one of the lower rooms of his house, being at most other times with his sister – who was also his housekeeper – in the upper rooms at the same dwelling place.

'His son en't the ordinary sort of munificent gentleman,' Hill was saying. 'A man out of the common track is Captain Harvey.'

He departed, and I turned back towards the window. The hangman's black cart had been drawn up on the white lawn. It stood, unattended and filling with snow, but ready to take Lund away to the Tyburn on the Knavesmire, the 'New Drop' behind the Assizes being still in the process of refinement. Only sacks of stones had been hung from there so far, evidently not very satisfactorily. The New Drop was being built according to the latest principles of engineering. It was, no doubt, a 'rational' gallows.

Diary of Fletcher Rigge.
Saturday November 17th.

'Tincture?' enquired Captain Harvey, leaning on his cane with one hand, as he poured port wine with his other.

'Tincture', I realised, was Captain Robin Harvey's term for a vast quantity of port wine, and the glass he handed me was brimming. It was the second one I had accepted. I own to a small weakness that way, inherited from my late father, and while incarcerated, I had been reduced to paying extortionate rates for the poor raisin wine supplied by the under-gaoler.

I had been admitted to Captain Harvey's ramshackle house by a dangerous-looking manservant: a squarish, dirty man with long grey hair. He seemed to be called Stephen. He was extremely familiar with his master – whom he referred to as Robin – and this same Stephen now sat on a slumped sofa in the corner of this gloomy, greenish room, lit by little more than a smoking fire and a wick drowning in dirty whale oil on the mantle.

The house was at the very bottom of First Water Lane. Therefore it was nearly in the river, which was half frozen but still for the most part flowed blackly on. It stood alongside the coal wharf, and men had been unloading bushels of sea-coal from a lighter named *Vulture* as I had pounded the knocker. Harvey, I had ascertained, was contracted to some of the mine owners in the country roundabout: he sold their coal in the city of York, and since the burning of the stuff, and the resulting befoulment of the air, was continually increasing, he must have got a decent income from the business, but he was not alone in it. There were two other agents on the same wharf, and his fortune would be nothing against that of the mine owners themselves.

Captain Harvey had bowed low as I had commenced the speech I had rehearsed in prison: 'Sir, I cannot express the sense I have of your kindness—'

'None of that,' Harvey had said, sweeping me into the house. 'You are in a condition to be of some service to me. You have forfeited your situation at the bookshop, I believe?'

'Forfeited' was not quite the word, but I nodded agreement. Soon after my confinement, I had received a letter from my employer, the bookseller, Skelton, saying that while he was sorry for my troubles, he must inform me that my situation was now being re-advertised.

'Yet in spite of your incarceration,' Harvey continued, 'you have held on to your rooms in – where is it, now? – Ogleforth?'

Ogleforth, that scruffy and unfrequented street full of barking dogs behind the Minster. I wondered how the Captain had come to know everything about me, but there was nothing to be gained by asking.

'Held on to them for now,' I replied.

'But how can you afford the rent?' asked Harvey, pointing me towards a faded couch.

'It is simply a question of not eating anything,' I facetiously replied.

Harvey smiled sourly. He was lounging against the mantle in such a way that took the weight off his bad leg. He removed a pipe from his coat pocket, and reached for his tobacco tin on the mantle; he inserted a taper into the fire and commenced to smoke.

Captain Harvey is perhaps in the late forties, with a good figure shown off by tight, grubby-white breeches. He is neat-faced, and he wears his own hair. He might get round to a periwig before long, since his own is somewhat thinning, but meanwhile still black with a tendency to curl. He wore a high collar, and a good – but old – black silk waistcoat.

'And you are against the enclosures,' he said.

'That is immaterial,' I said, 'since I do not have any land, either to enclose or to farm in the old way.'

'But philosophically.'

'Yes.'

'Explain your objection.'

'I do not think small copyholders should be made into labourers, or turned off the land altogether.'

'You hold the country life to be superior to the town life?'

'Yes.'

'Why?'

'Because the people are more closely connected. And the country is more beautiful than the town.'

At this, Harvey gave a shrug, and said, 'I daresay we'd all like a pretty little estate, if that's what you mean ...'

It *wasn't* what I meant, as he well knew.

'To come to particulars,' he said, 'I have had favourable reports of the way you penetrated to the heart of a certain matter.'

I frowned, perplexed.

'Do you know what I'm talking about, sir?' said Harvey. 'No, sir.'

Silence in the room. Snow was accumulating rapidly on the black windows, determined to block out the coal heavers and the dark grey sky of a midwinter afternoon. I thought of the estate, my late home: the crooking brooks, dark woods, cultured and fallow fields – all under snow, the robin the only bird singing.

There came a rattle on the door handle, and a woman entered, hatless in a thin red morning coat, with little more than a single petticoat beneath. I rose from the couch, and the newcomer gave in return the briefest nod and a 'How d'you do?' She was rather beautiful in a gypsy-ish way. She walked over to the mantle and tried to coax the wick – stirring it in its pool of oil – to give a better light. With a soft, sighing, 'Heyday' (for no greater illumination had been produced) she helped herself to port wine. She first sat – then lounged – on the same battered

15

sofa as the servant, Stephen; and so the picture composed: 'Three Libertines', the artist might have called it.

'You laid your hands on some missing books,' said Harvey, smiling through smoke at me, and I now recollected the matter to which he referred. 'It was a remarkable feat of reasoning,' he said.

'I wouldn't put it as high as that,' I said.

'I know you wouldn't, dammit. But to discover these extremely rare volumes . . .'

'In fact, it was only one. And it was obscure rather than rare.'

'I adore your rhapsodic style,' said Harvey. 'Do give us the tale. I don't think Esther's familiar with it,' and he nodded towards the lounging woman.

Fletcher Rigge, in continuation.

In the gloomy drawing room of Captain Harvey, I began relating the story of the missing book, which had seemed of such interest to that gentleman.

In the first days of May, when I'd lately commenced working at Skelton's Bookshop – a desperate stratagem to keep my creditors at bay – a certain Mrs Bryant, wife of a clergyman at some outlying village, had advertised in the

York Courant the loss of a valuable book. The finder, on delivering it to the printers of the *Courant*, would be paid two guineas. Bob Richmond, the other lad at Skelton's – happening to look over my shoulder as I perused this advertisement – mentioned that the book in question had been purchased from Skelton's a few days prior to my taking up my new post.

'What *was* the book, Mr Rigge?' Harvey asked, while removing himself to the green and greasy couch, on which I was sitting. 'I know the tale but do not recollect that detail.' The Captain stretched out full length on this, nearly touching me with his coal-dusted boot heels.

'It was called *A Key to the Symbolical Language of Scripture*,' I replied.

'Just the sort of thing I like to tackle,' said Harvey, from his recumbent pose. He propped his head on his hand. 'And who wrote the damned thing? I must ask these questions, sir, since you are rather sparing in your narrative.'

'A clergyman.'

'Mrs Bryant's husband?'

'Another one. The *dedication* was to Mrs Bryant's husband.'

'Is that what made it valuable?' asked Harvey.

'That and the quantity of gold leaf used in the binding.'

I explained that, by coincidence, this same Mrs Bryant – a great buyer of books – had turned up in Skelton's shop the day after that on which I had read her advertisement. I had used the opportunity to quiz her about the loss.

'You did so in hopes of the reward?' Harvey put in.

'No.'

'What then?'

'It was simply a diversion ... and I might be of some service to the lady.'

'Well, what did you ask her?' Harvey enquired. 'You will notice I'm giving you every opportunity of blowing your own trumpet, but you won't damned well oblige!'

'I asked her what she did after she'd bought the book.'

'And what was that?'

I explained how, on the day of the loss, *The Key to the Symbolical Language of Scripture* had been wrapped for Mrs Bryant in the black paper used at Skelton's. She had then continued her 'shopping', as she called it. Being rather flurried, and oppressed by the departure time of the coach that ran to her village, she had hurried along Stonegate to Carlin's the confectioner's, where she had set down her book in order to inspect some glacéd pears. She'd then hastened to Whitley, the glover in Spurriergate, where she had an appointment. It was in Whitley's that she discovered her loss. She hurried back to Carlin's, and asked if anyone had found a book. They had not.

'On hearing all this from Mrs Bryant,' I said, 'I asked precisely how she had couched her question at Carlin's. Had she asked after a book, or a black parcel?

She had asked for a book, and that was her mistake.'

'Oh, but why?' interjected Stephen, the servant. His voice was higher and more refined than I had expected.

'Carlin's,' I said, 'will deliver its chocolate to anywhere within the city—'

'Not to First Water Lane, I'll wager!' Stephen piped.

'Oh, do keep quiet for a minute, Stephen,' said Esther.

'. . . But they will not deliver without the city walls,' I continued. 'Therefore it seemed unlikely that Mrs Bryant, who lived a good way outside town, would know that all the chocolate they deliver is wrapped in black paper, the same black paper indeed (it comes from Barraclough, the stationer on Blake Street) as used at Skelton's. She would also be unaware that much of this chocolate – whether for eating or drinking – is moulded into tablets or slabs, the stuff being easier to consign in that form.'

'I think I'm beginning to see,' said Stephen.

'I gave Mrs Bryant a dish of tea,' I continued, 'and desired her to wait a little while on the sofa at Skelton's. I then walked along to Carlin's, whose back office, from where the chocolate is despatched, was, as usual, full of black packages. My surmise was that Mrs Bryant's parcel had found its way into that office.'

. . . It was Captain Harvey who concluded the story for the benefit of Esther: 'Then, my dear, it was simply a question of feeling the parcels for the tell-tale indentations of a book.'

Not so *very* simple, I recollected. I'd been the best part of an hour over the business.

'*I* know about the Carlin slabs, Mr Rigge,' said Esther, smiling sleepily in my direction. 'I had one for breakfast only the other day.'

'Naturally, you had the reward?' said Captain Harvey, blowing smoke towards the broken chandelier.

I shook my head.

'Why ever not?'

'I waived it.'

'Extraordinary!'

'You *waved* it adieu!' cried Stephen.

'I think somebody said, "Virtue is its own reward",' observed Esther, toying with her black hair. She looked up towards me. 'I mean, nobody in this *room* has ever said it, but I believe *somebody* did.'

It was Sir John Vanbrugh who'd written those words, but I did not think it worth mention. A silence fell. Was this the end of my interview? I looked the question at Harvey, who smiled back.

'We mean to show you six shades, sir,' he said.

'When?' I said, just as though I understood the remark, which I did not, at least not completely.

'Tomorrow, sir,' he said. 'Would you be willing to return here at the same time?'

'I am at your complete disposal,' I said, which was more or less literally true.

Derek Hill, Under-gaoler, examined at York Castle by Mr Bright, Clerk to Mr Erskine.

Mr Bright's prefatory note: Derek Hill, under-gaoler of the Castle, gave his recollections of Mr Rigge readily enough, once a ten-shilling fee had been paid over. I talked them out of him, the under-gaoler being 'no great hand at penmanship', and I kept up with his speech by writing in stenography, or short hand, at which I am tolerably proficient. I believe the fellow to have been in liquor at the time of the interview.

————

I would like to make this quite plain, Mr Bright: I don't get no wages. I must scrape a living as best I can from supplying the needs of those in my charge. Paper, chicken, snuff, wigs, feather mattresses ... and I'm half crippled from dragging sacks of coal up those stairs for the top storey debtors. Yet I'll go out of my way to do a service for any debtor. I recall one poor fellow: Crutchely or Critchley, his name was, for he'd been in the Castle that long – upwards of thirty years, I reckon, when I started here – that his very name had been forgotten. Well, I'll tell you this, Mr Bright – you won't hear it from the gentleman himself, since he's gone crack-brained – but I discovered his right name. Did it by hunting up an old punishment book. The fellow, you see, had been given two days' solitary soon after admission for laughing in chapel. He still had a bit of spirit in him back then, and I daresay he thought he might one day get out, and so could afford to laugh. Well, it was down there in black and white. His name was Critchley ... or it might have been Crutchely, I can't recollect just now, but either way he was overjoyed to learn the truth of it, and more than willing to offer a small gratuity to the finder.

[**Mr Bright's interpolation**: I suggested to Mr Hill that, since he was being paid for his time, he might come more speedily to the point.]

Yes, your Mr Rigge now ... I recall watching from the Day Room window, as that young fellow took his leave. November 16th it would have been, a Friday, and he was crossing the snowy lawn. He'd rolled his clothes into a blanket, and taken quite a time about it – always very particular about his wardrobe, was young Rigge. He'd first popped over to the women's prison, to collect three shirts he'd paid the ladies to wash and press – only coppers but a handy sum to them. Always very free with his purse was young Rigge, for a man who had no money.

I count myself an observant sort of fellow, and I'd made a study of Rigge. Interested me, did the lad. Now, when he got that letter from Harvey, he didn't seem exactly overjoyed at his stroke of fortune, but that was his disposition. Once, late on in the Night Room, I'd come upon him reading – alone and by a dying candle – a gigantic volume. I asked the title, and when he replied, '*The Anatomy of Melancholy*,' I said, 'That sounds just up your street, Mr Rigge,' him being so gloomy. At this, he glanced up from the pages to mention that it was really a comical work, at which I enquired, 'Why do you never laugh, then?'

'It isn't as comical as all *that*,' he said.

Tickled me no end, that did.

For all his cleverness, he was a rather muddled character, in my opinion. He was the son of a country gentleman who'd fought the enclosures being brought in round about. Rigge painted his old man as a kindly protector of the common people. Back-rents written off at the drop of a hat; shoemakers' bills paid, bakers' bills . . . But it was the worse for his tenants in the long run, because he'd taken more and more to drink and gaming, and he'd gambled away most of his fortune by the time he staked his whole estate.

He lost it, of course – to a fellow called Corrigan – and so he shot himself.

Young Rigge had been at the University when that happened. He returned home and was drawn into liabilities on his own account. I believe he tried to carry through some repairs to some workmen's houses, for, you see, the estate included the little village of Adenwold. These repairs had been promised, and young Rigge didn't think the new fellow, Corrigan, would feel obliged in the same way. I believe he borrowed upwards of a hundred pounds. Christ knows how he thought he'd pay it back – you'll forgive my language, Mr Bright, the two of us being men of the world. He'd somehow touched for the money from a fellow called Burnage. Now this Burnage had been a gaming crony of the old man, so perhaps his conscience was pricked, but it soon came *un*pricked, when he saw that Rigge had no expectations – and so the boy found himself on the end of a writ.

Talking to Rigge in the Night Room once, I brought up the matter of the suicide, in what I hoped was a delicate enough way. 'Your father succumbed to a . . . discontent of the mind?' I suggested. (It's what they say in the coroners' courts, you know.)

'He succumbed,' young Rigge replied, 'to a pistol ball.'

For he would not dissemble, Mr Bright. All part of his code of honour.

My thoughts were running along those lines, Mr Bright, as I looked down at Rigge from the Day Room window. By now, he was facing the prison and looking *up*, and I reckoned I knew why. He was observing the black flag that flew from the roof for Lund, the gallows bird. Rigge had offered every assistance to poor Lund; said he wished God speed to all sheep stealers (which was a queer thing for a landowner's son to come out with, but the enclosed meadows are generally turned over to sheep, you see).

As he turned and approached the Castle gate, the snow

was coming down pretty fast. The weather was unquestionably wrong. As I looked on, Rigge was raising his beaver hat to the men at the gate; then he was going through the gate.

I turned away from the window, thinking about how much I would miss the young gentleman, but also how it was even money he'd be back within the Castle walls before Christmas. You see, Mr Bright, I believed that nothing good could come of his involvement with this Harvey character. I then walked over to the fire, in order to kindle it up for some of the poor debtors sitting nearby. On the edge of the grate, I spied some unburnt scraps of paper.

Now I knew that, before taking his leave, Rigge had been sorting through his papers – of which he had a great many, since he was forever scribbling. Most of his letters were charitable applications, but these scraps in the fire were of a different sort; seemed to be a quantity of letters unsent to a certain young lady, and one of the scraps disclosed an address. I'm not one for snooping on the debtors – the felons, yes, you have to keep cases on that rabble – but the privacy of the debtors is respected in the Castle. I glimpsed an address before I'd had the chance to avert my gaze: Miss Lucy Spink, of North Bank Villa, Wellington Row, York.

Now he wouldn't be writing to a young lady unless he was engaged to her, would he? You couldn't throw any light on that little matter, I suppose, Mr Bright? You ought to be able to, with that name of yours!

Diary of Fletcher Rigge,
Sunday November 18th.

This afternoon, I resumed my acquaintance with Captain Harvey.

At half past three, the snow still lay thickly in First Water Lane, blessedly disguising the scenes of squalor I must pass before regaining the Captain's dropsical mansion. It being the Sabbath, I had not expected the coal heavers, but the carman was coming up the lane with a full load, and the rest were down on the wharf, unloading as before.

Once again, I was admitted to the presence of the Captain by the manservant, Stephen, but it appeared that today's business would be conducted in another house, for Stephen immediately quit the room, and returned carrying the coats and hats belonging to the household, all in a jumble. It didn't seem to matter who had which one. Esther put on a red military coat that had surely belonged to Captain Harvey. But the high-crowned-hat-with-feather must be her own, since it suited her so well, in spite of the feather being somewhat bent.

We quit the house, and commenced walking up First Water Lane, or at least Stephen, Esther and I did so. Captain Harvey was delayed at the wharf, talking to a coal heaver who wore a doublet made entirely of patches – and whose shirt was open to the waist on this freezing day.

Esther walked beside me. She enquired, in her sleepy way, 'What are you thinking of, Mr Rigge?'

'Oh – whether the Captain might prove the means of my deliverance from the Castle.'

'He already has done, surely?'

'For now, yes.'

'And you are thinking of some young lady, I'm sure?'

'Now that would be quite futile,' I said.

'Whatever do you mean?'

'A gaol-bird is not considered a very great catch, I believe. Not among the *bon ton*.'

Esther walked on ahead of me, picking her way through the snow in worn gold-coloured slippers, and with arms folded. But then she suddenly looked back, smiling. She had set my heart racing with thoughts of a certain person – and I believed she knew it. As she moved from left to right in front of me, to avoid the deeper snow, she slipped on a patch of ice, and I helped her to her feet.

'You are not hurt?'

'Not at all,' she replied, but now it was her turn to blush. A small blue book had fallen from her pocket. I would have been surprised to find she was a reading woman, had I not already noted her intelligence – which seemed to make her melancholy.

I returned the book to her, checking my curiosity about the title (which was printed very small). 'A precaution against the Captain's speechifying,' she said, 'but you, Mr Rigge – you would be well advised to pay close attention,' and she gave me a meaning look.

Stephen, who had been going on ahead, called back. 'Are you two commencing a flirtation?'

'Yes!' Esther replied with sudden spirit. 'So you keep out of it!'

Captain Harvey now came up behind, having been delayed by his talk with the coal heaver, and by his lameness.

'You know that my father was murdered in the Race Week?' he asked me, somewhat out of breath.

I nodded. 'I was extremely sorry to hear of it. I believe he was a man of great—'

'Skip all that. We're off to his house. It's not very far.'

First Water Lane was not thought worth illumination of any kind, but the lamps were lit on Coney Street (which we soon turned into) and here our shadows appeared on the snow. It was a quarter before four, but it might as well have been midnight. The street was deserted, apart from some chickens, puzzling over the snow in the centre of the road. It was the ringing day, but even the church bells had fallen silent. The three of us walked in front of the seamstress's place there, under the great wooden needle. I pictured it falling on my head, cleaving my skull in two.

We came to a forlorn grey mansion. Harvey knocked, and we were admitted by an untidy, grey-haired woman, evidently the sister – and housekeeper – of the murdered man. No introductions were made in this free-and-easy company, but I apprehended that she was called Susan.

She led the way along a cold passage of bare wood, and into the room at the back of the house where old Matthew Harvey had painted his shades. Susan went round lighting candles, disclosing a grey room, with one tall window overlooking a yard bounded by a low wall, and with only the river – or a dark void where I knew the river to be – lying beyond.

A long table held quills and paintbrushes, dirty feathers, strips of ebony wood, blackened pots of Indian ink and black pigments. There was a good deal of paper – oiled, white, black – a quantity of white and black stock card, and many bottles of beer – full, empty and everything in between. There were mounds of what appeared to be soot, daintily presented on white china plates; other plates held cherry and peach stones – and there was a sizeable ledger, bound in marbled boards. The fireplace was crammed with a jumble of crocks, cauldrons and kettles.

The walls were hung with shades, exemplars of the dead man's trade. These were mostly plain black on a white background, but some had embellishments of gold or silver around the edge of the figure, creating a kind of halo. The subjects were usually single individuals, but there was one family group, sitting on delicately made iron chairs – the very same chairs, I now saw, as those partly covered in sacking by the window. There was something salutary about this society of shadows. The meaning appeared to be that everyone's life was occluded – a notion I could very easily credit.

Besides the profiles, there were some watercolours of people and places, expertly done and signed 'M. Harvey, R.A.'. I recognised a couple of York scenes, but others were unfamiliar. As I contemplated these, the dead man's sister said, 'My brother travelled a great deal. He was always in search of physiognomical knowledge, you know.'

'And money,' Harvey put in.

If that fellow was distressed over his father's death he was very good at concealing it.

'There he is,' said Harvey, indicating with his cane one of the shades hanging from the wall.

I walked up to it.

'This was painted by some . . . friend of his?' I enquired.

'Some friend?' echoed Harvey. 'That implies one of many. It is a self-portrait.'

'Done with mirrors?'

'By no means.'

I beheld a handsome, neat-featured man, elegantly but plainly dressed, in a short-collared coat, no bows to the stock. He wore a neat, physical wig, tightly curled at the back. The impression was of an austere, controlled personage.

'You say he had not many friends?'

'Did I?' said Harvey.

'Who was at his funeral?'

Captain Harvey looked instinctively to Susan. He himself, it appeared, had not attended the funeral.

'It was a very private affair,' said Susan, with cast-down eyes. 'Mr Goodricke was present.'

'"Charles Goodricke R.A.",' as he likes to be known,' said Harvey. 'He paints portraits distinguished primarily by their expense – and he is an Academician!'

'As was your father?'

'Yes. Or so he always said.'

'Mr Cork came as well,' said Susan. 'He is connected with the York Theatre.'

'An actor?'

Again, it was the Captain who replied. Actor-*manager* – and more manager than actor. A money man.'

'Your father was a theatre-goer?'

'The regular – and solitary – occupant of the cheapest side box.'

Harvey approached the fireplace, where he commenced his upright lounging and smoking.

'Matthew was well known to the gentry at Bath,' Susan remarked, as if this might restore the social credentials of her brother, 'and he often took profiles at Brighton, although of course never on the Chain Pier.'

'God forbid he'd be seen on the Chain Pier!' said Harvey.

Esther came up to Harvey, and leant on his shoulder in a way that might have been lover-ish or merely companionable. 'Robin dear,' she said, 'do be quiet, and let your poor aunt speak.'

'He loved to be in this room,' Susan continued, 'although sometimes the smell was beyond anything. The fruit stones ... he burned them to get black pigment. He also got it from soot, which he made by burning pine pitch.'

'He was always looking for what he called a dead black,' said Captain Harvey, smiling sardonically. 'I reckon he's found it now.'

As Susan and Esther exchanged glances of exasperation, Harvey began relating what had befallen his father ...

———————

Matthew Harvey had turned seventy-three at the time of this year's races. In his younger days he might have booked a room in the grandstand and taken profiles during the meeting, for he was a skilled profilist, and versatile. He could create silhouettes with scissors, either by cutting white card (the void being then set against a black background) or black, which was then mounted against white. He could paint them on paper, card, glass or ivory.

But at the time of his death, Matthew Harvey was

on the point of retirement. He was pretty well situated, having always been careful with money; and he got something from his 'painting academy', which – according to the Captain – meant that he conducted two silly girls from one of the York villages around their own garden, pointing out paint-able flowers, before repairing to a shady tree with a glass of wine. But he had been in poor health throughout his final year, troubled by a racking cough, perhaps caused by inhalation of the pine soot.

It came down to this: the only profiles Harvey had painted in that year of 1798 had been done in the August Race Week. He had solicited customers by an advertisement appearing in the *Courant* in the week preceding. He had received six commissions; he had told Susan as much. The appointments would have been made by letter, but it was not his custom to retain this correspondence.

As the Captain spoke, I called to mind York in August. The race meeting . . . two hundred coaches drawn up near the new grandstand . . . The coachmen lying on the roofs, half dressed, basking in the sun.

Now in that week when so many people came *into* York, Matthew Harvey's sister, Susan, had unfortunately gone *out* of it, visiting a friend in Scarborough. Harvey had no other servant, and so was quite alone in the house, and it was not his habit to receive visitors, except for his sitters. For this reason – and another, to be explained in a minute – it was assumed that he had been killed by one of those sitters.

It appeared the attack had occurred on either Wednesday August 22nd, Thursday August 23rd or Friday August 24th, for Harvey had been seen at the service of Evensong at the Cathedral on the Tuesday. ('He attended church,' as Captain Harvey satirically put it, 'religiously.') His body was discovered by his sister on her return from Scarborough at about eight o'clock on the Friday evening.

Susan had shouted for the Watch, and the foot ambulance had been summoned. Harvey, his special scissors embedded in his stomach, had been carried by it to the police office of the Chief Magistrate of York, Mr Ralph Taylor. One of Taylor's constables, a man by the name of Joseph Miller, had then viewed the scene of the crime by lamplight, in company with a very distressed Susan. Miller had done about as much as any constable would in the circumstances. That was to say nothing, beyond establishing that the culprit was no longer on the premises. The room was disordered, and the relevant page had been torn from Harvey's ledger, in which he recorded all his sitters, but no article of value appeared to have been taken. The next day, Susan had swept up the spilled soot and broken beer bottles, and scrubbed the bloodstains away with hot saltwater.

Everyone in the room was now looking at me. My observations seemed to be required. It was as though we were involved in some drawing room entertainment and it was my 'go'.

I first walked to the table, and drew a candle over, in order to examine the ledger from which the page had been torn. I would reserve my remarks on this. I then turned towards Susan.

'Might I see the weapon, please?'

Nodding sadly, Susan reached across the table for a pewter, which had been covered over by a handkerchief. She removed the handkerchief to reveal a pair of scissors, propped inside. They resembled needlework scissors, having long shanks and short – evidently very sharp – points. I looked them over, and she returned them to the pewter, laying the handkerchief back on top.

'I like to keep the room as Matthew left it,' she said, 'but I can't bear to leave those on view.'

'Why are there so many beer bottles?' I asked.

'Not for making merry!' the Captain said, laughing.

'He mixed beer with the pine soot,' Susan replied. 'It made for a greater . . .'

'Opacity,' Esther supplied, half proud, and half embarrassed, and I recollected the novel in her pocket.

After an interval of silence, I rose from my chair, walked over to the window, and contemplated the snow-filled yard. I turned to face Harvey. 'Were *you* in York in that week, sir?'

The question seemed to create a *frisson* in the room.

'I was, sir.'

'And when were you informed of your father's death?'

'The next morning – the Saturday. By my aunt.'

I turned to Susan: 'After or before you had re-arranged the room?'

'After. I wanted to put things straight. It was such a very disagreeable scene. I *tried* to tell Captain Harvey before. I hammered on his door at about ten in the morning, but I couldn't rouse him.'

'I fear that we were all abed!' piped Stephen, who didn't sound the least bit fearful about it.

'The Captain finally answered the door about midday,' said Susan. She did not seem to reprehend the tardiness of her nephew – who was just then smiling at me while re-filling his pipe – but was resigned to it.

'He must have been murdered by the person whose profile he'd painted last,' I suggested.

'Most likely,' said Harvey, 'but we don't know which commission was the last one to be fulfilled. And it might be that the first sitter returned later in the week . . . perhaps to enquire about purchasing a duplicate, and that some argument blew up then.'

'A duplicate?'

'The shades we are about to show you are all duplicates, or so we assume. My father invariably made a copy, in case the sitter should want to re-order at a later date. He painted the first shade while the sitter posed. He might then offer them a glass of sherry . . . That is if he considered them people of quality – otherwise a cup of weak tea sufficed – and they would drink it as the paint or ink dried on the first, and the second was made. The oils took a little longer to dry than the inks or watercolours, but it was not above half an hour in any case. In the meantime he would be very solicitous, not to say servile in the case of the sherry drinkers . . . '

Susan and Esther frowned at this, but kept silence.

'I only mean,' the Captain continued, 'that he would engage them in conversation to while away the time. The sitters waited while the copy was made, and they were happy to do so. It was a sort of entertainment – a bonus, Mr Rigge, like the hornpipe given at the end of a play.'

'And he retained the duplicates, while the sitters left with the originals?'

'Yes. Which they paid for, of course. Nobody left without paying. My father would stow the duplicate in the top drawer of that bureau. He would lock it – and that would be the end of the transaction.'

I walked over to the bureau. There was a key in the drawer indicated.

'Why didn't the murderer remove the duplicate also?'

'Because my father had locked the drawer.'

'But presumably the key was about his person . . . and so could have been removed from him as he lay dying?'

Harvey shrugged. 'Evidently, the murderer's priority was to clear off out of it, double-quick.'

'The argument,' I said, 'must have blown up after

37

Harvey stowed the duplicates, since you say that we do *have* the duplicates?'

Captain Harvey nodded. '. . . Or reached its climax then, yes.'

'The overwhelming likelihood,' I said, 'surely *is* that he was killed by the last sitter: the one whose duplicate shade was put into the drawer last.' I eyed the Captain. 'It would have been on the *top*,' I said.

'But we don't know which was on the top of the pile.'

'Why not?'

'Because we were not able to lay hands on the key in time,' Susan said, wretchedly.

The Captain was smiling at my perplexity. 'We come,' he said, 'to the second outrage.'

Fletcher Rigge, in continuation.

The Captain nodded to Susan, giving her the floor.

'At ten o'clock the next evening,' she said, 'the key was returned to me by one of the attendants at the mortuary. It had been discovered in a pocket of Matthew's waistcoat.'

'A secret one,' Harvey interjected. 'He was that kind of a man.'

'I put it back in the drawer, and went to bed,' said Susan.

'You did not examine the shades?' I enquired, and she shook her head sadly.

'I was quite worn out,' she said, 'and I didn't think to do it.' She made an effort at self-control before continuing: 'Later that same evening this house was burglarised. I suppose it was done soon after midnight. The door was jemmied open while I slept upstairs.'

'You were not roused by the noise?' I asked, returning to my seat.

'I was *roused*,' said Susan, 'at two o'clock by the cry of the Watch.'

'Crying what?' I asked.

'"It's two o'clock, and a fine starlit night."'

At that, I could not forbear to give a small smile. I was aware of Esther (who had not yet resorted to her book) watching me do it, and smiling in her turn.

'The burglar took the duplicate shades?' I suggested.

Susan nodded, but even as she did so, the Captain was at the bureau, and removing what appeared to be the shades in question. He brought them over to the table, laid them out upon it.

It appeared that, while the first watchman of this police district – the one who'd cried the hour – had apprehended nothing of the burglary, one of his fellows, a certain Bernard Hodges, had seen from a distance a man carrying a leathern saddle bag along the riverbank soon after midnight. As Hodges looked on, the man – seeing he was observed – pitched the bag into the river, before slipping into the darkness of the town. The bag was not carried away by the current, nor did it sink. It was discovered, at five the next morning, by Hodges himself, entangled in some rushes on the riverbank just before the village of Fulford, where Hodges lives, and to which he was returning after his work.

'And the profiles were in the bag?' I enquired.

Harvey nodded. 'Together with my father's cash box, which had been emptied.'

'The shades were perfectly preserved?'

'Pretty well,' said Harvey. 'The bag was so well dubbined as to be effectually water-proofed.'

'Was any note taken of which was uppermost?'

'It was not,' said Harvey, 'and then they became disordered when Hodges examined them.'

With the shades on the table before me, I asked, 'Was there any resemblance between this man seen by Hodges and anyone depicted here?'

'Hodges couldn't make him out very well. He may not have been one of the subjects at all, but some ruffian, recruited to steal the evidence.'

'But in ordering the theft of the shades,' I said, 'was the murderer not identifying himself as one of the people whose shade had been painted?'

'I can only imagine,' said Harvey, blowing smoke, 'that the murderer would have thought it a risk to leave the shades, and a risk to take them. Keep in mind that he – or she – might have expected the fellow to come away with a greater number of shades. He was probably asked to collect every new-made shade in this room. Unfortunately for the murderer, this came down to only six.'

The First Shade

This was tiny – about the size of a penny. It looked all the smaller for occupying the dead centre of a sheet of white foolscap.

'A profile of that size was meant for a piece of jewellery,' said the Captain. 'This is the copy, as I say. The original would have been done on a small square of ivory or glass. My father did not do the settings. The sitter would have taken it away and got it fitted into a brooch or a locket. Then he would have sent it to his sweetheart ... A lucky lady!'

The profile showed a youngish man, bust-height. He wore a periwig, tied back with a ribbon. The knot of his cravat was distinctive, being of the (to my mind) indecently large kind called an Osbaldeston. He wore a frock coat, only the upper part of which was discernible, but this too was distinctive, since there were buttonholes (denoted by white slits) on the lapel turn. The subject had a weak chin. A higher collar would have disguised the deficiency, but it was as though the fellow were proud of it, the retardation of the chin making the rest of his features seem to be thrusting forward.

The Second, Third and Fourth Shades

This was larger, about ten inches across, and done on white stock card. As I contemplated it, Susan said, 'He took children equally perfect.'

Here were three shades in one: a mother (I assumed) and her two little girls. All sat on the delicate iron chairs. Both little girls' dresses were scored with rectilinear white lines, suggesting plaid, in a ghostly kind of way. The bigger girl held a triangle, and was in the act of striking it with a beater; the smaller had a dog on her lap. She was nuzzling the creature in a most affectionate manner, even though the beast was far from beautiful. I know a little of dogs, but those of my boyhood were all useful – or at least sporting – dogs, whereas the one sitting on the little girl's lap had no utility and was applicable to no sport. It was, in short, a pug dog, and Matthew Harvey had (perhaps by scraping away at the blackness) depicted the creature's body in the same semi-luminous, silvery white – the nearest thing to a colour that his palette allowed – as had been employed on the little girls' dresses. In the case of the dog's muzzle, however (insofar as pugs have a muzzle), Harvey had reverted to his customary black.

'This pug dog,' I asked, 'whose is it?' (For I had thought it might be like the hats and cloaks in the room, kept on hand to 'dress' the sitters.)

'Theirs,' said Harvey, who had resumed his upright lounging, only now by the window. He meant that it belonged to the sitters.

I looked closely at the supposed mother. She wore a small, round cap, and a simple, robe-dress with a low neck. The hair beneath the cap was fashionable and short – *à la Brutus*.

The Fifth Shade

This again was on foolscap. It showed a respectable woman, age perhaps in the thirties. Again, bust-height. She had regular, elegant features. Her hair hung in tumbling bangs at the back, and was curiously – but fetchingly – offset by a rather severe riding hat, cocked like that of a man, so the effect was a combination of prettiness and practicality.

'We have nothing much to say about madam,' said Harvey, 'except that the hat's out-of-the-common.'

It's Robin Hood's hat, I thought.

'. . . And she's pretty,' said Esther. 'I like her, and I'd rather she didn't swing.'

The Sixth Shade

This – on card – was that of a man, perhaps in the late fifties or sixties. Bust-height, yet again.

'Now this fellow's from London,' said Harvey. 'You can go there and look for him.'

'There are a million people in London,' I said.

'Observe the nose,' Harvey said.

I had already done so. It had a tendency to the bulbous: the kind of nose associated, justly or not, with a tippler. The man wore a wide-brimmed hat, curled at the side, and with a low crown – a luxurious hat, signifying vanity. But it might have been meant to obscure the nose.

'In this case alone, we have the identity,' said Harvey. 'He's a famous author. Well, not famous *exactly*. But notable enough for my father to have mentioned him to my aunt in advance of his visit.' He nodded towards Susan, who supplied the particulars:

'Matthew told me on the Monday of the Race Week, which was the day I left for Scarborough, that a well-known literary gentleman from London had made an arrangement to have his profile taken.'

A writer given to drink, I thought, looking at the nose . . . That did not tighten the focus to a significant degree.

But Harvey was saying, 'My father told Susan the fellow's very *name*. He was apparently quite full of it. Samuel Gowers. Mean anything to you?'

It did. Samuel Gowers was an inhabitant of that metaphorical Grub Street, in which it seems likely that I myself will have to seek lodging, assuming I remain a free man: turner-out of catchpennies; books written for the printer instead of the muse. But Samuel Gowers had scored one small success that meant his fame had just about staggered as far as York. I said as much to the company.

'And what was his success?' Harvey enquired.

I pronounced the title: *'The Reasons, Plainly Stated, Why Not to Purchase the Works of Samuel Johnson.'*

'Encapsulate this work for us.'

'Peevish.'

'Be so good as to enlarge on that.'

'Samuel Gowers is obviously jealous of that other, more eminent, Samuel.'

'If it was Dr Johnson who'd been murdered,' Stephen piped up, 'we would have our man!'

I eyed Stephen. 'Dr Johnson has been dead these past fifteen years,' I said.

'Well, if you *say* so!'

I thought of Johnson's famous *Dictionary*. Under 'Gamester', he had quoted Bacon: 'The greater master he is in his art, the worse man he is.' By that measure, my father was a very great man indeed.

I turned towards the smiling Captain, asking, 'You are quite sure there were not *seven* shades?'

Fletcher Rigge, in continuation.

I seemed, by my question, to have created another *frisson*.

'Why seven, sir?' asked Harvey, tense at the dark window.

I said, 'Things tend to come in sevens, wouldn't you say?'

'Not particularly.'

'Seven days of creation,' I said, 'seven plagues, seven planets, seven wonders of the world; there might as well be seven shades.'

'You are becoming mystical,' the Captain said, not smiling.

It was the catchpenny hack in me that was coming to the fore. I had been thinking that 'Seven Shades' would be a better title for a romance than 'Six Shades'. But this idle thought had immediately given way to another, more substantial. I took up the ledger. The pages prior to the torn-out leaf were inscribed with the names and addresses of previous subjects. These lists had stopped in June of the previous year: 1797, the date on which Matthew Harvey had effectually commenced his retirement. An altogether new page, it appeared, had been started for August 1798, and this was the missing one. Certainly, there were signs of tearing, and I did not doubt that the page had been so removed. But Matthew Harvey's nib had left an impression on the new page beneath. The impression was not strong enough to show what precisely had been written, but there were seven lines of impress, and not six, as I pointed out.

Captain Harvey had been eyeing me from the window. He now advanced in such a way that I apprehended a blow from his cane. But he commenced to smile, and, fishing in his coat, came out with a pocket-sized square of stock card, which he handed to me. 'He took mine into the bargain,' he said, 'on the Wednesday of that same week. Naturally, he did not want to show his son a cripple.'

The card held a good, black likeness of Captain Harvey, depicted full-length, and with his cane, but looking dapper in full regimentals. I remarked on his attire, but the Captain said, 'I was dressed as you see me now; but my father preferred to depict me in uniform.'

My surmise was that everyone in the room knew the father had taken the son's likeness, and that seven, not six, shades had been discovered by the constable called Bernard Hodges in the stolen bag. Hodges would no doubt have sworn to that before a magistrate. Harvey knew that it was hopeless to conceal that he himself had been the subject of the seventh shade. He had made the attempt nonetheless, but in a half-hearted way.

'I wanted to see whether you'd find it out,' he said, mustering another smile of sorts.

'Why would a father, taking his own son's shade, feel the need to enter it in a ledger?' I asked.

'Oh,' said Harvey, 'he made quite a performance of it. Writing the entry gave him the chance to read out my address, "Captain Harvey, of Bottom House – he always called it that – First Water Lane!" He did not care for my address. I would say to him, "Sir, if you think First Water Lane is bad, you should see the *Second*."'

(Most of Second Water Lane had long since tumbled into the river.)

'Also,' the Captain continued, 'he wanted to make everything above-board. He had painted my shade before, when I was a boy, but always informally, so to speak. He would make a quick sketch, then colour it with lamp black. I was a rebellious child, I'm afraid, and when he handed over the finished work, I . . . well, I would regard it pretty lightly. I might use it as a taper to light my pipe . . .'

'The Captain smoked a pipe when he was a boy, you see,' Stephen put in.

' . . . Or I might twist it into a corkscrew, and drop it out of the window,' Harvey added.

I asked, 'What did you do with this latest profile of yourself? The original of it, I mean, if that's the copy.'

'Oh, it's somewhere about,' said the Captain, with a smirk. 'It has caused me a good deal of trouble. I might almost think he painted it to ensnare me.'

'You are not suggesting suicide?'

Harvey shook his head. 'I am not, sir. I jest.'

'Mr Rigge,' said Susan, with a new severity, 'Robin loved his father, even if he is not sentimental enough to say so, and I remind you that he has staked a very large sum to discover his murderer.'

'Who will inherit?' I asked.

'That does not signify,' snapped the Captain. 'It is quite beside the question.' But I held his gaze until he made a small concession: 'Susan was the principal beneficiary, as we all expected. She came in for this house – which is her home, after all. As for me, I assure you that my expectations were adequately met.' I continued to eye him, and he added: 'Damn it, sir, you can go and read the blasted will in the Registry if you've half a day to waste.'

That was a dispiriting prospect. There is a fee for searching the wills. And a long wait in the Registry – that worm-eaten shack attached to the Minster (the wills coming under the Archbishop's care) – is always involved.

'Your mother, sir?' I asked.

'Dead these twenty years.'

I asked, 'Did not any of the sitters come forward after the murder? They must all have heard of it.'

'Come forward to say what?' said Harvey. 'To declare they didn't murder him? In that case, they might have been accused of protesting too much.'

I said, 'I take it you want to me to discover the murderer?'

'I want you to find the subjects of the shades, sir. Which will amount to the same thing.'

'And what then?'

'What then? You will gather your evidence. If there is a reasonable cause of suspicion against any one of them – which there must be, in light of the circumstances – we will begin a prosecution. We will make our depositions before the magistrate, and get a warrant for the arrest of the man, woman or – come to that – the child. Because sharp scissors go into a man's stomach as easily as knife into butter. One of the subjects, of course, we already know, and you are to go to London to examine him. I don't doubt that you, a Cambridge man ...'

'I kept a single term.'

'More than any of *us*, sir. I don't doubt you will gain his attention. The London coach lets out from the Black Swan on Wednesdays.'

I mentioned that it cost twelve shillings to sit on the roof, at which Harvey advanced towards me again, this time removing his pocket book. He handed over five pound notes drawn on the York Bank. 'I've only York notes at present. They might not do in London, but there's an agent will exchange: Wentworth & Co, on the Strand. Ever been to London, Mr Rigge?'

I shook my head. It would be absurd to mention that I disapproved of London, so I merely remarked, 'It's a tedious ride, I believe.'

I had heard about a new class of constable there. They take up the supposed scent of any crime and follow it anywhere, like bloodhounds, even when nobody has come forward to prosecute. They are likely to be an interfering class of men, tyrannical and unconstitutional – in it for what they can get. I dislike the idea of this sort of organised spying but it seems that – on the strength of having found a single missing book – I am being recruited to play a similar part.

Fletcher Rigge, in continuation.

Out in Coney Street, I hesitated. I had been entrusted with the six shades (Harvey having retained his own), and had them in my greatcoat pocket. The three libertines had departed for First Water Lane. It struck me that I had rather enjoyed quizzing Captain Harvey about the circumstances of the crime, but I am decidedly not engaged in some amusing parlour game. I am required to hunt up some stranger, and drag them to the gallows. Yet I have no choice but to accept the commission; the price of declining will quite likely be a lifetime's confinement in the Castle.

In that silent street, I thought of the York Tyburn:

51

the 'government signpost', as the felons call it. I pictured snow descending upon the great wooden frame; poor Lund suspended from it, turning silently; at once cold, yet released from the cold.

There was still nobody about, only the chickens in the road. As I looked on, they stopped pecking in the snow; they seemed to become watchful, contemplating each other with some apprehension of danger; and then a great roaring started up, and they began to squawk and scatter. The row seemed to be coming from beneath the very cobbles. Suddenly two black thoroughbreds burst into the road not ten yards from where I stood, followed immediately by two more; then came the giant black and white coach, bouncing on its steel springs as it turned hard left out of the drive leading up from the stable yard of the Black Swan. It hurtled away from me, raising up a snow cloud all the way along Coney Street. Only the coachman and the guard had been on top, and they had looked desperate characters: the coachman muffled but hatless, the shotgun of the guard plainly visible. There had been two men inside. I had seen their profiles through the carriage door. They inhabited a world of danger, as did everyone in this cold and colourless world.

I commenced walking; my boots commenced leaking. The black swan painted on the white door panel of the coach had been a bird in flight, whereas the iron black swan dangling from the door of the inn before me was sitting down. *This* black swan I could apprehend, and I might as well do so, for I needed to book myself onto the London coach; I also required a glass of port wine.

A notice was propped in the window between the door of the inn and the wide, dark mouth of the yard: 'Travelling in general,' I read, 'has been very much obstructed by the late fall of snow.' But squinting at the smaller print beneath, I saw it was mainly the short stages to the North Riding that were disrupted, and not the London run.

A minute later, I stood by the Black Swan fire, resting my most waterlogged boot on the fender, while sipping a glass of port wine. The recent departure of the coach seemed to have left the room eviscerated and silent. The barkeeper scratched his ear; a greyhound lay on its side; a slumbering, half-dead-looking man reposed in a distant armchair.

I took down from the mantelpiece a copy of the *York Courant*, a week old. I have it before me as I write this entry. It appeared – from the lists of wretches named under 'Bankrupt', and the notices baldly beginning, 'WANTED: MONEY' – that the city had been running on its usual grim course during my confinement.

I turned to the news from London:

'Yesterday the two Hamburg mails which were due arrived in town. The news contained in the different letters was that every appearance of peace is vanished.'

The badness of the times ... Strange to think that any person imprisoned for debt was deemed unfit to be at large in such a society. Seeking to lighten my spirits, I looked for, and found, the heading 'ASSEMBLY ROOMS':

'There will be a BALL, on Monday next at the Great Assembly Rooms. Tickets 5s each, to be had at the Rooms.'

In other words tomorrow. Miss Lucy Spink, I mused, will very likely be there. Thanks to Captain Harvey, I can afford a ticket, and I *will* afford one.

But to continue the story of Sunday ...

I glanced over to the counter, where the barkeeper was making marks in a wide black ledger. The fellow suddenly looked more official than previously. I re-approached him and, yes, it seemed he was in a position to take a booking for London. I would not have to go into the cold yard.

'Inside, is it?' he enquired.

I knew that my gentlemanly looks had earned the question, but it was not a success to be long savoured, for I had to reply, 'Outside,' so proving myself a gentleman in looks *only*. I handed over one of Captain Harvey's pound notes and five shillings of my own on top, the cost of the journey both ways. The barkeeper made a note.

'You're on the bill, sir,' he said, handing over a shilling in change, and a billet. 'Tuesday morning – five o'clock sharp.'

'Where does it go to?' I asked.

'Why, London,' said the barkeeper, perplexed.

'But where *exactly*?'

'The Black Swan. Another one.'

'. . . Which is in?'

'High Holborn.'

'Is that near St Paul's?' I asked, for I had the idea that all the bookmen of London clustered near St Paul's.

'Near enough,' said the barkeeper, and he nodded, but this was directed at a new arrival. I turned about to see a small, pinkish man with a snow-dusted coat of a nicely calculated grey shade, and lacier shirt cuffs protruding beneath than are usually seen in the common room of an inn. The man removed a tall, silken hat. He next removed his wig and scratched his bald pink dome, which was surrounded by a halo of white hair. He had a very flat nose. He was accompanied by a small dog, which also had a flat nose. I saw that it was of the breed depicted in one of the seven shades, namely a pale-coloured pug with a blackish face; but the animal depicted by Harvey would be unlikely to turn up only half an hour after I had seen the depiction. That would be too providential, not to say miraculous. And the depicted dog had been attended by three human females, whereas I had the idea that this new man – like Captain Harvey's servant, Stephen – wouldn't have much to do with human females.

He looked a merry sort of fellow. Perhaps he had taken

a drink, but he wasn't after one now. It was the pug that was drinking, from a bowl kept a little way inside the door for use – gratis – by the customers' dogs. The sleeping man stirred in his armchair as the greyhound approached the pug. The greyhound studied his smaller and stubbier brother, with an amused cocking of the head.

'Good evening, Dash,' the new man said, in a courtly way, to the greyhound, which commenced wagging its tail. At this, the pug left off drinking – which it had been doing with a great deal of snuffing and spillage – to begin yelping at the greyhound, which looked quite put out.

'Tum-Tum!' exclaimed the man. 'A little decorum, please,' and he was smiling at the barkeeper as he added, '. . . Not so thirsty today. He's been eating snow all the way from Jubbergate.' His eye now fell on me, and lingered for a moment or two as he righted his wig and set his hat back on his head.

'Allez, mon petit,' he said to the pug, 'we will leave these gentlemen in peace,' and he quitted the inn.

I made a swift calculation. How many live pugs had I ever seen in the city of York? One: the specimen of a moment before. I thought it likely that one pug owner might know another in a town of twenty thousand. The barkeeper – who would certainly know the pug man – had gone from sight. I quit the parlour, and turned into the yard in hopes of discovering him there, but I found only the silent, stabled horses, a half-dismantled coach, and the falling snow. I ran back out into Coney Street. Faint footmarks, rapidly disappearing under new snow, led away to the left, then went right, so indicating that man and dog had turned into New Street.

Therefore I entered New Street, which seemed composed entirely of windows shuttered more tightly than was needful. I turned into Davygate, another street of small shops, and churches of equivalent size, all sleeping after their one day of work. Davygate gives onto Thursday Market Square, which looked abandoned, as it always does except on Thursdays. I was starting to think the pink-faced man very intrepid to be abroad on such a dismal night. I then heard a dog bark from far off. I hate to hear a dog bark in the city: the sound echoes so futilely off the stone and brick; and this was not the bark of a pug.

The distant, hoarse bark came again. The next minute, an actual word was formed in the frosty air, and this was much closer to hand: '*Et voila!*' – a surprisingly happy sound in the moribund dark. It must be the Frenchified, pink-faced man. Walking fast in the direction of the noise, I came to two warehouses intersected by an alleyway. At the head of the alleyway, a black turd lay in the white snow, surely a production of the pug's, and no doubt the result of strenuous effort, hence the owner's triumphant '*Voila!*' The snow fell rapidly on the turd – a frantic attempt to restore decency.

I followed the alley, which came out in Back Swinegate.

Here are more small shops, but these are at odds with the coarse name of the street, being more select, jewel box-like. I walked past a perfumier's, then a wigmaker's, whereupon I heard the bark of the pug. Its owner was unlocking the door of a shop that – I saw as I came alongside – was another perfumier's, and an apothecary's into the bargain. In the window, baton candles burned. All through the lonely night, they would illuminate a jumble of fantastically coloured bottles. I read the name above the window: 'M. Garencier'. I must have walked past this window many times, but I had never remarked 'Garencier'. The man himself was looking back through the swirled door-glass at me, and so I endeavoured to speak through the glass:

'Forgive the intrusion, sir. Might I have a minute of your time?'

I knew that a minute of anyone's time does not come cheap when the request is made by a stranger late on a Sunday, yet Garencier's expression was not without amiability. I was obviously not a footpad, or any sort of ruffian. He seemed minded to admit me.

'What is it concerning?' he called back through the glass. 'The shop is closed.'

'Am I addressing Mr Garencier?' I called through the glass, attempting to put the conversation on a civil footing. The man called back, 'Monsieur Garencier is deceased. I am Mr Hurst.'

My interlocutor was clearly still in two minds about whether to open the door. Some sort of dumb show was required. I took the roll of profiles out from my pocket, and riffled through until I came to the one showing the three females and the dandled pug. But Mr Hurst was shaking his head, and withdrawing into the dark recesses of his shop.

Quite alone in the street I looked up again at the sign: 'Garencier'. I usually ignore such overly genteel shops. I prefer the tack shops, the gun shops and boot makers', and others signifying the life of the country gentleman.

As I turned away from Garencier's, I pondered my own foibles and affectations. Yes, I look in the tack shop windows, but I am an indifferent horseman. As for the gun shops, I have been after pheasants or rabbits no more than half a dozen times – and with marked lack of distinction. I pictured myself in feverish study, a week after father's suicide, bent over *One Hundred Points of Good Husbandry*, and taking in barely a word, being nothing but a *pretended* country gentleman.

Stowing the shades back in my pocket, I returned here to Ogleforth, to my own cold bedchamber, and the writing of this journal.

Diary of Esther, Sunday November 18th.

I sit here on Sunday evening with my brandy, and my writing box. In this house it is brandy and water before six, thereafter pure brandy – the ball of fire. A fire of the literal sort burns in the grate (there is never any shortage of coal in this house) but I fear I have a chill coming on, and I have retained my coat and hat. The Captain is upstairs in a hot tub near another fire, occasionally singing. Stephen lies on the couch opposite to me. It is high time for him to put on his greatcoat and walk up to the Spread Eagle on Micklegate for his own nightly tincture, and to collect the mutton he took there earlier on for roasting. Instead he is reading. He is dressed – according to his evening custom – in nothing but his shirt, from beneath the forelap of which his member protrudes intermittently. In former times, he might have invited me over to meddle with it a little, and I might have complied, if only to please the Captain, who would amuse himself on his own couch at the sight. But now Stephen must do the meddling himself; or the Captain does it, willingly enough.

I know the book in which he is so engrossed: a directory of London whores called *Taylor's Index of Covent Garden Ladies*. Of course, an index of Covent Garden *gentlemen* would be of equal if not greater interest to Stephen.

I will go up to see the Captain in a minute. In the

past, I would bathe with him, which required – the tub being so small – my sitting directly on top of him, which was fortuitous for the Captain. But these days I am more likely to soap his back from without the tub. All that side of things has fallen away. I mean, the Captain is not so familiar with what he calls my Low Countries as once was the case. It is idle to think I will ever forsake him, but I do think about it – and pretty often, even though he rescued me from an existence that was insupportable.

He was handsomer then. I noticed last night, as he leant to put a taper in the fire, how sparse his hair is becoming; in places it is like a memory of hair, a quick and careless sketch of it. But he is clever, and when we met in London he told me point blank that I – daughter of a sophisticated gentleman (if a country-town vicar may be so described) – must have a clever consort. Today, as he held forth before his new 'friend' Mr Rigge, I found myself wondering just how clever the Captain is, and whether he has met his match in young Mr Rigge. I also found myself weighing my lover in the balance, with an objectivity that would have been impossible in my early, smitten days.

He has given me steadiness, in a way. He has set me up in a grand house, albeit one that is falling down. He has restored me to a world of books – albeit the most indecorous kind – and of pens and paper . . . but in London I saw what use he made of those articles and I believe he is about the same business again. He paces his bedchamber at night, and his kneehole desk has been brought back into use. As he writes, he keeps his pistol on his desk. I believe this signifies the dangerous content of the writing, which takes the form of correspondence. I am not supposed to see these letters, or to know who receives them. He might walk up to the post-office himself, even though it is a trial for him to go so far; or he gives the letters to Stephen, or the coal heavers who lodge on the Staith.

I break off to note that Stephen has evidently found a whore whose specialisms he approves of. He is smiling at me, and with a question implied, but *only* implied. He knows of my deepening anxieties, and is curious to see how I will resolve them, but he is pretty sure I never will. He himself is a walking contradiction: a manservant who is the frequent bed-mate of his master; a man with a great knowledge ... of matters that may never be mentioned in any respectable company.

I have just taken another glass, to fortify myself against my own unmentionable, numberless anxieties. Here is one. Every time I unlock this lap desk to take up my pen, it occurs to me that it contains all my earthly treasures, everything that I really love, and all these things are quite anterior to my life with the Captain: this journal, the locket of my mother's hair, my gold brooch, my poems, in their blue silk ribbon (the ribbon, of course, having far greater artistic merit than the literary contents), and the reference from Mrs Griffin. Were it not absurdly pompous,

I would like to have told Mr Rigge that I was once found to be satisfactory governess to three children in a very learned household, for I noticed his surprise on finding me in possession of a novel, although he attempted nobly to disguise it. I would like Mr Rigge to think well of me, and not only because he is – as Stephen has already remarked to me – 'a provokingly pretty boy, and dressed just the right side of foppish'.

Will the Captain prove a plain-dealer with him? I doubt it, and I am sure trouble lies that way. Did the Captain kill his own father? I cannot quite believe him a murderer, but whether he has *caused* people to be killed, or caused them to kill *themselves* – that is another matter again. In any event, he has lately become bored, and I fear Mr Rigge will prove a victim of this dangerous boredom.

I can hear the Captain's uneven tread on the stairs. If only I did not know how he was lamed, for it makes me laugh even now and in spite of everything to think of it. In a moment, he will enter the room in his nightshirt and robe, wine glass in hand. After a pause he will come towards my sofa rather than Stephen's, and I will be pleased at that, but I have often wondered, of late, whether this glass of brandy might not mean more to me than the close presence of the man I used so readily to call 'my Captain'.

Memorandum from Mr Erskine, Attorney, to Mr Taylor, Magistrate.

Precentor's Court, York.

On the next day, the Monday, our Mr Rigge was busy indeed, in pursuit of his commission. He went first to Bainbridge's, the milliner's on Nessgate, seeking information about the distinctive type of cocked hat worn by the woman Harvey had depicted. He then called in at the York Registry in pursuit of Harvey's will. Afterwards, he returned to the premises called Garencier, which visit gave rise to a pursuit culminating in a famous location of the city, as will be disclosed. Some time after these exertions, he called at Skelton's Bookshop in Stonegate, where he had been employed.

In the evening, he attended the Assembly, after which occurred a shocking fatality, such as might have merited half a sentence in the *Courant*, but evidently not. (Although my eyesight worsens at approximately the same rate as that journal's print size reduces, so perhaps I do the editor a disservice.)

Our young protagonist seems to have spent most of the next day writing up these events in his diary. But in the cases of his visits to Mrs Bainbridge's, the Registry and

Skelton's I choose to introduce other voices. So I bring forward Mrs Bainbridge herself, followed by Mr Thaddeus Myers, Deputy Under-Registrar at the York Registry; and then young Bob Richmond, resentfully retained as the 'lad' at the principal bookshop of our city. I assure you, my dear Taylor, their accounts correspond in all important particulars with those in Rigge's diary, and they have the benefit of throwing sidelights on his character.

It is necessary to mention, however, that Rigge's own description of his visit to Mrs Bainbridge's is much taken up with his regret at having to dissemble before the formidable proprietress. He pretended that his mother was still alive, whereas Mrs Rigge died of a cancer some twelve years ago at the family estate. (It was, he writes, a 'sordid stratagem', disrespectful to the memory of his mother.)

But here is Mrs Bainbridge's own account, as transcribed by Mr Bright, who provides some preliminary remarks.

Mrs Bainbridge, Milliner, examined by Mr Bright.

Mr Bright's prefatory note: Mrs Bainbridge submitted to my interview with the greatest reluctance. When I visited her premises in Nessgate, she was 'stock taking', which is to say she was incessantly hurling a variety of bonnets, turbans and tricorns into and out of pasteboard boxes. Apparently, these were all 'last season's' hats, but the amount of dust thrown up suggested they dated from a good *many* seasons ago, and at the conclusion of the interview I embarked on a coughing fit that – as it seemed to me – Mrs Bainbridge observed with a good deal of satisfaction.

———

Your Mr Rigge came into the shop at about eleven in the forenoon on that Monday. If you say it was the 19th, Mr Bright, then that's what it must have been. I was not as busy then as I am just now, but getting on that way. When I heard the bell ring, I was down below – in the basement, but we just call it 'below' – making up orders with the girl. The girl is called Peg, if you must know.

'I'm interested in a hat like that,' Mr Rigge said, pointing to one of the cocked hats we have in the window.

'It's a ladies hat,' I said.

He said he knew that.

'We don't sell hats for gentlemen,' I pointed out, and he told me he knew that as well. He was polite enough, and a well set-up young man, I suppose, but I was suspicious of him, for he seemed embarrassed, and not in the ordinary way of a gentleman being in a ladies' shop.

'It is a riding hat,' I told him, and that, I believe, he did *not* know.

'Therefore,' he suggested, 'it would likely be of interest to any keen horsewoman?'

I pointed out that it was not compulsory to ride in such a hat.

'I'm thinking of it for my mother, ma'am,' he said at length. 'But I'm not sure it will quite suit her.'

'She's a pretty lady, I assume?'

'Very,' he said, which is what all men say of their mothers, but I could credit it in his case.

'The style is a little severe,' I said, 'but any pretty lady will carry it off splendidly.'

He said, 'It might help if you could mention some of the more eminent, fashionable ladies who sport this style.'

'Why?'

'It would . . . commend the hat to my mother.'

Thinking she must be a very weak-willed creature indeed, I asked, 'Is she a fashionable lady herself?'

At this, he seemed lost in some sad reflection, and so I repeated the question. 'Is your mother a fashionable lady herself?'

'Indeed so, yes.'

'Well then, she would *know*, wouldn't she?'

He bowed, rather shortly, and was about to take his leave, when the girl – yes, the same girl, there is only one – came up the stairs and appeared in the doorway. You can lay your life she'll take a good look at any young man who comes into the shop. I was about to suggest that she go back below, but before I could do so, your Mr Rigge made so bold as to ask her directly whether she knew of any York ladies who favoured that style of hat. I would not suffer such impertinence, and so I answered for the girl. 'She can't think,' I said. 'Neither of us can.'

He bowed again, respectfully enough, before departing.

Letter from Mr Thaddeus Myers, Deputy Under-Registrar of the York Registry, to Mr Erskine, Attorney.

The Registry of Wills and Probate,
The Minster,
York.

Thank you for your communication about a Mr Fletcher Rigge. The date of your letter, I fear, cannot be made out but if this reply comes to you belatedly, please bear in mind the great weight of correspondence bearing down upon this office.

I regret to say that the Registry does not command the capacity to record every single visit, and I have been unable to discover Mr Rigge's name in the Search Diary. But Mr Rigge did have occasion to visit the Searching Office of the Registry on the date you mention, viz. the late morning of Monday November 19th, as I am able to attest in person. In spite of being in the midst of an important commission for the Dean, I myself was in the Searching Office at the time, endeavouring to assist the Chief Clerk, Mr Wilkinson, in dealing with the great hurry of business.

I recollect the visit of Mr Rigge because he sought the will of Mr Matthew Harvey, the artist who was murdered. In answer to your question, he did not say why he wanted to see it, and I assumed it was out of morbid curiosity, or perhaps he was a relative in hopes of discovering a legacy. I enjoined Mr Wilkinson to perform the actual search, and he was not instantly able to lay hands on the deed in question.

I recollect Mr Wilkinson explaining to Mr Rigge that he might request a Full Search be undertaken, with the usual conditions applying. In the first place, his guinea would be retained. Secondly, he must know that we have often to spend one or two months in finding a will; and thirdly there could be no guarantee of a successful outcome. Mr Rigge declined to request a search. Instead he asked whether he might himself look over the shelves to seek the will. At this, I once more intervened, explaining the total impossibility of allowing any member of the public to enter the actual repository. The Archbishop himself would not dare make such a request. Mr Rigge then suggested to Mr Wilkinson that he would probably return and 'try his luck' *(as he somewhat sardonically put it) at a later date. I need hardly say that, where the Registry is concerned, it is never a matter of luck, but of methodical work carried out by its servants in the face of the great impatience of so many of the enquirers.*

Whether Mr Rigge ever did return, I am presently unable to say. No subsequent entry appears in the Search Diary, but that in itself may not signify. There has been no opportunity to ask Mr Wilkinson whether he attended to Mr Rigge on any later date because that gentleman, long in a broken-down state of health owing to the demands made upon him in the Registry, has recently been incapacitated altogether from work, and I believe it unlikely that he will return to his post in the near future, if at all.

————

[**Mr Erskine's postscript to the above:** The inadequacy of Mr Myers' letter will be startling to any right-minded reader – any one, that is, who has not been so presumptuous as to seek a will at the Registry, which benighted warren we will be compelled to revisit.]

Diary of Fletcher Rigge, Monday November 19th.

The Cathedral bell was chiming two, and light snow – like so many feathers – was swirling, as I walked from the

Registry to Back Swinegate and the shop called Garencier. The streets were packed, as the Registry had been, and after my futile morning, I could see no prospect of discovering six significant people among twenty thousand.

Regarding the Registry, the obvious question is whether I was turned away innocently, or as a result of some conspiracy to conceal the will. I discovered that a clerk must always intermediate between the public and the wills, but whispers of corruption do surround the Registry. Perhaps the will was never deposited there? But then probate would not have been granted. Susan Harvey would not get her house. Had the Captain invited me to search for what he knew I would not find? For all his bravado, I am not inclined to think so.

As I stepped into the warm and perfumous interior of Garencier, the bell on the door tinkled. It did so very delicately, yet the pug came barking loudly from the rear. Hurst came up to shush the dog, by picking up and kissing it. The animal accepted this compliment begrudgingly, while continuing to growl at me, as I made a show of examining a bottle of something called Cordova Cream.

'For soaking and washing leather gloves,' Hurst said, indicating the bottle. He then recognised me: 'Weren't you the young gentleman who followed me home last night?'

'. . . Didn't mean to alarm you, sir; I was interested in the dog.'

'*The dog?* I think you mean Tum-Tum!'

'Delightful little fellow,' I said, as Tum-Tum broke into another fit of yapping.

'Thirty years ago,' Hurst said, above the din, 'the breed was almost lost. Imagine what a disaster that would have been! Note his tail,' he continued in a lower tone, the dog having quietened down again, 'the double curl.'

This, I thought, anticipated the shape of the faeces that would emerge from beneath it.

'And his legs,' Hurst continued. 'See how well under they are.'

It appeared that the appropriate place for a pug's legs was *beneath* the animal.

I contemplated the shop, which I consider preposterous. It sells most of the things the *belles* and *beaux* could require, including cosmetics such as Tincture of Pearls for removing freckles; perfumed water in various outlandish colours, but always called *Eau de Charm* ... soaps ... snuff, snuff boxes, hair powder. I almost gave a start when my eye fell on the slogan of a skin cream: 'Self-Preservation is the First Law of Nature.' The fate of my father suggests otherwise. (Once again I hear the gunshot echoing down the stairs of the house. I see myself racing *up* the stairs, entering the bedchamber, and seeing father slumped forward in a curious posture. That slight, sad-eyed man had been sitting cross-legged when he pulled the trigger, like some Hindoo of India.)

Hurst was inviting me to stroke the dog's ear. It was pleasantly velvety, like a fine quality slipper.

'The rose ear,' Hurst said, fondly. 'In harmony with the wrinkled face.'

'Charmingly . . . snub-nosed,' I ventured.

'*Retroussé*,' Hurst corrected.

'It . . . he . . . has somewhat the aspect of a bulldog,' I suggested.

Hurst shook his head primly. 'The pug is the very reverse of that savage race.'

We were standing by the window display, which meant we were only about four feet from the window itself. This commanded a good view of the bright and snow-dusted street and – the window being bowed – the view went on a little way forward and behind, with the result that I saw people parading in an arc: a succession of low hats and high coat collars.

The pug wriggled in Hurst's arms.

'I wonder at the origin of the name,' I said, and indeed I really had done. 'Something to do with the Latin *pugnus*: a fist?' (For the profile of the head is somewhat like a clenched fist.)

'I call that learned nonsense,' said Hurst. 'I believe a pug is so called because he is short and thick-set. It is the kind of name given to anything that is tenderly loved. Note the mole and three hairs,' Hurst ran on, indicating the dog's cheek, 'those are specified by the Pug Dog

Club . . . The neck is not an important part of his anatomy.'

It certainly was not.

'They are noted for cleanliness,' Hurst added. 'They have no smell.'

But you wouldn't smell a dog in that place if it *did* smell, I thought, the shop being so complicatedly odiferous.

It was time to get on to the pug Harvey had painted. I contemplated bringing the shade in question from my coat pocket, and asking Hurst, 'Do you know this dog?' But having decided not to make any linkage between my questions and the murder of Harvey, I proceeded elliptically:

'How many pugs are there in York, do you think?'

'I couldn't possibly say. Not many. You must consult the stud books.'

'They are more often black, I believe.'

'Yes, or half black. Smuttiness is a *very* common fault . . . the black of the mask leaking down along the body.'

'Whereas this . . .'

'Tum-Tum is his name.'

'Tum-Tum, yes. He's sort of . . . yellowish.'

I knew this to be the wrong word even as it passed my lips, and I might not have spoken it out loud, had I not just then spied a certain interesting person walking past the window. He was a young-ish man; he wore a periwig tied back with a dark ribbon. His greatcoat had buttonholes on the lapel turn. He had not much chin.

'Yellowish?!' Hurst was exclaiming. 'Tum-Tum is *apricot fawn*!'

'Of course, not really *yellowish*,' I said, still watching the passing figure. 'What I meant to say was . . .' Here, I hesitated. What *had* I intended to say?

The chinless young man would soon arrive at the kink in the street, whereon he would disappear entirely, very likely forever. I could only see his back now. He had a rather proud, strutting walk – somewhat chicken-like – and his elbows were overanimated. When I forced myself to turn away from the window, I saw that Hurst's face was very close to my own, and that he was waiting expectantly. The fellow combed his eyebrows, I noticed; either that or they grew vertically. He no doubt sold eyebrow combs in his absurd emporium.

'I was about to say . . . *light* . . . *caramel*,' I extemporised, which apparently mollified Hurst, for the eyebrows seemed to relax. I craned towards the window. The chinless man had come to a halt just before the kink. He was inspecting a shop window, evidently a boot maker's, for a giant boot depended from a kind of gibbet above him.

As the pug recommenced yapping, I embarked – I regret to say – on an out-and-out lie:

'Mr Hurst, I would like to possess one of these charming creatures. Do you know where I could obtain an apricot fawn pug dog puppy?'

'I know of only one other light-coloured pug in the vicinity,' Hurst began ... but now the cursed shop bell tinkled again, admitting a pernickety-looking woman. Hurst bowed to her, and she nodded back curtly.

'I'm told you sell Essence of Myrrh,' she said, 'for preserving the teeth.'

Hurst now commenced what threatened to be a prolonged exchange with the lady about teeth. I looked again through the window. The chinless man was still in sight, but a brewer's cart was approaching from the extreme right. Ten-to-one that would force the man to move aside, so continuing his walk, and taking him away from me. I couldn't be sure whether he was the man Harvey had painted. There must be plenty of young fellows with weak chins in York – more than there were white pug dogs certainly, and Hurst had not yet yielded up the important intelligence regarding any such creatures. Therefore I ought to wait for Hurst to put his hands on the Essence of Myrrh.

He had now retreated into an ante-room to find it.

I remained at the window. The cart had indeed dislodged the chinless man, and he was moving away, as Hurst returned from his ante-room, holding a paper packet (along with Tum-Tum). He was showing the contents to the customer, who was nodding, acknowledging that this was indeed the correct essence; but still their conclave continued.

'Now it ought really to be kept in a rosewood box lined with tinfoil . . .' Hurst was saying, and a search for such an article was obviously about to commence. But no! For Hurst exclaimed, '*Comme ça!*' He had located the right box, in the window. As Hurst reached in to pick it up, I laid a hand on his sleeve.

'The light-coloured pug, sir.'

'Yes, yes,' said Hurst. '*Un moment*, if you please. I am in the middle of . . .'

I re-doubled the grand manner I had affected. 'I am in rather a hurry, sir. I require only the name.'

'The Kendalls,' said Hurst, annoyed. 'They have a new house at Clifton Green, directly opposite to the horse trough. You know the spot, I'm sure. They have a certain Swizzle.'

'What?'

'A dog called Swizzle.'

'It is light-coloured?'

'*He* is a light drab, yes. Or stone.'

'And are there any daughters in the family?'

'Two young ladies, yes.' Hurst hesitated. 'And I'll thank you to keep my name out of it, sir . . . Come to that,' he continued after a pause, 'I would advise you to tread very carefully yourself. They're a pretty queer lot, the Kendalls.'

I gave a bow – wasted, since Hurst had already turned his back on me – and dashed into the street. I ran beyond the kink and a moment later I was clear of Back Swinegate altogether and standing at a loss in the next street, Stonegate. Skelton's Bookshop lay immediately to the right. The Cathedral bells were beginning to chime en masse, as a new snowfall commenced, and the pedestrians increased their speed, all these events seeming somehow interconnected. I looked the other way, and there was the chinless man, walking cross-wise to the main flow of pedestrians; walking – in fact – in a circle, much to the irritation of those intersecting with him. He held a paper in his hand, and was muttering to himself, heedless of the snow falling on him. At a certain point in his perambulation he came face-on to me, and I saw that his cravat knot was of the wide and flamboyant sort called the Osbaldeston. I also noted that his black waistcoat, like his top-coat, was of a peculiar cut, being much vented and buttonholed. Everything was overelaborated. He had a long, rapidly tapering face, somewhat old-fashioned ... But now he had turned away again.

As I looked on, the chinless man unwound himself from his orbit, moving quickly towards the west end of Stonegate, where he turned into Blake Street. I hurried after him, along Blake Street and into the place called St Leonard's, where he passed the old, half-ruined hospital, and came to the building by which all – or at any rate a good deal – might be explained.

Fletcher Rigge, in continuation.

The York Theatre Royal always puts me in mind of a cluster of outsized churches. On the snowy Green alongside stood the horse that is somehow connected with the theatre. In between Green and theatre lies a covered walkway. The chinless man entered it, and I followed, my boots rattling on the flags; but the chinless man did not so much as give a glance behind him. Theatre-goers promenade here during the interludes, drinking burnt wine and eating sweetmeats; and here too is the office for the purchase of box tickets. I spied some silhouettes painted on a playbill. It advertised a performance of shadow puppets. Chinless, who had paid it no attention, was now making an enquiry at the box office. He gave a rather bitter laugh at the response (whatever it might have been) before proceeding with a proprietorial air, stopping every now and again to declaim something possibly Shakespearean. He was making for a propped-open door that I – having been in the theatre once or twice – had never remarked before. It proved to lead into the principal auditorium.

As I followed the chinless man through the door, I heard the banging of the box office door. The clerk, bespectacled, wearing a small squirrel wig and with a cash box under his arm, had emerged, and was falling into step alongside me.

'Sir,' he was saying, 'the theatre is presently closed . . .'

In the auditorium, another, rougher-looking man was engaged in picking up debris from the pit: rotten apples and oranges, hunks of bread, broken bottles. The viewing boxes on either side seemed incredibly vertiginous with no crowd in attendance: two towers of babel, decked with discarded food. The whole place smelt of paint. On the stage were the remains of an Arcadian scene – a couple of primitive wooden trees. (Well, trees *are* wooden, I confusedly thought.) A great barn door (usually hidden by scenery, and, I supposed, kept shut) stood exposed and open, revealing falling snow and a high brick wall. That unfamiliar visitor, daylight, came in from there; also coldness.

The chinless man was walking, declaiming, through the auditorium. I watched as he departed through another door, which banged behind him as he disappeared from view – banged so emphatically that I put my question to the clerk in the past tense:

'Be so good as to tell me, sir: who was he?'

'That gentleman, sir?' he said. 'Well now . . . This is not Liberty Hall, sir. The public are not allowed in here outside the performance times.'

'Then he is not a member of the public?' I asked, indicating the door through which the man had departed.

'No, sir, but *you* are.'

I took a coin from the pocket of my breeches. I had been trying to fish out a shilling, but had got hold of half a sovereign. I gave it to the clerk anyway, who regarded it as though stunned. He seemed to be revolving whether to put it in the cash box under his arm.

'The gentleman's name,' said the clerk, 'is Jeremiah Smith. Now can I ask your business?'

'He is an actor, I assume?' I said, thinking this would explain the declaiming and apparent lunacy.

The rubbish picker now spoke up, glad of an interruption to his drudgery, I supposed.

'En't he just,' he said. 'Member of the second Company here. The touring lot.'

I said I thought that the good old days of strolling and barn acting were all over.

'Not for him,' the rubbish picker called out, indicating the door through which the man had departed. 'He's a stroller all right ... Didn't you see the way he strolled through *here*?'

'What sort of an actor is he?' I enquired.

'What do you mean?' asked the clerk, with some asperity.

'A Garrick in the making?' I suggested.

'You will find a uniformly high standard in this—'

'He's *loud*,' offered the rubbish picker. 'There was a near riot in here last night – above a joke, it was – fruit raining down, pint bottles ... quart bottles ... but you could hear young Smith clear as a bell.'

'But you said he was a stroller.'

The clerk, clearly irritated at the interventions of the

81

rubbish picker, was now attempting to usher me towards the door. 'The tours are off, at present,' he said, 'on account of the weather. So he has a role here just now.'

'What's the play?' I asked.

'Never mind what it is,' said the clerk. 'It's coming off.'

A literal truth, for just then a third workman appeared, to remove one of the wooden trees from the stage.

'It must *have* a name,' the rubbish picker called out, 'but I'm blowed if I can remember what it is . . . Give you the jist of it, though.' He blew his nose before continuing. 'The fair Clarissa—'

'Celia,' the clerk corrected, testily.

'The fair Celia,' said the rubbish picker, 'is about to marry the villainous Squire Badger—'

'Sir George *Trifle*,' the clerk corrected again.

'When the faithful young . . . somebody-or-other—'

'Young Mr Lovermore,' said the clerk, exasperated. 'When *he* arrives disguised as a serving man—'

'A country clown, I thought it was,' said the rubbish picker, who by now had climbed onto the stage, and was frowning down at some particularly disgusting object. 'Bloody performing dogs,' he said.

I had got the picture: something along the lines of *She Stoops to Conquer*, by the estimable Goldsmith. Some pale imitation thereof.

'Smith,' said the clerk, 'is Young Mr Lovermore. Or should I say he *was*.'

'Because it's coming off?'

'Yes.'

'This fellow Smith,' I said, 'he would have been out of York in the Race Week, I suppose?'

Silence for a space; but I pursued my theme. 'He would have been tramping through the countryside in that week, I assume?'

'I would have to consult the diary,' said the clerk. 'But why is this of any—'

'The touring lot stay in York for the crowds then,' the rubbish picker put in. 'They'd have been down at the Cock Tavern, doing the—'

Just then a great crash came from beyond the door through which Smith had exited; then came another, this one redolent of splintering wood. These were accompanied by shouts.

'*What?* How now, sir!' came from a youthful-sounding man, presumably Smith. 'By God, I will knock you down, sir!' came from an older. There was then some bandying of the two words, 'That lady'. At issue appeared to be the question of whose lady she was.

The door burst open, and Jeremiah Smith reappeared, his long face now red, his cravat, coat and waistcoat disordered. He had acquired a cane, perhaps from the properties box. He swished it as he walked, disregarding all our stares, but it seemed to me that he was not unaware of those stares – he was an actor, after all – as he marched across the pit, kicking out at such of the debris as the rubbish picker had not yet collected up, and shouting, 'That *gentleman*! That *gentleman*!'

Apparently, he saw the necessity of embellishing this speech as he stomped diagonally through the auditorium: 'That *gentleman*! The very one who put me to trudging through the country like a gypsy, sleeping in a baggage wagon while the muse expires nightly in this place!'

I approached him, only to be waved aside. 'Out of my way, sir.'

'I would like to speak to you about—'

He raised the cane menacingly, and I was braced for a set-to. 'If you wish a consultation about a private reading, or an audition, or . . .' and here he paused briefly to assess me, apparently discerning some literary bent, ' . . . or an assessment of your play . . . kindly leave a message with Mr Hardcastle.' (He indicated the clerk.) 'There is a five shillings reading fee,' he added.

I spied a new-made cut above the left eye of this Smith, who resumed his walk, with further histrionics. 'That infernal Cork . . . who secures the failure of all works he is associated with! Stale plays and stale performances! Takes all the witty things away!' At this he smashed his cane against one of the pillars that supports the lower gallery. It broke clean in two, the end of it skittering over towards where I stood. Smith pitched the other end away. He then marched out through the door, clattering along the flags of the walkway, heading out into the darkening city.

In the shocked silence that followed, I recollected the following: a man named Cork, manager of this theatre, had been a friend of shade-maker Harvey. He had been one of the few mourners at his funeral. Jeremiah Smith was clearly at odds with this Cork. It appeared that he had, indeed, come to blows with him only a minute before.

I turned to Hardcastle and suggested as much. He seemed lost for any answer, eventually mumbling, '... An artistic disagreement.' It seemed to me that Jeremiah Smith had certainly wanted to give that impression, but there had been a hollow ring to his protestations. I thought of the miniature portrait Smith had commissioned from Matthew Harvey. It had been of the kind fitted for insertion into a locket: a gift to a lover.

I asked Hardcastle, 'Is Smith a married man, sir?'

The question echoed, but there came no echoing reply, merely a look of mortification, not only from the clerk but also, I saw, from the rubbish picker.

Notwithstanding, I put another: 'And Mr Cork? He has a wife, I assume?' which did earn a reply of sorts from Hardcastle:

'I must ask you to take your leave, sir. This is not Liberty Hall.'

'You have already told me that, sir,' I said.

He advanced towards me, holding out the half sovereign.

'It is quite impossible for me to accept this,' he said.

'Put it in your money box, sir,' I said, 'consider it a donation to the theatre.'

'All donations must be accompanied by a letter,' said this fellow, who was about the least theatrical 'theatrical' I have ever encountered.

I took the proffered coin, only to pitch it, spinning, towards the rubbish picker, who caught it overhanded. Making a formal bow to each in turn, I quit the building.

Mr Erskine's prefatory note, concerning a letter he received from Mr Bob Richmond.

A week after the denouement we are working towards, I received a letter from Mr Bob Richmond, sometime colleague of Rigge's at Skelton's Bookshop. It details the visit Rigge made to the shop – the place of his former employment – in the early evening of the Monday with which we are concerned. Richmond also disclosed a further action of his, performed some three weeks after the visit, and I have reserved that account until its appropriate chronological place.

The account of the bookshop visit is effectually two letters, despatched together but written, I believe, some few hours apart. All has been presented in the smooth and seamless transcription of the excellent Mr Bright, but I noted on receipt of the originals that the handwriting of the second differs somewhat from the first, suggesting a greater urgency, a greater heat, as compared with the attempted restraint of the first – and perhaps also the consumption of a good deal of the port wine to which, for all their differences of character, young Richmond and young Rigge were equally partial.

Extract from a letter sent by Mr Bob Richmond, Bookseller's Assistant, to Mr Erskine, Attorney.

Skelton's Bookshop,
Stonegate,
York.

'Well, it sounds a Tom Fool errand to me,' I said, after Fletcher Rigge had described something of the queer undertaking he had set about. Whether he would have related any of it at all without my asking what he had been up to since his release from the Castle I cannot say. What I do say is that he disclosed the information not exactly grudgingly – Rigge was always too gentlemanly for that – but sparingly, so that he and I were in our usual roles: I the agitated petitioner, he the indulgent object of my fascination.

It was about half after five, and that gentleman and I were alone in Skelton's. Dark had fallen outside, but the shop – which would be open for another hour – blazed with the light of the hundred candles that I must keep lighted every single day of business. By one of these candles, Rigge was glancing over the first page of An Account of the Kingdom of Nepal, by a certain Colonel Kirkpatrick. The title is irrelevant, but I always remarked the books he picked *up, thinking I might learn something, for I was – to speak plainly – in awe of Rigge, which I resented most strongly, as will be seen.*

As you know, Skelton's shop is really one long, high room with bookshelves all along the lower walls, and two galleries of books overhanging on either side. One holds old books, the other new. The door to the street – Stonegate – is at one end, with the stone bible hanging above. On the evening in question, a good fire roared in the wide stone hearth at the other end. It always roared when 'Skinflint Skelton' was away, I made sure of that. There was one customer in the shop just then, a man in a patched black coat who prowled the upper gallery. He was a well-known impoverished bibliopolist, name of Martin Andrew.

Rigge and I sat at the long table that ran down the middle of the room. We had dishes of tea before us.

'I believe I've heard of this Captain Harvey,' I said, continuing in the soft tone we had been using, to prevent the bibliopolist from hearing.

'Heard what?' said Rigge in his usual, languid sort of way, now picking up a History of Scotland that – as he remarked – Skelton had seen fit to price at two shillings, even though the boards were falling off.

'Some pretty scandalous reports,' I said.

I own there was a deal of bluff here, for, while I knew Harvey had the name of a reprobate, I could not have said exactly why.

Rigge probably guessed that I was bluffing, but he did not stoop to say so, or to answer my remark. He now caught up a sermon that some vicar had paid Skelton five guineas to print: An Address to the York Methodists. *He began reading it – and he would read faster than any man I ever met. At length, irritated by his silence, I asked his opinion of the work.*

'Seems to be an opinionated fellow,' he said, turning the pages, '... bigoted as well as opinionated, for it appears he's telling the Methodists to leave off Methodism ...'

I was provoked into asking about his confinement in the Castle: 'What was it like ... in the clink, I mean?'

'Pretty disagreeable.'

'Well, I'm mightily pleased to see you at large,' I said, which was not strictly true, but Rigge nodded his thanks. We two were friends in theory, but Rigge knew I resented his gentlemanly credentials. He must also have known I would have taken a measure of satisfaction in his confinement for a large debt.

He picked up another volume. The title amused him for he read out loud, 'A Treatise on the Culture of the Pine-Apple and the Management of the Hot-House, Together with a description of every type of insect that infest Hot-Houses, with effectual methods of destroying them. The second edition, with additions. By William Speechly.'

'You're to be a sort of thief-taker for this Captain,' I observed. 'You don't want to acquire the name of an informer, you know.'

Rigge merely nodded, infuriatingly.

'You'll do well to carry a pistol,' I said, although to the best of my knowledge Rigge possessed no such article, the guns belonging to his father having all gone the same way as the family house and lands.

'And now you'll to London?' I said, for he'd told me that part of the commission.

He nodded.

'It's the dearest season,' I continued, just as if I'd ever visited London myself. 'Parliament still sitting; all the main families in town. Have you a letter of introduction to this author fellow? I don't see that he'll entertain you if not. That's if you get to London at all, because the roads'll be in a pretty shocking—'

Rigge stood up. It seemed he'd recollected the reason he'd called into the shop.

'Do we have anything by Gowers?' he asked, and we both took up candles and prowled around the shop for the next five minutes. (During which time Martin Andrew took his leave, no doubt having read whatever chapter or poem he'd been after without troubling to make a purchase, as was his wont.)

I myself discovered the book by Gowers that Rigge had mentioned: The Reasons, Plainly Stated, Why Not to Purchase the Works of Samuel Johnson. It had been poorly printed in London, with the cheapest marbling, and the type too faint. Rigge ignited a spill and lit several more candles to inspect it, I looking over his shoulder as he did so. On the title page, a little engraving appeared beneath the author's name:

91

a jewel, with lines emerging from it to indicate radiance.
Yet the jewel was coloured-in; shown as black, in other
words. Rigge flicked through the pages, reading out passages
at random. It proved to be one long assault on that other,
better-known, Samuel.

"If Sam Johnson," Rigge read out loud, "had held his pen
as well as he held his bottle, what a charming hand would
have been observed." Or, "When his little phase of notoriety
has passed, he will be seen in his proper perspective."

'Vicious, en't he?' I said. 'I shouldn't be in the least
surprised if he had killed that poor painter.'

The thought that Fletcher Rigge might be heading for a
dangerous encounter in London so cheered me that I said,
'Fancy a tipple, Fletch? Skelton can spare a jug of claret, I
reckon.'

As I made towards the cellar, Rigge called after me, 'How
do you fancy the Monday Assembly?'

I hesitated. 'What day's today?'

'Monday,' said he, 'all day', which was a typical Rigge
remark. Droll, I suppose you'd call it.

I paused at the cellar door. 'I'd been thinking of going,' I
said, 'but Skelton docked me two shillings last week. I spilt
tea on an octavo Samson Agonistes. So I'm a bit short of the
readies.'

'I'll sub you,' said Rigge, and I recalled that he had been
paid an advance by Captain Harvey.

'Well now,' I said, 'it's hardly fair to ask—'

'You haven't asked,' said Rigge, *magnanimous and maddening as ever.*

'Then I accept,' I said. 'That's d----d civil of you, Fletch. And we'll start the festivities with a little wine, shall we?'

Bob Richmond, in continuation.

At half after six, I locked the shop door, and turned to face the thousands of silent, sleeping books. Authorship in these times is not a very exclusive club, and yet it has always seemed that membership was barred to your humble servant, while Fletcher Rigge had been invited to apply at his earliest convenience; and when he had shown no enthusiasm for joining, he had been positively dragged across the threshold.

It irritated me no end that he should have written his books for Skelton with such disdain, as though he'd been put to sweeping out a grate . . . And to have knocked them out so speedily, in despite of those prolonged interludes when he would barely move or speak, but simply sit staring into a fire, a dish of cold tea on his lap, sunk in some deep – but no doubt poetical – mortification, the likes of which a mere Bob Richmond could never hope to understand. 'Languishing', that's what it's called in the literary circles.

I began snuffing out the candles in the shop interior, cursing myself for having accepted from Rigge the price of admission to the Assembly. All evening, I would be out-danced and out-dressed, and all under the eyes of Miss Lucy Spink. We were competitors for her, not that Rigge knew it. He would never have entertained the idea of me as a rival. Even now, he would be reclaiming his dancing pumps from Bulmer's the pawnbroker's. Or he would be pressing his best shirt with a smoothing glass. He would do this in a tea tray placed over his washstand, for I'd seen him about the task in his lodge on Ogleforth.

I own that I would like to have put all of his d----d finery on the dunghill by Layerthorpe Bridge. Or I would have burned them on that bonfire of shavings that smoulders perpetually on the opposite bank. I would have burned the dancing pumps first. Rigge would not wear boots to a dance like any ordinary Yorkist. He maintained that anyone doing so looked as though they had left their horse outside. But for all the rest of the time, he aspired to look as though he had done exactly that, affecting, by his looks and manner, to have returned from a run with the York Harriers.

If I, Bob Richmond, am a mere demi-beau, then Rigge was a demi-squire; or not even that. Yes, he was born on a large farm. Very well then, an estate. Yes, he had been away to some pretty grand school or other in the Midlands. But he had been at the University only for a term, so that he had not been able to write 'M.A. Cantab' on the title page of the books he had written for Skelton, and would not be able to do

94

so until he returned to complete his degree, or got an honorary one. (You see, I looked into all this.) But Rigge probably wouldn't have written 'M.A. Cantab' even if he had been so entitled. It would not have been quite gentlemanly, by his code.

I moved over to the window, snuffing out the short candles, and lighting the batons that would display the books through the night, also illuminating the window cards, such as the one reading, 'Periodicals and new publications secured with expedition.' That card, sir, was the bane of my life. 'Secured with expedition by Bob Richmond,' it ought to read, 'no matter what else he might have on hand at the time.'

Then there was the card reading, 'Wanted: A Youth of Character', advertising for Rigge's replacement. A number of applications had been received, none satisfactory to Skelton. I moved the card to a more prominent place. It was imperative that Skelton should take on another assistant before he relented and re-employed Fletcher Rigge. The ideal applicant for the post, from my own point of view, would be a reading man – for the sake of decent conversation – but not by any means another writing man. Not that I thought it very likely that Rigge would be re-engaged, having been imprisoned for debt.

I crossed back to the long table, where I drained off the last of the claret I'd shared with Rigge. I am not generally one for boozing, but I planned to sink at least another bottle at the Assembly, all refreshments being included in the ticket price. I mention this simply to show the tormenting effect Rigge had upon me. I was curious to see how Miss Lucy Spink would react to seeing him again, in light of his sojourn in the Castle. She had surely heard of it, and if she had not then he would surely tell her, being all for plain-speaking in his apparently honest, and yet I believed artful, way.

The shop was now pretty dark, aside from the yellow glow from the window, and the redness of the fire. My last job of the day was to bank it up, as instructed by Skelton, who bemoaned the cost, but a bookshop must perforce be heated, against that dangerous enemy, mildew. It had often occurred to me that if Skelton's shop burned down one night . . . well, that would be perfectly explicable: a spilled coal from an overloaded grate. Or the soot might catch in the chimney, for Skelton got the sweep in too infrequently, and would not fork out for fire insurance, so no engine would come. Perhaps it might be thought that Rigge had burnt it down, as revenge for his dismissal?

Yes, Mr Erskine, it is all most unbecoming, and don't think I don't know it. But this all goes to show that Rigge had far too great a hold on my imagination, while I was perfectly certain that he hardly thought of me at all. Standing alone there in the darkness, I felt myself to be a creature of darkness, a benighted soul, and so, I fear, it would prove.

Diary of Fletcher Rigge, entry for Monday November 19th, resumed.

Amid the innocuous chattery preceding the Assembly, I had heard a young woman exclaim, 'This is elegance! This is taste!' Well, she had been *very* young, and small (almost entirely enveloped by her own robe); also, no doubt, a newcomer. It was an ordinary Monday Assembly; the dandy set of York, nothing more or less. The dancing is always fairly conducted, the people are always decently dressed. But the flambeaux in the portico smoked badly as Bob Richmond and I approached.

Bob – a little boozy, I thought – was marching through the icy snow in his boots, whereas I was rather picking my way in my kid-skin pumps. (I well know that Bob Richmond disapproves of these shoes, and I in turn reprehended his red and green waistcoat, but of course nothing was said on either side.) He does not seem any better suited to life in a bookshop than any spirited young man ought to be. It seems to have turned him pettish.

The principal Assembly Room itself seemed smaller than I remembered it, perhaps because the dance floor, illuminated by a dozen swaying chandeliers and bounded by marble pillars (it is the very height of the Grecian taste), is margined in darkness. Here stood the servants, giving attendance to the dancers, or simply looking on, which they are not supposed to do. To commence proceedings, a Miss Somebody-or-Other – daughter of *Sir* Somebody-or-Other – danced a bolero, and did it pretty well, but with occasional cross expressions fired at the band, who were not yet quite in tune. I ended by feeling rather sorry for her, and so applauded all the harder.

Here indeed was the 'pink of the ton'. Merchants, manufacturers, squires, squire-parsons (a busybody class, of whom there are too many on the Justices' benches), and more down below, gaming in the undercroft. Soon after my arrival, a whisper buzzed through the Rooms at the arrival of a party who'd looked surly and disaffected enough to be truly fashionable. It proved merely the family of a bishop, yet minus the actual bishop, as a second, more contemptuous wave of whispers testified.

Occasionally, a face in the crowd gazed back at me. I received some cautious, grave inclinations of the head from men who had known my father, and what had befallen him. Presumably they felt themselves unable to encompass with sufficient delicacy not only the suicide of the father, but the imprisonment of the son, for none of them came up to me. Suicide is ill-mannered, perhaps also contagious. Therefore I myself might be dangerous, for perhaps the madness runs in the blood of the family.

Bob Richmond had gone seeking wine, and I had not yet set eyes on Miss Spink, but new people were coming in all the time.

The opening dance was a quadrille. I turned aside, to observe it being conducted on the walls of the room — conducted by shadows, which flowed over the niches of those walls. I saw the shadow of a chinless man revolving, but it was not that theatrical youth, Jeremiah Smith. I saw a young woman of real, floating grace, but it was not Miss Spink; and then my eye fell on the shadow of a man *not* dancing; he leant on a cane. I turned sharply about to verify the seemingly impossible. Captain Harvey amid the dandy set? But no; merely a grinning *demi-beau* with a bandaged foot.

I felt the tap of a fan on my shoulder. I turned about and saw the wife of one of my father's gaming friends. They had an estate somewhere west of York. She said, 'And how fares young Mr Rigge?' only to walk on, not waiting for an answer, doubtless because she *knew* the answer.

Still no sign of Miss Spink; but she never missed an Assembly, as far as I knew. I thought of a worse eventuality than her non-appearance: her appearance in company with an eligible male.

I was in need of port wine. I strode along the margins of the dance, passing the watching and gossiping servants. I heard the loud bucks, bantering over the music: 'Confounded flirt . . . Needn't have bothered coming . . . It'll perk up at about ten . . .'

I entered the refreshment room, where the vapour of

warm wine contended with that of cinnamon, coffee and tobacco. I took a glass – and then I saw Miss Spink. She was at the far end of the refreshments table, with her sister, Jenny. They wore simple, white muslin gowns with sashes, Lucy's blue, Jenny's red – two pocket Venuses, or idealised emanations from the French Revolution. Their chestnut-coloured hair was teased into bouncing ringlets. Her father and mother were also present, together with a wiry, bald man I did not know.

Miss Spink saw me, and seemed to take a deep breath. My own heart was pounding, as though I'd just that minute left off dancing. Surely this was a momentous glance on both sides. But then the people with her closed around her, as though sealing her off from me. But Miss Spink still looked fixedly towards me as those environing her seemed to become involved in an animated discussion of which I was clearly the subject. 'You will come away this minute,' I fancied – or perhaps merely imagined – I heard her mother say. Then came a most unexpected development: the human barricade dissolved, and Lucy, smiling, commenced walking towards me. It was a moment of such piercing pleasure as to be almost an assault, and I was quite confounded.

She gave me her hand; I bowed.

'We haven't seen each other for four months,' she said, 'and yet you seemed on the point of darting away from me.'

'I thought your people might object to our meeting.'

'I don't see why they would object.'

'Because I was lately in gaol, perhaps?'

'You have lost nothing of your former gaiety, I see,' she said, smiling, almost laughing. She had such a lot of light in her eyes. Her ears, half hidden by the ringlets, were slightly too large, and therefore perfect.

'My father is a respectable man, would you not agree?'

I agreed: her father (who, I perceived over Lucy's shoulder, was speaking to the little bald man, with occasional glances thrown our way) owned some very opulent furniture shops, and had a mansion on Wellington Row.

'And do you know how many of my father's friends have become a little overextended, requiring a short stay in the same place you were in?'

'None, I should think.'

'Two. And do you suppose he disowns them now that their difficulty is passed? Has it occurred to you, Mr Rigge, that your time in the Castle might come to seem a very trifling interlude?'

'If it is succeeded by a great many worse things, you mean?'

'A great many better, is what I meant. I know that's fantastically improbable.'

In the dancing room, the Master of Ceremonies was announcing a quadrille.

'I suppose we should have a little hop,' said Lucy, smiling. She was suggesting that we dance, I believe, but she was also, by that particular phrase, invoking the circumstances of our first acquaintance.

———————

It was about a year ago, my father lately dead, my own heavy season just beginning. Vaguely apprehending my want of spirits, a fellow called Tom Milner, who had been at the University with me, had invited me to his place at Pocklington. Milner's father is an extensive farmer, and Tom – a very amiable fellow – knew all the country people east of York.

On that sunny Saturday morning, horses had been announced soon after breakfast, and our party of about a dozen commenced driving about in three carriages, with Tom at the helm; and yet he had no fixed aim for the day. We called in at some houses, sometimes collecting their occupants, including Miss Spink (with whom I fell in love the instant she climbed into the carriage). At the next house, there was a re-arrangement, causing her to move directly next to me, and so, for the remainder of the day, all my troubles were forgotten. I entered a magical realm: everything out of perspective. The houses we visited, connected by dusty white roads, all closer together than they ought to have been, just as Miss Spink – frequently turning to speak to me with a great ardency – was closer than I had any right to expect. But while the houses came up quickly, we sometimes seemed to rumble through orchards that lasted for miles (it was all unenclosed land) and the butterflies flitting among the trees seemed amazingly large.

Tom's principal aim had been to reach the house of some people who, we were informed by a servant on pulling up in their driveway, were out on a jaunt of their own. Tom then fixed on the idea of visiting a Mrs Aspinall, who turned out to be a tiny widow sitting in a circle of her unpromising elderly friends in the back parlour of a tumbledown cottage.

A little collation was served out, and everything was meant to be serious but nothing was. The conversation went in fits and starts. One man kept taking snuff, and trying not to sneeze. Another – a man of about seventy, who wore a threadbare wig of a greenish shade, and was clearly in some way Mrs Aspinall's adversary – kept proposing a musical interlude.

Mrs Aspinall said, 'I do wish you would drop the subject, Mr Lazenby, the spinette's locked.'

'Can you not unlock it?'

'With what?'

'The key.'

'The key is lost.'

Mr Lazenby left the room at a certain point and Mrs Aspinall said, 'Who wants music? We will put it to a vote. I am obliged to warn you that Mr Lazenby has brought his contra-bassoon.'

The vote was taken and the motion for music was passed, by a majority, Mrs Aspinall observed, 'of all those who have never heard Mr Lazenby perform'.

When Mr Lazenby returned, Mrs Aspinall reluctantly unlocked the spinette, taking no trouble to disguise the fact that the key had been about her person all along. Throughout these proceedings, Lucy Spink kept shooting me looks of the most delightful humorous incredulity.

The contra-bassoon – a sort of black drainpipe with sinuous attachments – was sent for, and Mr Lazenby took up a position next to Mrs Aspinall, who made one last attempt to dissuade him from playing. 'Mr Lazenby,' she said, 'I have taken the trouble to learn an instrument that provides its own harmony.'

But he was quite undeterred, and when Mrs Aspinall embarked on some slow bagatelle, he commenced a wandering accompaniment of extraordinarily low and mournful notes, at the conclusion of which everybody clapped, and a petite young woman said, 'Might I sing, mama?' thereby revealing herself to be Mrs Aspinall's daughter.

After a conference with her mother, from which Mr Lazenby and his bassoon were forcibly excluded, she commenced some ballad, but it was obviously awry.

Lucy Spink, favouring me with a look of the most picturesque alarm, whispered, 'I fear she has started on the wrong note.'

Gravely shaking my head (I had already divined that Miss Spink enjoyed mordancy, as complimenting her own exuberance) I said, 'I'm afraid she's set off in the wrong *key*, and that will not be so easily corrected.'

It *was* corrected, with a sudden plunge (Miss Aspinall had been too high), which caused Miss Spink to gasp, and involuntarily grab my knee in mortification, at which I merely raised an eyebrow, thereby, it seemed, compounding the hilarity. Mrs Aspinall made no comment on her daughter's performance, but uttered the famous words, 'I suppose we should have a little hop.'

There followed one of the happiest interludes of my life. The wine began to flow; a carriage brought new, and younger, people; Mrs Aspinall proved herself a fine rhythmical player – and a loud one in spite of her diminutive size – while Mr Lazenby's elephantine grace notes pointed up the joyful comedy of the dancing, in which Lucy Spink was my constant partner.

――――――

After these happy reminiscences, we stepped through to the main room of the Assembly, where quadrilles had given way to country dances. There are no cards with the country dances. It is simply a matter of getting the attention of the Master of Ceremonies. It was the York Maggot that was about to be called. Three couples only were required, and several were jostling about, waiting to be called, but Lucy Spink was actually whispering in the dancing master's ear, requiring her to stand on tiptoe. It was very touching to see the discrepancy in their heights, and perhaps the dancing master thought so too, for he now called me forward at Miss Spink's behest, and we were in the dance, albeit separated to begin with.

I would be in the couple designated 'first'; Miss Spink was in the third. Her opening partner – I saw with indignation – was Bob Richmond. He had sheered off from me the moment we entered the Rooms, but I had glimpsed him looking grimly over as I spoke to Miss Spink in the other room. My own first partner was a rather too tall and white-painted woman. But no matter, because by the scheme of the York Maggot, the first man and third woman converge more often than any other two.

There was a moment of anticipatory silence, as when somebody is about to sneeze; but it was the entire Assembly that was anticipating. This was the optimum moment: enough drink taken, but not too much, and for the first time in the evening, the two fiddle players in the band stood up from their chairs. They smiled at each other and, with a laughing swoop, began to play.

I held the hands of the first female, and we began to turn. We cast down the middle, my two hands in hers, where they surely belonged, and we were both turning and smiling, and Miss Spink, indeed, was *laughing*. She was such a small person; she would be so very easy to enfold or enclose.

We cast down the middle again, and I would like to have danced her through the main door and out of the Assembly altogether, but we must turn again, and now I was *not* holding Miss Spink's hand, but that of some other person. It bothered me greatly when Miss Spink was at the opposite end of the line, as much as five yards away. The scowls that Bob Richmond flashed my way bothered me much less. All the same, it was a good thing the York Maggot did not require me to hold the hand of Bob Richmond. He must be sweet on Lucy Spink. That would explain a good deal.

Two turns later, she and I were together again; I was grinning at her in a manner positively imbecilic, and the York Castle was quite banished ... But then she was far away ... And yet now beginning to return ...

As we moved, I watched the dancing, bobbing shadows – all continuing safe, none resembling the shades painted by Matthew Harvey; none signifying a person I must confront, and who would surely want to confront me, if they knew the task I had undertaken. I glimpsed Miss Spink's father in the watching crowd.

I could not read his expression. It was certainly not one of unalloyed delight, but that might not signify. He had a naturally frowning face, being a thin, pale, handsome but predatory-looking man; a sort of white hawk of a man.

The music was finished amid loud applause. I came off the dance floor by Miss Spink's side – we were the only pair to go off together. Her family – and the mysterious small, bald man – were all within a close radius, again flicking glances towards the two of us, the meaning of which I could not make out.

'Do you realise you are perpetually talked about, Mr Rigge?'

'That is what I feared.'

'I believe you are now off on another adventure?'

'What do you mean by another?'

'You are to London?'

'Only for a few days. But how do you know?'

'Bob Richmond, from the bookshop, told me.'

'When?'

'Just now. When we lined up for the dance. He said you are to undertake a secret mission for a certain crippled Captain. A man who lives in First Water Lane. He paid your debt, or some of it . . . Can that really be right, and how can somebody from First Water Lane afford it?'

I was glad that she doubted Bob Richmond's word, even if what he'd said happened to be true.

'I'm going to London to interview a man on behalf of . . . a certain Captain, yes.'

'And who is he, exactly?'

'He is not known to the world at large.'

'And it is a secret mission?'

'Evidently not,' I said, at which moment I glimpsed Bob Richmond out of the tail of my eye. He shot me a darkling glance before turning away.

'Well,' said Miss Spink, 'I knew you wouldn't be doing anything as tedious as . . .'

'As what?'

'Teaching Latin. Going for long walks. Practising moderation and economy. You have gone from writing romances to living one out, Mr Rigge.'

'I never wrote a romance.'

'But you are forever scribbling. Are you sure you didn't toss one off under a *nom de guerre*?'

'*Nom de plume*. A *nom de guerre* is a name under which a man fights.'

'Well, perhaps that's exactly what I meant.'

'Only you can say what you meant, Miss Spink.'

'I have every confidence, Mr Rigge, that you need not rely on the benefactions – if indeed that is a word – of this lame Captain. I know that by your own efforts, you can dispel your present troubles, but you must believe it; you must believe there can be a termination in gladness.'

'Well, I am notoriously optimistic, as you know.'

She fluttered her fan for a while, looking all around the room, raising the awful possibility that our conversation, absurd though it certainly was, might be on the point of termination. But having nodded to a couple of friends in far corners of the Assembly, Miss Spink asked, 'Now, Mr Rigge, do tell me, is there any news at all of your father's estate?'

'It is no longer my father's estate,' I said. 'For the

moment, it is in the hands of my father's steward, Mr Knight. But it will soon be the possession of Mr Corrigan, who is probably gaming down below. My father's solicitor, Mr Pullman, has transferred the deeds.'

'But that cannot be countenanced. Surely something will happen to prevent it?'

I smiled, making no reply, and reflecting that Miss Spink appears to regard my life as a sixpenny romance ... in which case would not the recovery of the estate make a fitting end to it? (Is it possible she sees herself by my side at that 'termination in gladness'?)

'Do tell again,' she said, 'the story of your father and the terrible man who built the wall. I was saying to my sister that it was like the fable of Robert the Bruce and the spider in reverse, but I couldn't quite recollect the details.'

'Sir Patrick Procter ...' I began.

'Who lived next door to you, so to speak?'

'His place was about five miles off, yes ... About fifteen years ago, he made his park and enclosed it with a wall, so obstructing a right of way between two villages on my father's estate and the road to York. Once a year my father, attended by some men from the village, would take his coach, come up to the wall and pull it down before driving through the breach.'

'Pull it down?'

'It was made of loose stone.'

'Very good. Then what?'

'Then they'd all go off to the inn, and get drunk.'

'All except your father?'

'No, him as well.'

'While Sir Patrick . . . ?'

' . . . Built the wall back up again.'

'And how do things stand today?'

'The wall is built up. There's no one to knock it down.'

'But the right of way?'

'It fell into desuetude.'

'Then how do the villagers get to York?'

'Oh. By another road.'

She looked down at her slipper-like shoes, smiling. 'What a sad diminuendo – don't you dare say that's the wrong word, by the way – and how very typical of the speaker.'

She turned; her sister was at her side. The family, it appeared, were departing, and Lucy Spink was being fetched away.

'I am sorry, Mr Rigge, but my sister has the vapours, and must go directly to bed.'

'What are the vapours?'

'Something my sister has when a certain idiotic boy called Jack Bennworth is not at the Assembly.'

'Do you still go along the New Walk on Thursdays?'

'I was just about to tell you that I do. Thursdays with my mother, who has excellent hearing, Fridays with my aunt, who is deaf – which is so very unfortunate,' she added.

111

I smiled, and Miss Spink hit me quite hard on the arm with her fan. 'I don't know what is so amusing!' she said.

But we understood each other very well, and it was settled that I would be walking along the river a week on Friday, in order to be accidentally discovered by Miss Spink and her companion, in whose company our speech need not be too circumspect.

'I will be back from the Bennworths by then,' she said.

'The Bennworths?'

'Yes, they're out at Thirsk. The family has a large assortment of muddy sons. My mother wants one apiece for Lucy and me.'

'Which one for you?' I asked, appalled.

'Oh, she doesn't much mind about that, since they've all got about two thousand a year. There are three older candidates beside the boy, and they're all up from Oxford next week.'

Down from Oxford, I thought miserably, as I kissed Lucy Spink's hand prior to her departure, but this she delayed, standing before me and eyeing me conspiratorially.

'Mr Rigge,' she said, 'on Friday next I will tell you how to get back your estate.'

She turned, and was gone. If it were her intention to leave me in a state of bewilderment, with joy and depression contending, she could not have succeeded better. I am sure I ought to disregard her remark about the estate, although I am not yet able to do so; still less can I dismiss the vision of the Bennworth squirearchy. I must cling to her use of the epithet 'muddy'. Is that compatible with any sort of esteem?

Having no further interest in dancing, I advanced with quickness along the dark margins of the room, and descended by the back stairs into the undercroft of the Assembly Rooms.

Fletcher Rigge, in continuation.

Two great fires gave the main illumination, and not much of it. In the centre of each green-topped table, two or three candles drooped and dropped wax, as if weary of the small repeated scenes they illuminated. Every man smoked, and every man played as if his whole life depended on the game; there were many wide-brimmed hats, occluding faces. I remarked those players who took up their cards instantly, with a trembling hand, as soon as they were dealt round. My father had got like that. Others again waited before collecting up their cards, perhaps draining a glass, or offering a remark on some extraneous matter. In nine out of ten cases, it was a pretended casualness. The sound of music and dancing, reverberating overhead, seemed intolerably whimsical.

I found myself alongside the faro bank: the cards of the 'set-up' were laid out like graves in a graveyard. There was no talking at all, only the click of the cards, like so many locks being engaged, as the banker took them from the dealing box.

I must quit the undercroft, but the place also fascinated me, for here rationality was refuted, and in the very heart of the town. I surveyed again the green islands. Each table was crowded around, for besides the gamers there were the men who bet on the gamers: the 'woodpeckers', they were called. They looked like bystanders, but every so often they made an important intervention. There were also the patrolling men who kept order, the Clerks, as they were known, who carried pistols in their pockets.

I was searching in particular for my father's nemesis, Mr Corrigan. It was a matter of finding the *vingt-et-un* table ... and there it was, in the far corner, and there *he* was, in the banker's place. I saw him sidelong, and it was as though Corrigan felt the weight of my stare for, in the process of taking the Excise band off a new pack of cards, he turned towards me. We locked gazes for five seconds, and it was Corrigan who looked away first, as he could well afford to do. His Christian name, I recollected, was Victor, and that was apt. He was a large, pale man, with a white smear of a face, all features small and somewhat skew, therefore unreadable. He was shuffling the cards, as he was about to shuffle the lives of the villagers, labourers and farmers of Adenwold.

I contemplated going over and laying him out. Instead, I caught up a glass of port wine, tossed it off, set it down; I immediately did the same with another. By now, Corrigan had dropped his gaze back to the game, but another man looked towards me from that corner – a man who stood behind Corrigan, observing him. It was the small, bald man, who had been in company with the Spinks.

I had had my fill of the underworld, and I made towards the front stairs. These brought me up into the portico, where I found myself standing directly before one of the smoking flambeaux. This uncertain flame, battered by the wind, cast wavering shadows of the people awaiting their carriages and hackneys, and I fixed on one particular shadow: that of a hat. It was the impertinent, cocked hat commonly associated with Robin Hood, and I was sure I had seen it before: in a shade painted by Matthew Harvey.

Fletcher Rigge, in continuation.

I turned my head to see the original, so to speak. A pretty female ... regular features with a trim nose ... chestnut hair in tumbling bangs at the back ... the rest concealed by the hat. She was older than her painted profile had suggested: in the early forties rather than thirties as I'd thought. She had a look of amusement in her clever, dark blue eyes, which were the colour of the night. I bowed to her, muttering the word, 'Ma'am', which she obviously didn't much care for.

Beyond the portico, the snow was falling again, streaming diagonally before the Cathedral. The woman was scanning the street, obviously waiting for a carriage. But she now re-fixed her gaze upon me and, having studied my face, she lowered her inspection to my dancing shoes.

She said, 'You're not proposing to walk in those, I hope?'

It had been somehow inevitable that we two would fall quickly into conversation.

I said, 'My lodge is only half a mile off.'

'Half a mile will do for those shoes. I have a carriage coming in a minute – or so I have been repeatedly told over the past *ten* minutes. May we offer you a ride?'

A man was coming up the stairs from the gambling hell – portly, in a crooked wig, puffing and blowing a good deal; perhaps twenty years older than the lady. She addressed this person, evidently her husband. 'Are you up or down, dear?'

'Down fifteen guineas,' he said.

'Ah well,' said the woman, 'that's the price you pay for mixing with the people of quality,' the entirety of which sarcastic remark was addressed my way. She smiled at the man, but she had certainly not been pleased to hear about the loss of the money.

A hackney now rolled up beyond the portico; a footman of the Assembly was holding the door open. The woman said to her husband, 'We're taking this young gentleman with us, Harry,' at which he nodded abstractedly, having fallen to staring at a pretty young woman who was collecting her cloak.

'Oh?' Harry said. He was being helped into his coat by another footman, and what with this and the young lady, he seemed a good deal distracted.

As we approached the carriage, there were confused introductions in among my declarations of regard and thanks. The couple were Mr and Mrs Sampson. As we climbed up into the carriage, I heard a familiar idiotic, wailing street cry from some distant alleyway, 'How's your poor feet?', and then the smashing of glass.

'Dangerous town this,' said Mr Sampson, continuing distracted, groping in his pockets. He was not as refined as his wife, his accent pretty broad. 'Three murders so far this year.'

The footman called up to the driver, 'Monk Street. Number three.'

I remarked the address: respectable, but nothing more, a little way outwith the city walls; and the pair didn't have their own carriage, but must use a hackney.

'We're stopping on the way,' Mrs Sampson called up to the driver through the open window. 'At . . . ?'

I supplied, 'Ogleforth.'

Mrs Sampson repeated the name for the driver. She smiled at me, perhaps mockingly, for she must know that Ogleforth was a far from fashionable street. She had excellent teeth. Perhaps she used Essence of Myrrh, but I doubted she would be taken in by such quackery.

The street cry came again, and the smashing of more glass.

Mr Sampson was looking at me. 'Where are the gentlemen – so-called – of the Watch?' he enquired. 'That is what I'd like to know. They ought to be here when the Assembly lets out.'

There was no heat in this, however; he was a pretty amiable fellow, possibly complacent.

The brazenness – and, I fear, dishonesty – necessitated by the Captain's commission now came into play.

'I know a poor fellow who was killed this year,' I said, eyeing Mrs Sampson directly, 'Matthew Harvey, the profilist or shade painter.'

'Yes,' she said, looking evenly back at me, 'he was. In the Race Week, and only a matter of days after he'd painted *my* profile.'

My heart was racing.

'It's said he was killed by one of his sitters,' I said.

'What on earth are you suggesting, young man?'

'You're an undergraduate, I suppose,' Mr Sampson enquired unexpectedly.

'I kept a term at Cambridge.'

'A brilliant scholar, I suppose.'

'Nothing out of the ordinary.'

'Only a term, you say?'

'Circumstances were not favourable to my continuing.'

'The trouble being?' Mr Sampson enquired.

'Debt, I expect,' Mrs Sampson put in, hitting the mark precisely. It was her revenge for an accusation of murder, but I didn't mind this tussle, rather relished it, in fact. I felt a tug of attraction towards Mrs Sampson.

'Well, I wasn't exactly *swimming* in money,' I said.

'And nor are you now,' said Mrs Sampson. 'I saw those very shoes in the window of Bulmer's last week.'

'In hock?' Mr Sampson interjected, surprised.

'Everything in Bulmer's is in hock, dear,' said Mrs Sampson. 'It is a pawnbroker's.'

'I'm afraid so,' I said, 'and they'll probably be back there before long.'

Mrs Sampson, evidently a very sharp customer indeed, sat back. She looked through the window for a while, as I glanced down at her own shoes. They were kid pumps of yellow and white, and of good quality; or they had been. They were patched on the instep with a gold-coloured heart, and this heart – betokening a girlish sentimentality – seemed incompatible not only with her age, but also her character, as I had so far apprehended it. I looked up at her, encountering again the steady, assessing gaze.

'Do you like my hat?' she enquired.

'It's very charming,' I said.

'Had to say that, didn't you?' chuckled Mr Sampson.

I said, 'It's a riding hat, I think.'

'Mmm,' said Mrs Sampson, 'but I never ride. I walk about a good deal.'

That would explain her knowledge of York, and I was willing to bet that this very autonomous lady walked alone. She leant forward suddenly, touching my knee with her glove. 'You were asking about this kind of hat in Bainbridge's, the milliner's. At any rate, a young man of your sort of stamp was doing so. Mrs Bainbridge herself told me.'

This fairly took my breath away.

'What did she tell you?' Mrs Sampson asked, laughing.

'That she couldn't think.'

Mrs Sampson smiled a tight, quick smile, for of course Mrs Bainbridge could think perfectly well, and had been protecting the identity of a regular customer. Even so, it seemed to me that Mrs Sampson had done a good deal more 'detecting' than I myself. She deserved the truth.

'I will speak plainly, Mrs Sampson.'

'Good. About time.'

'I have been contracted to investigate the circumstances of Matthew Harvey's death.'

'Good God!' said Mr Sampson, and a smell of wine came gusting from his mouth.

'I am to discover the identities of the people who sat for him in the Race Week.'

'You must be working from the book – the ledger – in which he wrote down the names.'

I explained what had become of that, and the lady gave every appearance of being surprised at the news, while Mr Sampson, by contrast, slumped forward, having dropped asleep.

'Then it must be my hat that gave me away,' said Mrs Sampson, 'on the duplicate shade? Are you working for the magistrates?'

'I am working for Matthew Harvey's son, Captain Harvey.'

We were now going along Petergate. The snow whirled confusedly, trapped between the overhanging houses.

'The *Captain*,' Mrs Sampson was saying. 'He's the one who lives by the coal wharf on First Water Lane, isn't he? He is not quite respectable – to say the least. Have you considered the possibility that he himself was the murderer?'

'. . . The enquiry he has asked me to conduct being an elaborate charade, you mean?'

'Exactly.'

'Yes. I have considered the possibility.'

There had been a couple of drunkards on Petergate, but Goodramgate, which we now turned into, was quite deserted, and I heard the cry again, 'How's your poor feet?!' It came from the direction of the Cathedral. It was the regular cry of a certain wandering lunatic of the city, which was sometimes taken up and echoed mockingly by passing drunks. Mrs Sampson had heard it too; she smiled again, but rather tightly now. Mr Sampson had begun a gentle snore. College Street – a white-whirling void – was passing on the left. Next would be Ogleforth.

'No need to go along my street,' I said. 'I'll climb down here.'

Mrs Sampson opened the window and called a halt to the driver, which did not wake Mr Sampson. I climbed down.

'Might we speak further about Harvey?' I enquired, standing in the snow, and addressing her through the open window of the carriage.

'Which one?'

'The father.'

'You may,' she said.

'Then I may call on you?'

'Yes, and it might be perfectly seemly, since this is a professional matter – I mean, I assume you are contracted to this Captain; I assume you have something in *black and white* . . . in which case it might be seemly if I were to call upon *you*.'

This was meant to be disconcerting, I believed, and I would not *be* disconcerted. 'I would be honoured to receive you,' I said, and I gestured along Ogleforth, indicating the shambling parade of irregular houses and workshops. 'My lodge is above the violin maker's at the far end.'

Mrs Sampson was smiling and holding a card in her gloved fingers. It could not have been plainer: 'Mrs Maria Sampson, Number 3, Monk Street, York.'

'Thursday or Friday afternoons suit best,' she said. 'But run! Your poor feet!'

As the carriage rolled away, I did not run, but turned and watched the snow spinning down Ogleforth.

I began walking towards my lodge, perhaps finally ruining my shoes, reflecting that, if so, I will at least be spared the indignity of trying to hock them again. Is there something in me that wants to bring everything to the same disastrous end? Lucy Spink seems to detect this tendency, and it appears to amuse her, which is better than mawkish and false solicitation. Mrs Sampson had also seemed amused, as well she could afford to be. She knew she could not seriously be suspected of murdering Matthew Harvey. But I have reason to think her not quite so sanguine as she tried to appear . . .

Like most of the ladies at the Assembly, she had been carrying a reticule. No frippery nonsense for the forthright Maria Sampson, but simply a square of black velvet; a sort of detached pocket. She placed it on the seat by her on first boarding the carriage. When she realised I was the person who'd been enquiring of Mrs Bainbridge about the riding hat, she had taken it onto her lap and held it there as if it were in danger of blowing away. When I declared my true connection with Captain Harvey, she had taken it in her two hands, and begun kneading the thing. This was by no means her normal habit, for her husband had remarked it by the raising of an eyebrow . . . before succumbing to the effects of liquor.

As to her seeing my shoes in the window of Bulmer's . . . How had she come to see them? Conveniently for its shame-faced customers, the shop is set back in its own private court – Lady Peckitt's Yard, by name – and so its window would not naturally be encountered by anyone merely browsing.

As to Mrs Sampson's own dancing shoes, they were somewhat cracked. I believe the patch to have concealed a hole, and that it has been a long time since she did any dancing in them.

Fletcher Rigge, in continuation.

The above, somewhat uncharitable, observations on the character of Mrs Sampson might have marked the end of my entry for Monday November 19th, but there is a further incident to report.

(I write this, incidentally, on the Tuesday, with a whole day in hand before I board the London coach. I sit with my journal and my pen in the empty choir stall of the Cathedral. My ink pot is on the shelf before me, intended for the choristers' music. The ink is diluted with snow and I write with the reverse of the nib – and so both are eked out. It is cold but dead quiet and I am in a writing mood. I will be still more so when I repair – as is my intention – to the Tiger Inn on Jubbergate for a glass of port wine.)

Before entering my lodge last night, I visited the necessary house in the yard to the rear of the violin maker's. I do not think I have made mention of this fellow before. He is pleasant enough, but no violinist, judging by the intolerable scraping that sometimes comes up from the workshop. He is called Buckley, and his wife brings me a pitcher of hot water every morning at seven, and a hot dinner every *night* at seven. She sweeps my room daily; brings my letters from the posting office, and sometimes takes them there.

The Buckleys lodge alongside their workshop, and were tightly asleep on my return, judging by the blank blackness of the workshop windows. The necessary place is an almost comical hovel, full of back numbers of the *York Courant*, some of the pages partially burnt, for it is Mr Buckley's habit to make narrow tapers of some of the pages in order to read *other* pages while he performs his nightly ablutions.

[**Mr Erskine's interpolation:** the following paragraph had been scored out in the original document.]

Well then, in this necessary place, I performed two necessary acts, the second – even more shameful than the first – accompanied by contending mental images of Lucy Spink and Mrs Maria Sampson. As a result of the act, both females were temporarily displaced from the front of my mind.

I walked over to the yard pump and washed my hands. The contraption was not frozen, but creaked badly, and I watched the Buckleys' back windows with anxiety. The watchman's cry came from far away, 'One o'clock and all well!', the fellow evidently taking the fast-falling snow in his stride. A row of pewter jugs was kept by the pump. I filled the one containing the least amount of ice, and carried it up the stairs – which creaked similarly to the pump – and unlocked my chamber. The first room is the bedchamber (it contains my bed, anyhow), so that if I ever do receive Mrs Sampson, I must suffer the excruciation of leading her through this, into what I suppose must be called the sitting room, on account of its single, small couch. (At Aden Park, my bedchamber was referred to as the Tapestry Room, which is what it had been three hundred years before. My wide, canopied bed was like a room within a room. It took exactly twenty of my mother's soft, slippered footsteps to traverse the distance between door and bed, and when she arrived at the bed, she would – in my early boyhood – set herself down upon it, and read to me from one of the 'old favourites', *Robinson Crusoe* being the oldest favourite of all.)

I sat down on my humbler bed in Ogleforth, and lit a candle. I removed my shoes, and took from my pocket some pages of the *Courant* that I had pocketed in the necessary house. I stuffed them in the shoes. They must be left to dry like that, and on no account be put near a blazing fire, not that I have ever had a blazing fire in my present lodge. I laid my coat, shirt, necktie and breeches on the bed and ran my candle over them, looking for marks, as is my habit. They had come through pretty well. I hung them in my wardrobe. I washed myself quickly in the icy water, and put on my nightshirt, which still smells of distemper from the Castle, even though I paid Mrs Buckley sixpence to launder it, and another sixpence to launder it again. With the candle in my hand, I contemplated my reflection in the tall mirror that is the one opulent feature of the room. I perceived what appeared to be the ghost of a young gentleman.

A pot of port wine stood on the mantelpiece. I drank down about half, put out the candle and climbed into bed. I was cold.

[**Mr Erskine's interpolation**: the following sentence had been scored out.]

I had hoped the port wine might warm me, but it only

brought Miss Spink and Mrs Sampson floating back into my brain. I sat up and re-lit the candle. I caught up the page of the *Courant*, but it was all bankrupts and mortgaged estates. The window being un-curtained, I watched the relentless snow. I got up and went over to the wardrobe. Taking out my coat, I laid it on top of my two blankets. I could not find my nightcap, which I begin to think I have left in the Castle. The under-gaoler will have auctioned it off by now. As I tried to settle down again, I thought I heard a distant cry – not the regular lunatic who enquires about one's feet, but a more agitated voice. It was far distant, however. I blew out the candle, and drifted into a state that was equal parts sleep, dream and memory.

... When I was aged about eight years, there had come a strange October day on the estate. I had insisted on helping one of the tenants, Ned Brown, with his ploughing. Of course, I had done nothing but plod behind the plough – all the while pocketing stones in order 'to use them later' for, as I repeatedly announced, 'improving the road'. Presently, Ned Brown forced me to empty out my pockets (since the stones therein would ruin my clothes) and sent me home. But I did not return directly to the park. I had unaccountably decided to 'sleep out under the stars', and so flopped down beneath a hedge. I slept soundly at first, with my parents and the entire household frantically searching for me. But I woke after perhaps an hour to discover – with fascination and horror – that I had become Jack Frost, being limed all over with it, even to my hair and face.

In my dream state, the white blanket that provided my immediate covering in the Ogleforth rooms had become somehow analogous to that liming of frost.

I sat up in my bed, but still with my mind on that childhood escapade . . . I had been left in no doubt by my father's gamekeeper that had I not woken when I did, I would certainly have died before morning. But what had woken me as I slept beneath that hedge? It was concluded – at a sort of inquest held later on, as I sat in a steaming bath before the kitchen fire – that I had been roused by the sound of badgers screaming in the woods, for badgers can scream like women if distressed.

I could hear screaming at that very moment.

I leapt to the window, and opened it; snow came in – and more screaming. I turned away from the window. I couldn't see my Hessian boots, so I dragged the newspaper out of the dancing pumps, and put them on. Throwing my top-coat over my nightshirt, I dashed out into the street, commencing to run – and heading left, since I thought the screams came from Goodramgate. But it was possible they were from further off. Perhaps Monk Street? Was it the self-possessed Mrs Sampson who was screaming? That I could not credit. On Goodramgate, I turned right, seeming to be running into the streaming snow, running into pure whiteness.

At the end of Goodramgate, I had the choice of Petergate or The Shambles. The screams indicated the latter. I turned left, and was still running into wind-blown snow when a man came hurtling towards me, apparently borne on the wind and the snow. I could not make out his features, but he wore a coat with three capes attached, which flew out behind him like three pairs of wings. Was he connected to the screams? He must hear them, yet was running the opposite way. Moving over to check him, I slipped and smashed the side of my head on the cobbles. I lay confused on the ground as the snow commenced trying its best to bury me. I arose, groggy and half frozen. The screaming had been replaced by shouts – the ineffectual shouts of two York watchmen. It was a simple matter to follow the sound, and I picked my way to the beginning of The Shambles.

In this street of shuttered butchers, a piece of butchery had occurred independently of any shop. A man lay along the gutter. He was perhaps in the late fifties. His wideawake hat was crushed under his head; his wig lay to the side, like a dead animal, and the man himself was quite dead but with eyes open, as though closely inspecting the cobbles. I realised at length that the dead man's snowed-upon brown waistcoat had a patch of crimson spreading about the stomach. The body was being attended by one watchman; another attended – equally ineffectually – a young woman, who screamed again, as if by way of proving her identity as the one who had been screaming all along. The first watchman was removing a pocket book from the dead man's coat. This had been no robbery, therefore. A quantity of papers was folded inside the pocket book, and the watchman meekly passed these up to me, whereon I read the following: 'At the Theatre Royal, York will be performed a comedy, called *The Rivals*.' Sheridan's play. They were forever putting that on. The next paper announced, 'A brand new comedy for the New Year, *The Midnight Hour*'; the next again spoke of a burlesque, *Humours of the Green Room* – the frivolity of which projected entertainments contrasted horribly with the pallor of the dead man's face, which was gradually blending with the snow around him, the colour gone even from his lips.

'Fellow by the name of Cork,' the watchman pronounced, presumably having discovered the name in the pocket book. But I had already guessed the man's identity. The curtain had, by this deed, been rung down on the feud between the actor Smith – whose shade had been painted by Harvey, and who may well have been the man I had seen running away – and the theatrical manager Cork. I wondered whether I would need to look very much further for the killer of the profilist himself. I told the watchman that he and his fellows would do well to look out for a certain Jeremiah Smith, connected to the Theatre Royal.

'Why?' the dolt asked.

'I'll lay odds he did this.'

The flying snow seemed to carry away our converse, but I gave the fellow my address and told him I would willingly go before a magistrate to explain further. (But I doubt that any such summons will arise, unless some individual connected to Cork seeks a prosecution, and to the best of my understanding that will not be his wife.)

The young woman had finally left off screaming. This was because she was running fast away, having escaped the clutches of the second watchman. I alone gave chase for a while, but she disappeared into the darkness of the Market Place. When I returned to the scene of the crime, the two watchmen were standing silently over the dead body, like two inexperienced undertakers. They seemed transfixed by the sight, and hardly looked at me as I attempted to quiz them about the young woman, who was – it appeared – the only material witness to the crime. All I could get out of the watchmen was that her name was Melissa, and she was a woman of the street, 'an unfortunate'.

But she was not, just then, as unfortunate as Mr Cork.

Mr Erskine's prefatory note concerning a letter sent to him by Mr Saul Handley.

There follows a letter sent to me by an old friend of mine, Mr Saul Handley. I include the date as being material to our story. As the letter shows, Handley and I were aware at the time of the loss that Rigge had suffered, and we had discussed the matter between ourselves. This, indeed, marks the beginning of my own – and Mr Bright's – direct involvement with the fortunes of that young man.

Mr Saul Handley has forty years on our young Mr Rigge, and is a good deal less refined (as I know he will not mind my saying), but there are echoes of the Rigge characteristics in his own personality. Like the younger man, Mr Handley affects to be a straightforward country gentleman – he farms out at Wetherby – but his native intelligence repeatedly draws him to the allurements of the town, as will be seen.

Letter from Mr Handley to Mr Erskine.

Skelton's Bookshop,
Wetherby.
Tuesday November 20th

You can't expect a poor farmer to know the difference between libel and slander, but I give you fair warning, John, that I'm about to commit one or t'other, so you might want to pitch this missive into the fire once you've looked it over. As you know, I game a trifle, which is why I came to be in the undercroft at the Assembly last night. At the start of proceedings, I was moving between the tables, taking a little wine and placing a few side bets while Ruth and the girls were prancing upstairs.

Shortly after the 'off' Corrigan appeared, together with his henchman, that evil-looking fellow, Cracknell. There was no fanfare, as usual; the pair simply slid into a table of vingt-et-un. I strolled over that way myself and observed the play. Nothing untoward, from what I could see . . . and why might there be, you ask, being an amazingly charitable sort of fellow (for a lawyer, anyhow)? Well, that brings me to the actionable part of this letter.

There's a good deal of talk about Corrigan in town, as you know. When he cleaned out Rigge senior . . . well, that was the start of what has proved a very lucky streak indeed. I don't believe he's come by another country estate, but he's bled some pretty rich fellows pretty freely. On top of that, there's his rapid rise from surgeon to physician, and with hardly a patient in sight. It is said that money changed hands over that swift elevation, and so here I am, putting myself in the way of a writ from the Royal College of Surgeons, or whatever that parliament of quacks is called. It's said he wanted to be a physician for the sake of the brass plaque on the door of his big new mansion in Micklegate, and for the equally grand doors that would be opened to him.

To repeat, I saw nothing amiss at the vingt-et-un last night. Corrigan and Cracknell dipped a little, if I counted aright. They then moved over to the faro table, and here they dipped a little more. In fact, I'd swear that Corrigan, as *banker, was playing with a design to lose. You see, my dear fellow, I think he knows the name he's getting in the world at large, which – libel be damned – is that he is a clever cheat. There are plenty of poor gamesters in this town, and the ones who know they're poor gamesters – a minority, I admit – are growing wary of sitting down with Corrigan and his unsavoury friend – for Cracknell is most certainly not considered an innocent bystander. The two do not go about in society as a pair. Corrigan dare not foist the uncouth Cracknell on the refined hostesses of York, but they are always paired up when it comes to the gaming.*

The latest I've heard is that Corrigan wants to initiate a bank, so his growing notoriety will do him no good at all, hence his carefully contrived losses at the Assembly. But that charade comes too late for the unfortunate lad you and I were discussing, namely poor Rigge's son. I had heard that he'd been taken into the Castle for a large sum, but he must have got a reprieve somehow, for he was at the Assembly last night, and it chanced that I spotted him a little later in the refreshment room, where he was being closely observed by the family of Carl Spink, who keeps those upholstery shops, and in whose company I passed much of the evening. It seems that Spink's eldest daughter, Lucy (a very fetching creature indeed), had on some previous occasion formed an attachment to young Rigge. I admit that, having taken a fair bit of wine, I gave them the benefit of my opinion about Corrigan, speaking almost freely as I do in this letter, and they were all most interested to hear it. Afterwards, when the Spinks had left, I saw the boy again, in the undercroft, where I was resuming my study of Corrigan. He did not join the play, but looked on with a sort of pale-faced mortification, occasionally taking up a glass of wine in an attempt – I suppose – to recruit his spirits. Our eyes met, but the boy doesn't know me from Adam. He knew Corrigan all right, though, and was looking very dangerously in that gentleman's way. I was behind Corrigan, so I could not see his return glance, if any, but he leaves the darkling looks to Cracknell, and whether Rigge is aware of that knave's existence I cannot say.

Now you told me that your brother lawyer, Mr Pullman, was the late Mr Rigge's man of business, and that he was in the process of transferring the deeds of those lands up at Adenwold to Corrigan. You said he was doing so with a heavy heart, but unable to see any loophole. Have we not now found one?

I do not know the boy Rigge, but I put it to you that if we do something for him – by checking Corrigan – we will also be doing something for York.

Letter from Mr Erskine to Mr Handley.

Precentor's Court,
York.
Tuesday November 20th

Your letter intrigues — yet does not entirely surprise — me. I would like to do something for young Rigge. His father was reputedly a decent fellow, who looked after his people very well up at Adenwold. I assure you also that my brother attorney, Mr Pullman, would be glad to see this apparently watertight contract of honour fatally holed, for you must know, dear Saul, that the parties are bound by honour alone, a gambling debt above ten pounds being unenforceable by law. But as regards the cheating of Corrigan and Cracknell, I must ask for further and better particulars, otherwise we come up short evidentially.

Please don't trouble yourself about slander or libel. It is libel, by-the-by, when the content is written, slander when spoken. But I am becoming lawyerly, for which I apologise, and justification will be a perfectly good defence, in the unlikely event of your letter falling into the wrong hands.

Letter from Mr Handley to Mr Erskine.

Linton Manor,
Wetherby.
Wednesday November 21st

I was just coming on to the question of how the cheating is done, when my man came in and told me the well was frozen, and that the clod-headed groom was trying to answer the difficulty by pitching in big stones. And so I forgot to put in the important detail.

Some people don't care for Corrigan's particular manner of throwing the dice out of the box. They observe that he rather stamps it down on the table, but the plain fact is that the dice are only a side line with him. Therefore I believe it is to the card games that we must look, and to those games unsupervised by the official – and sometimes, I suppose, honest – gentlemen who patrol the tables of the Assembly and other public events.

I have twice observed Corrigan and Cracknell at play in York mansions. The addresses don't really signify, but I might as well tell you that the first occasion was under the roof of the Sandersons in Walmgate, the second at the Parkers' place on Tadcaster Road. On both occasions, only Corrigan played, while his sinister colleague looked on.

The game in each case was loo, which is commonly played between five, but it is fashionable in York for there to be only three at the table, and this, I believe, is highly convenient for Corrigan and his man. The hands at loo are small – only five cards – and so may be apprehended at a glance by anyone standing behind the players. There are always a few onlookers, and Cracknell was not so conspicuous in their number, except for his surly demeanour, and some personal habits that began to strike me as more disgusting than was needful. I am not – you will agree – excessively genteel, but as I looked on, Cracknell's coughing, nose blowing, snuff taking and pipe sucking seemed more fitting to a tap room than a drawing room, and as the evening progressed, I fancy that I began to detect a code of communication; a sort of masquerade between him and his master. Whether the coughs corresponded to a good hand in the possession of Corrigan's opponents or a bad one, I cannot now recollect. Perhaps the taking of snuff indicated a high flush, the loading of a pipe a low flush, but I'll lay my life that some such intrigue was afoot, and I need hardly add that Corrigan won handsomely on both occasions.

I am not alone in having suspected such devilry in that pair . . . Damn it, I do not suspect, I am certain, and so are both Sanderson and Parker, both heavy betters and not lightly deterred by losses, but neither one will entertain Corrigan on any future occasion. I am not one for such passive measures, however. I am minded to have it out with the fellow, but we both know that I lack diplomacy and so it will end – if he has any unsuspected shred of gentlemanliness – in his calling me out. We will meet at dawn on the Knavesmire and I will be obliged to blow the villain's brains out, but (and do please give me your professional opinion) I suspect that would not stop the transfer of the Adenwold lands to his heirs, such as they may be. Corrigan is unmarried and childless, and the dread prospect must be that of the man Cracknell getting hold of the lands, which will be an even worse lookout for the people of Adenwold than if Corrigan becomes the squire.

Letter from Mr Erskine to Mr Handley.

Precentor's Court,
York.
Wednesday November 21st

I am persuaded by your letter of today that it is worth our holding a little conflab – two of them, indeed. I will endeavour to persuade Mr Corrigan to pay me a call here in my office, but we had better summon young Rigge first. I have discovered that he lives at Ogleforth, and at half after one today, I wrote and despatched a note to him, or rather, Mr Bright did so. (You know very well, dear Saul, that nine times out of ten when I say I have done something, it is the good Mr Bright who has performed the action.)

Mr Bright returned – his deeply dented tricorn full of snow – at two, with the news (imparted by Rigge's landlady) that he departed this morning on the London stage. He is projected to return 'towards the end of next week'.

Mr Erskine's memorandum to Mr Taylor, concerning Fletcher Rigge's departure for London.

We now, my dear Taylor, come to the writing of Mr Villiers, a London author and member of the 'Black Diamonds' (a literary society). He is not an attractive man, but honest, I suggest. The following letter, the first of three from him, was received after our denouement, in response to my written enquiry.

Letter from Mr Villiers, Author, to Mr Erskine.

4 Bride Lane,
London.

*The person who is the subject of your enquiry appeared at
our regular meeting place, Cuthbert's Ale House, on Friday
November 23rd, in company with Mr Samuel Gowers.*

*I did not at first know how they had got acquainted, but
anyone enquiring after Gowers in the bookish parts of London off
the Strand will soon be directed towards his illustrious personage;
and I was not particularly surprised that he should have a young
gentleman in tow. Strange to relate, Gowers would attract his
share of bookish acolytes: ambitious – if usually craven – young
fellows who had perhaps received poor marks or reviews for some
essay on Johnson, and so had sought out the anti-Johnson, the
author of a book condemning his works.*

*It goes without saying that no other member of our club
may introduce an outsider. Samuel Gowers reserved that
privilege to himself, as the founder of our society, the Black
Diamonds, and the pre-eminent jewel among them – for so
he undoubtedly considered himself. In this particular case,
I found that I didn't mind the intrusion. The newcomer –
his name, I had gathered, was Fletcher Rigge – seemed a
person of condition, not overly opinionated, and his approach*

towards Gowers himself was novel: interested, yet not sycophantic. Shortly after my arrival at Cuthbert's, he was stating a fondness for Sterne's Tristram Shandy, *a fairly unexceptionable position, rousing nothing more than a slight peevishness in Gowers.*

'But do you not think, sir,' Gowers enquired, 'that while that work diverts, it suffers from the utter lack of any noble or dignified character?'

'But the work does divert, sir,' said the newcomer, 'and that is a rare thing, not to be mentioned merely in passing,' which remark rather confounded our principal.

I should now explain that I tended to keep my own counsel at the meetings, every remark being likely to provoke some slighting response from our bumptious founder. I had in fact been meaning to resign from the Black Diamonds (I have since done it), whose meetings were always carried on in Cuthbert's, which lies down an alleyway off the Strand. I daresay its fame has not carried as far as York, so I will mention that the front of the ale house pokes out somewhat from the shops on either side, like the prow of a ship, so putting itself in the way of the winds that race up from the river, rattling the little window panes of the upstairs room, some of which are decorated with stained glass depictions of ships, and some of which are missing entirely – so that you might see a real ship through the gap; and these sudden draughts make the fire in the grate a rather cowed, flinching thing.

Little Edwin Bird, another member of our club, began joshing the newcomer, while pouring out porter. 'Congratulations, sir,' he said, smiling broadly. 'You have met the constellation of genius in one mass.'

'Might I ask why the "Black Diamonds"?' Rigge enquired.

'The name is my own invention,' said Gowers, taking a sip of wine. (He alone would disdain the rough porter of Cuthbert's in favour of wine.) 'It denotes talented persons of dingy or unpolished exterior; rough jewels . . . The blackness fittingly suggestive of . . . shadowy eminences in the literary world.'

This sounded like modesty. It was false modesty, of course.

'It was that or the "Blackguards",' Edwin Bird put in, 'which wouldn't quite have done.'

Bird, too, seemed rather taken with the young man, hence the frequency of his satirical interjections, which the newcomer rewarded with a gracious inclination of the head.

Bird sat on the same side of the table as another of our regular Diamonds, namely Mr Noble. Gowers, naturally, sat at the head. He asked Rigge, 'And how is the printing and publishing in York in these benighted times?'

'In a pretty poor state, sir,' said Rigge, which was undoubtedly the correct response. Naturally, the book trade was faring badly in York, without Gowers on hand to oversee it.

It appeared this Fletcher Rigge was from York, and this was the foundation of the connection with Gowers – forged

144

between the two of them that very afternoon – for Gowers had himself passed a few years in York as a young man, doing I know not what, but on the strength of which he had now set himself up as a sort of ambassador for that city, ever-willing to receive, and more especially to give, opinions on it . . . And if Gowers were the York ambassador, then his house, in a quiet court off Fleet Street, was the York Embassy, and he had been known to take in stray Yorkshiremen of literary inclinations.

As the young man described the iniquities of the York libraries and book clubs (it appeared they were demanding unsupportable discounts from all suppliers) Gowers gave the occasional nod of acknowledgement. Otherwise he looked straight ahead. It was his custom to do so, with an expression of perplexity, brought on by the necessity of enduring the ramblings of some lesser intellect. Or it might be that Gowers did not look at other people because he did not want them to look at him.

'But I trust,' said Gowers, 'that the good people of York resist the pretended learning of that late charlatan, Johnson?'

'His Dictionary does pretty well,' Rigge replied, thereby – as it seemed to me – testing the extent of Gowers' prejudice.

'Then the city is damned to hell,' said Gowers, smashing his fist onto the table.

'Very likely,' said Rigge, when the vibration had subsided; and so he had found out his answer.

'I believe,' Rigge continued, after an interval of silence,

'that you gentlemen include mention of your society on the title pages of your publications?'

Gowers nodded rather stiffly. 'An engraving of a black diamond appears above our names.'

At this, the conversation had taken a turn I found very interesting, and so at last I spoke up: 'The diamond is accompanied in most cases,' I said, 'by a silhouette of the author . . . I can furnish an example. I think I have one of my own works about me.'

'Not that he carries them everywhere!' Bird interjected in his teasing way.

I reached into my pocket and took out my latest production: A Commentary on the Works of Pope, *the literary merit or otherwise of which is irrelevant here. I turned to the title page, and showed Rigge the shade, or silhouette, of myself, as painted by a fellow in Seven Dials. I had then taken it, together with the manuscript, to the printer. The profile is pretty well done, I think, and I turned side-on to demonstrate its accuracy to Rigge.*

At this, Gowers swivelled smartly towards Noble. 'Sir,' he said, 'I think that when we adjourned last week, you were about to give an interesting opinion on our greatest poet.'

Plainly, he was intent on a total change of subject. Unfortunately, Noble – a worthy fellow but none too clever in my view – took the bait, and embarked on a small speech. 'I was on the point of saying that when I read Paradise Lost, I am quite confounded by the genius and imagination of Milton, to the extent, indeed, of giving way to despair at contemplation of my own artistic efforts.'

'Indeed so,' said Gowers, nodding and happy, as ever, to confirm the inferiority of Noble.

But Rigge was equally intent on the question of the shades.

'Sir,' he said, addressing Gowers, 'I have had the pleasure of looking through your own work, the study of Johnson, and I saw no profile or shade at the beginning of the book, but only the engraving of the diamond.'

Now this observation interested me very greatly. It was perfectly true that while every member of our little club had commissioned a profile of himself – Bird's had appeared in the small collection of comic verses he had recently brought out – Gowers had never got round to doing so. Or, if he had done so, he had never mentioned it. At first, this had aggrieved me, for while I admit that it was Gowers who first suggested the name of the Black Diamonds, I had been the one who proposed carrying the theme through to the painting of shades, which would make the works of the authors instantly recognisable, and perhaps in time collectable.

Gowers, blushing brightly (especially his nose), said, 'My Johnson book dates from a time antecedent to the suggestion of the silhouettes.'

A lie. The first production to include a shade had been Birdsong, *Edwin's little volume of comic verse, published almost a whole year before the tirade on Johnson had appeared.

Gowers now drained his glass, and stood. He was for the back yard, and the necessary house. His preparations for such visits were by no means genteel, and I watched with distaste as he rolled up the sleeves of his grubby cambric, and took from the pocket of his coat a small volume. He collected a candle from the table, and departed.

Edwin Bird and I leant towards Rigge.

'You will have observed—' I began.

But at that very moment, Gowers returned, in order to collect a narrow leathern case from his coat pocket. He departed again.

'Forgot his glasses,' I explained, having divined the reason.

'Calls them his barnacles,' Bird put in.

'You will have observed—' I began again.

'He'd forget his arse if it was loose,' said Bird.

'If it were *loose, Edwin,' I said. 'We are meant to be a literary club, after all.'*

(A rather coarse exchange, granted, but I include it as being indicative of the bitter tone that Gowers had engendered in our group.)

'You will have observed,' I said, resuming my address to Rigge, 'the proboscis.'

Rigge nodded, saying, 'Does the defect trouble him very greatly?'

Bird nodded. 'His Achilles heel is on his face . . . It has, at least, preserved him from the dangers of matrimony.'

'You will not find a mirror in his house,' I put in. 'You are stopping at the house, I gather?'

Rigge nodded again. 'This night only,' he said, before giving a few words of explanation – not enough, for the young man spoke rather sparingly. It appeared that he had called on Gowers that very afternoon, saying that he was fresh in town from York, and had heard that he would find a great friend of Yorkists in the august personage of Samuel Gowers.

I could make a hazard at how things would have gone from there. Gowers would have sighed and demurred. The young man would no doubt have discovered him 'extremely busy just at present, making up an important article for the London Magazine' or going over the proofs of his (actually non-existent) latest work. Young Mr Rigge would have bowed deeply in apology. He would have made to withdraw, begging Gowers to forgive the intrusion, the like of which he must often experience, being just about the most famous literary gentleman in the locality. At that, of course, the door would have been thrown wide open, and a glass of Gowers' staple – and rather cheap – sherry would have been proffered.

'You have read the Johnson book, you said?' I asked Rigge.
'I have looked it over. It was a great hit, I gather?'
'By no means, sir,' I said.
'It is what is technically called "out of print",' Bird put in.
'How does he maintain such an animus against Johnson?'

Rigge enquired. 'The Doctor died in eighty-four, I think? And while Gowers has not Johnson's fame, he is at least alive.'

'That's not sufficient compensation,' said Bird.

'He began on his book when Johnson was alive,' I explained. 'He said he was heartbroken when the fellow died, since he avoided seeing his inadequacies set out in cold print.'

'But we think Gowers was pleased,' said Bird, 'because any danger of a libel suit was removed.'

'But was there any one particular event that set him off hating Johnson?' Rigge enquired.

'A very good question,' I said. 'The two of them met once, you know.'

'It was at Lackington's,' said Bird, 'the bookshop on Finsbury Square.'

'A veritable Temple of the Muses,' I put in. (I own that the excitement of talking so freely about Gowers had made me rather facetious.)

'Anybody in there after eight is usually blind drunk,' said Bird. 'They sell porter at discounted prices, you see.'

'And what passed between them?' Rigge enquired.

'Can you not guess?' I said, and my high opinion of the newcomer was confirmed when Rigge replied, 'Johnson, perhaps . . . made some remark about his . . . ?'

'He mentioned the unmentionable,' said Bird.

'Or so we surmise,' I added.

'But that doesn't square with what we know of Johnson

from Boswell's life,' Rigge mused. 'That's a hagiographical work, of course, but by all accounts Johnson really was a kindly man, sympathetic to the infirmities and afflictions of others. He himself was badly scarred by—'

'The scrofula,' I interjected. 'Just so. And therefore our speculation runs on the following lines. Imagine the scene. Johnson and Gowers clash glasses. They're getting on famously over supper and beer in the back room of Lackington's. There are some mutual expressions of regard. Johnson suggests they have much in common: well-stocked minds . . . '

'Uncombed periwigs,' Bird put in, grinning.

'A refined taste in poetry and prose . . . prodigious industry, a valuable experience of life in the provinces . . . all of which, Johnson makes so bold as to say, have allowed them to rise above a certain lack of physical comeliness. "I," Dr Johnson says, "must bear the cross of my poor complexion, while you must brave the wondering glances directed towards your . . . "' And I looked about me, making sure Gowers was not yet returned, before uttering the significant monosyllable.

'I suppose,' said Rigge, after a moment, 'that while Gowers made no immediate response, the remark festered?'

I leant closer towards young Rigge. I was whispering now, for even a Gowers evacuation could not go on much longer. 'Whether he made a remark at the time or not we cannot possibly say, but we have it on very reliable authority that he picked a knife from the table, and menaced the good Doctor with it.'

Just then, Cuthbert Long the landlord came up from below, to recharge the fire, and bring more pitchers of ale and porter. Some other fellows came in with him, three of them Black Diamonds, known of old to Bird and myself. All three had produced books in which their shades appeared, as I mentioned when introducing them to Rigge.

A few moments later, Gowers himself returned, and I noted that the lower parts of the great anti-Johnson's shirt were a good deal smeared with snuff. At least, I hoped that's what it was.

Mr Villiers, in continuation.

Gradually, the talk in Cuthbert's became general, and I circulated the room, avoiding the conversational orbit of Gowers, but observing him as he commenced his pompous, wine-fuelled pontifications, most of them directed to the new arrival. Gowers had never yet met his Boswell. Perhaps he had hopes that young Mr Rigge would fulfil that role. But Rigge seemed rather more watchful than admiring, it seemed to me.

'But your metropolis of the North, sir,' Gowers was asking Rigge, 'how do you find the society? I lived there for five years when I came down from the University. I lodged in Godramgate. You know it?'

'It is more often called Goodramgate,' Rigge corrected, and Gowers instinctively touched his nose, a sort of unconscious acknowledgement of a fallibility that would never be admitted to explicitly. I had often observed this tick or mannerism, and I believed that Rigge was remarking it just then.

'I have friends and acquaintances in some of the principal families,' Gowers continued. 'Do you know the Peacocks? Old Mr Peacock is chaplain at the prison. A good man, and the author of some theological works, although of course he's not to be heard of in the regular trade. Now the last time I was in York, he invited me to tour the prison: the Castle, as I believe it's known, and I talked to some of the poor felons in the cellars, as it were—'

'The Lower Grates?' Rigge cut in.

'Indeed so, indeed so. I observed to Peacock that the inmates seemed entirely uninstructed in Christian principles. He was grateful for my frankness, I believe. He then introduced me to the Master, who was very interested in my opinions and wanted something written up. He kept a journal himself, but it was a poor thing, deficient in style to say the least, and by no means fit for publication, as I took the opportunity of telling him. Well, he fairly plagued me with letters for months afterwards, but the proposed subject was rather well-trodden ground, as it seemed to me. The Castle has earned the good opinion of many authors. Defoe, in his . . . now I forget the title . . .'

Rigge supplied it, with some severity. 'A Tour Thro' the Whole Island of Great Britain.'

'Quite so,' *said Gowers, and he touched his nose again.* 'He described the Castle in that work as the most stately and complete as any in the whole kingdom.'

'In any intelligent abridgement of the work that opinion is omitted,' *said Rigge with considerable asperity.*

'And Smollett,' *Gowers continued, touching his nose,* 'gives a description of the prison in* The Expedition of Humphrey Clinker.' *Gowers began quoting, for which he put on his quoting face:* '"It stands in a high situation, extremely well ventilated, and has a spacious area within the walls for the health and convenience of all the prisoners, except those whom it is necessary to secure in close confinement." I believe he considered it the best prison that ever he had found at home or abroad.'

'He had seen the inside of many prisons, I suppose,' *Rigge observed, and it seemed to me the young man was leaving off politeness where this subject was concerned.*

After an interval of silence, Rigge asked Gowers, 'You say you visited the prison when you were last in York, sir.'

'I—'

'When was that?'

I observed Gowers touch his nose not once but three times before replying to that apparently straightforward enquiry. 'Oh, I don't think I've been north in seven or eight years,' *he said.* 'I'm a good deal busied . . . simply haven't had a *moment's leisure to . . . ' And so saying, Gowers simply walked away from Rigge.*

Come the end of the symposium, however (when the liquor ran out), the two of them set forth together, Gowers' desire for an audience trumping all other considerations.

It is now late, and I must to bed. I therefore reserve for a second letter my description of the dramatic postscript to the events described above.

Diary of Fletcher Rigge. Friday November 23rd.

'You will have noticed,' said Gowers, as he and I walked along the Strand together, 'that I remain civil in spite of constant provocations. That is the lot of any literary man who has risen above the common place. Take Edwin . . . '

'The jolly fellow?' I said.

'On the face of it. It would be more accurate to say the pinched, atomy man—'

'The poet,' I said, recollecting.

'Self-declared. Now he is a particular trial to me, and my most devout wish is that one of his collections of poems might sell more than a couple of dozen copies, so that his bitter humour might be sweetened somewhat. *Nimium ne crede colori,*' Gowers added, and he flicked a rare glance directly at me to see whether I understood. I did, but forbore to give the translation. It seemed it was being demanded, however, for Gowers repeated the Latin.

I obliged him with, "'Trust not too much to a complexion.'"

Gowers nodded approval, but this was directed inwardly, so to speak. He was perhaps congratulating himself on having offered bed and board to a sufficiently learned visitor; but I feared I would soon have to prove myself an ungracious one, for I must probe an untruth he had told some two hours before: namely that he had not been in the city of York these past eight years.

'As for Villiers,' said Gowers, 'what did you make of him?'

'He seemed sagacious.'

'You thought so?' said Gowers. 'His books are never heard of in the trade. You will have observed his very evident chagrin?'

I had certainly noticed that Villiers did not care for Gowers.

'He has all but stopped talking to me, and I fear I must tone down my wit, or his jealousy will make him quit the society. Have you viewed the shops, sir?' asked Gowers, before launching into some speech about the dedication he proposed for his new work.

It was half after ten, but the lights of all the passing

shops blazed forth. Each building seemed to harbour several of them. If one line of merchandise didn't 'take' then perhaps another would do: jewellery, silverware, engraving, boots, cloaks, clocks, lottery offices, coffee rooms.

[**Mr Erskine's interpolation:** In the original, the following paragraph had been scored out.]

Many of the women appeared to be for sale as well, judging by the brazenness of the looks directed my way. (I recollected the one time I paid for a woman: it was in Cambridge, in Queens' Lane to be exact – not a spot known for that sort of dealing. I had been on my way to collect some laundered shirts when the woman stepped out – seemingly, if improbably, from the lodge of Queens' College – and made the suggestion, to which I immediately agreed. She led me onto the Backs. At first, I had assumed we were walking to her lodge, but she suddenly lay down and pulled me on top of her. It was a beautiful and sultry summer's evening . . . But I fear I did not put up a very creditable performance, and the embarrassment of the memory had decided me against a similar dalliance in London, even though it seemed more or less obligatory for an unmarried young gentleman. I also consider myself consecrated to Miss Lucy Spink – an absurdity, since she is no doubt consecrated to the muddy brothers in Thirsk.)

Many raucous gentlemen were also coming forward,

usually in twos, the one usually saying to the other something uncivil like, 'What the devil do you mean by that?' yet the two continuing side-by-side. The whole place was one ceaseless, flowing dispute. The streets were all dirty dark ice. There was no snow here, and I found that I missed it. On the journey from York, it had left off somewhere about Stamford. The people here, like the ever-flowing carriages, chaises and drays in the road, seem all to *rattle* about the place, like the iron balls in bagatelle or the dice in the dice box. Their boots or pattens rattle on the pavement, their voices rattle in the cold air. The city is such a very jarring place. I want to cover the ground with corn and cattle, and put everybody to work upon it.

I was in tolerably good spirits at that moment, however, and when Gowers and I passed a beggar, I dropped a shilling – rather than the looked-for penny – into the wretch's outstretched hand. I was beginning to feel munificent – dangerous, of course, but I felt that Captain Harvey's commission might not be so impossible to carry through after all. I was thinking of Johnson's poem, *The Vanity of Human Wishes*, which had been provocatively brought up earlier by the fellow Bird. At first Gowers had refused 'to waste breath discussing that confounded doggerel', but then he gave a good ten minutes to its denunciation, concluding, rather inevitably, 'The greatest vanity was that of the author himself, in attempting to assume the mantle of poet.'

But the point had substance, as I now remarked to my companion.

'Was not the philosophical pessimism of the poem an unconscious product of his failure to soar in its lyrics?'

'Of course it was,' said Gowers.

'If so, it might be disregarded.'

'What might?'

'The pessimism.'

'Of course it might,' Gowers said, shortly. It appeared that he alone was permitted to formulate criticisms of 'The Great Cham' and so I kept my next thought about the poem to myself. It concerned the line: 'Fate wings with ev'ry wish th' afflictive dart'. Why must that be so? Some endeavours are successful; otherwise there would be no endeavours at all. The consideration arose from my being able to perceive a 'termination in gladness' to the Captain's commission.

It was this way . . .

The murderer of Matthew Harvey must surely have been the actor, Jeremiah Smith. Had he not proven himself a murderer almost before my very eyes? If he could do it once, he could have done it twice, and his method was the same in both cases: the bludgeon. True, I had not *quite* been witness to the act, which in itself was fortuitous, since I had not been called on to sign any affidavit before any magistrate. I could reserve my speculations, which ran on the following lines: Jeremiah Smith had entered a romantic liaison with the wife of Cork, the theatre manager. I seemed to have hit the mark when I hinted as much to the two theatre men. The self-regarding Smith had resolved to present a likeness of himself to the lady in question. Therefore he had visited shade painter Harvey, who had somehow heard of this illicit affair. Being a moralistic – indeed pious – man, and a friend of Cork's, the artist had disapproved, and expressed his disapproval, and threatened to divulge the secret. A row had transpired. The hot-blooded Smith had seized the special scissors and struck out at Harvey, with fatal consequences. Mr Cork himself had, nonetheless, come to hear of the liaison. He had clashed in the street with Smith – at that hour of the night they were both, no doubt, in liquor – and Smith had gone to work with a blade again, this time one of his own.

Smith had then absconded, and was now at large in the city of York or, more likely, the county of Yorkshire. It was all up with him as far as the acting profession was concerned, but he might yet evade capture. He may have embarked already for the Continent. Therefore I could point the Captain to the culprit, without being the cause of a hanging.

There remained, however, the outside possibility that my walking companion was the true murderer, brought to a pitch of fury by some injudicious mention of his bizarre physiognomy.

We had now turned off the Strand, and entered one of the unfathomable London mazes – unfathomable even though I had emerged from it some three hours before, in company with my host. We were approaching his house. Gowers lived, as far as I could tell, among traders, printers, lawyers, the unfashionable sort. The houses were big, functional boxes, each with its 'area' to the fore: a matter of six or eight black flagstones, mostly covered with orange peel, broken glass, old newspapers or other debris, and with a strip of railings to ward off the riotous city.

Where the shutters of these dwellings remained open, I generally observed literary production: bespectacled gentlemen reading or writing before guttering candles or low fires, and looking up with dazed expressions at the passers-by. Occasionally, Gowers would offer comment. 'The fellow you say there ... Leadbetter. He once sold a Bible commentary for fifteen guineas. That was twenty years ago, but you'll never hear the last of it if you meet him.' Or, 'See there, Dashwood, obituarist. I'm surprised to see him at home.'

'Where ought he to be?'

'The King's Bench Prison, sir. He was arrested for twenty pounds last week.'

We passed one house with nobody visible inside, but firelight coming through a crack in the shutters. 'That's

Fawcett's place,' Gowers said. 'He once got fifty guineas for a history of India.' I waited for the bathetic rider, and none was immediately forthcoming. Could it be that Gowers actually admired this lucky Fawcett? But after we'd turned another dark corner, he confided, 'Fawcett doesn't run his household on the proceeds of authorship, however.'

'Oh?' I said. 'What then?'

'His wife's a whore,' said Gowers, 'and there's an end on't.'

Gowers' hat was the very same one – or at least the same sort – as he had worn when his profile had been taken by Matthew Harvey. He wore it low, then as now, over his bulbous nose. I have often observed that vain men (and I hope I am not so vain as to *exempt* myself from that category) are vain about all aspects of their appearance. Nobody wears well-cut breeches yet a raggedy top-coat. But Gowers appeared to be the exception. His scruffy and stained raiment suggested a lack of self-regard, but he could not so easily disregard his deformed nose. It was plainly a trial and torment to him. Its dimensions dictated a face about a third bigger than that from which it protruded, and he was perpetually squinting down at it, which would send him momentarily cross-eyed.

It struck me that Gowers' nose stood for all his shortcomings. He would touch it whenever he was uncertain of himself, and in particular when he lied. I was revolving putting the question point blank: 'Did you murder the shade painter Harvey?' for the truth might be signified pretty quickly by his response.

Yet, monstrous though Gowers might be, I had reprehended the way his fellow Black Diamonds had slighted him behind his back. There was a bracing quality to Gowers, whereas I found his supposed colleagues, Villiers and Edwin, to be sinuous, feline, embodying all the duplicity I associate with life in the capital.

We had long since left the thoroughfare, and were deep in the labyrinth. Every other house seemed untenanted, or at least unlighted. We must soon approach Gowers' own place.

Two more turns, a low-burning lamp illuminating a sign – Blue Lion Place – and we were upon it. There came a small flash of illumination from the black door, as if a glow-worm had alighted there. Gowers' servant – a little Sottish fellow called Duncan – had flicked back the peephole, and was now proceeding to unlock the door, as signified by a rattling of chains. This gloomy court, I considered, was the very opposite of Adenwold village, where no door was ever locked; where, indeed, the houses were not lockable.

The presence of the servant emboldened me, and I turned to Gowers as we waited before the door. 'Sir,' I said, 'you mentioned that you had not been in York these past eight years.' Gowers grunted. He had removed his hat in anticipation of stepping into his warm hall, and was growing impatient with the delay. 'Is there any possibility,' I asked, 'that you misremember?'

'Not the slightest, sir. Do you take me for a halfwit?'

'I've been meaning all evening to mention—'

'What, sir?'

The door was opened. Duncan was bowing; we stepped inside. Gowers commanded the servant, 'Bottle of the claret, sirrah.'

As Duncan took my coat, I came out with it in a flurry: 'Only that I believe I saw you in York in the Race Week of this year.'

Gowers touched his nose, and there was now a decisively different expression in his eyes. He had been well disposed to me. That was now over. He made an attempt to regain some of his old, booming bluster.

'The Race Week, you say? That is the one se'enight I would certainly *not* be in York. That *rout*. The city becomes a positive stew at that time. All the reading and writing men are driven out, unless we count the readers of the Turf Registers!'

'The Assizes are held at the same time, and—'

'And what of it? The lawyers come to the trough, too.'

'Perhaps I am the one mistaken.'

'It's a surety, sir!'

'It was only that I thought I saw someone who somewhat ... resembled you.'

I had now – albeit elliptically – brought the nose into

things, and so was doubly damned. (I wonder, as I write this, whether I have deliberately damned myself.)

We entered the drawing room. Duncan had set two chairs by the fire and a bottle of wine stood on a little table in between. If the house was a brick box, then here was a wooden box within, the room being darkly wainscoted in the old-fashioned style. No looking glass hung on the wall, nor any picture, and the room was cold, in spite of the fire. Duncan took two more logs – not enough – from the narrow cabinet set into the panel alongside the mantelpiece. He placed them on the fire. Gowers indicated that the servant should return into the hallway; he followed him. The two began a conflab in the hallway, and after a moment, Gowers closed the door, so that I might not be privy to the conversation. A moment later, I heard the front door open and close. I knew that, had the shutters in the drawing room been open, I would have observed the departure of Duncan. He had been given the night off, or otherwise despatched. He presumably had a family home to return to in the vicinity. He couldn't possibly live with the intemperate Gowers all the time. There was no other servant, and so I was now alone in the house with Gowers – who had not yet returned to the drawing room.

I heard the creaking of the staircase. Gowers was ascending, not descending; his slow movement set the whole house creaking, like a brig in a high swell. Apart from the fireside arrangement there was but one piece of furniture in the room: a cabinet of drawers. A burning candle sat atop it, another on the mantle. I could hear Gowers in the room above, where he seemed to be opening a drawer or a cupboard. I simultaneously rose from my chair and did likewise.

In the first drawer that I pulled back, I saw a hairbrush, matted with the hairs of a periwig, and with some other, reddish ones that I presumed came from Gowers' own head. I turned the hairbrush over to see, on the reverse, a small mirror, or anyhow the remains of a mirror, for it had been smashed, and only a couple of slivers remained. I felt thoroughly ashamed for having looked; and yet, after closing that drawer, I slowly pulled back the next one down. It held a mass of torn and crumpled papers and cards, everything monochromatic. I unfolded a piece of screwed-up white stock card. There was lettering I couldn't read. I dashed over to the mantelpiece, caught up the second candle, took it to the cabinet. In the re-doubled light, I read, 'Likeness by Mr Higgins, Seven Dials'. I turned it over, and there was the shade of a big-nosed man.

The same, or more or less the same image (the hat came and went but the nose was obstinately repeated in its true dimensions), appeared on all the pieces of paper and card. Some had been torn clean through, some half through.

Evidently none had been deemed suitable for the title page of a book, and I wondered how many more had been pitched onto the fire. Gowers was snagged on Villiers' proposal that the Black Diamond authors should include their profiles in their books, and I wondered whether the insidious Villiers had proposed the idea specifically in order to embarrass Gowers. An unworthy plan, if so. A man ought to confront his enemies directly, not undermine by subterfuge.

Gowers still moved about upstairs. I shut the drawer full of shades, and opened the next one down. It held a pistol. My own fault for looking. The creaking on the stairs being renewed, I shut the drawer and I had regained the chair by the fireplace a moment later. I listened as Gowers locked and bolted the front door, making a prisoner of me. When he finally re-entered the room, I saw that I had stupidly left the mantelpiece candle on the cabinet, and so the two candles stood side-by-side in incriminating alliance. Gowers, of course, glanced that way immediately.

Fletcher Rigge, in continuation.

I passed the next hour in the room with Gowers, but I might as well have been there alone.

The candle flames – Gowers had carried the mantelpiece one back to its proper place without comment – wasted uneasily in the diverse draughts as I attempted to draw Gowers out in conversation. I mentioned Milton, but Gowers cut me off: 'It is far too large a subject.' Gowers would not be drawn out even on the question of his own art. Asked whether he had a book in hand, he grunted, 'Of course. A man must live, mustn't he?' Asked the title, he muttered something like, '*Observations*', and I had to make do with that, as he resumed his staring into the middle distance, or down into the flames of the fire.

I attempted to get back to the personalities of the Black Diamonds, or the literary men in the houses roundabout, but Gowers simply said, in a low tone, 'It is a wonder we are all alive.'

Presently – and while drinking a good deal more wine than my host – I began speaking of the coach ride from York, and Gowers let me ramble on, while never once looking at me.

We had left York in a white fog – I told him – which had mercifully obscured the Tyburn at the start of the Great North Road. The land had been enclosed almost all the way, but in Lincolnshire – where the wind had fairly screamed at us – the fields had been bare of sheep, the creatures presumably huddled in the brick pens that I would see occasionally. The sheep – a stupid, but liberty-loving creature – only seeks indoor refuge in the vilest weather. The snow had given out around Peterborough, while the trees had stopped at about Royston, to be replaced by thorn bushes, and then, in Highgate, by houses.

Gowers showed no interest in this topography, but still he let me run on. Therefore I explained how I had become fascinated by the driver, and I attempted to fascinate Gowers about him . . .

The fellow always made the stages on time, with only occasional consultations of his watch, which he called his 'clock'. He called the coach the 'drag'. On boarding at York, I had noticed scratches all down the sides, and I first saw the reason for these somewhere about Doncaster. The driver enjoyed giving any other vehicle on the road ahead the go-by. 'Ought to just shave past,' he'd say, and I would tense as the fellow whipped the horses on prior to some reckless manoeuvre. I had come to quite enjoy these spurts of speed after a while.

The coachman knew all the inns, which he called 'Jerry shops', and on each of our two nights of laying over, he let me – as the outside passenger – have the first hot bath. In those inns he drank gin, which he called, quite unfathomably, 'ribbon'. He and I had usually shared a table: two dishes apiece, two pastries and a penny to the waiter. We would eat in companionable near-silence. The landlords of the inns he called 'Bungs'. He didn't much care for the guard, whom he referred to without his hearing as 'that bladder of lard', the guard being rather fat . . .

But now I broke off, for Gowers was rising from his feet. He took the candle from the mantelpiece.

'I will show you to your bedchamber, sir.'

Just then, I took heart from the sound of a commotion in the court outside, but the shouts soon died away, and I was left alone once again with Gowers. I would have given a good deal to hear the lunatic's cry of 'How's your poor feet?' for that would have proved I had woken from a dream and was back in the city of York whose attendant dangers are perhaps more easily negotiable.

Gowers began walking towards the door, and I, draining my glass, meekly followed.

Fletcher Rigge, in continuation.

I write this sitting on the bed provided for me in Gowers' house. The writing calms me somewhat. I have just heard the cry of the Watch. 'It's midnight, and . . .' the rest was lost. The fellow was too distant for my liking. My thoughts are running upon the pistol I discovered in the drawer below, but I saw no powder, and I believe I once heard that Londoners kept powder-less pistols to wave about in hopes of scaring off intruders.

Is it possible he is waiting for me to drop asleep?

On showing me up to the room, Gowers closed the shutters very firmly, stoked up the fire, pulled back the blankets on the bed, and departed with barely a goodnight, agreeing only with the greatest reluctance to leave behind a candle. Now that I think of it, he did everything but slip me a sleeping draught. As he took his leave, I rather cravenly hinted that I would like to use the necessary house – for that, of course, would be outside, and *once* outside I need not come back in – but Gowers pointed out a pot cupboard behind a screen in this room.

When he had departed, I re-opened the shutters, to see that two of the four panes of window glass were cracked and two missing entirely. Beyond lay nothing but the shadowy court. How can the middle of London be so silent? But it appears I have entered the eye of the hurricane.

I am revolving the idea of demanding, point blank, to be allowed to depart, but I will not stoop to that indignity. In any case, I might thereby provoke Gowers to an act that may, at present, be only in contemplation. Either way, my anxiety comes as a well-merited punishment for thinking Gowers an irrelevance in light of Jeremiah Smith's actions.

Is it possible that two murderers were numbered among Matthew Harvey's sitters?

The candle is guttering, and will expire before I reach the foot of this page.

My host is certainly not abed. I hear him pacing below. Assuredly some act seems in preparation, unless the pacing should signify indecision? Ought I to descend the stairs and have it all out with him, demanding to know why he lied about being in York, and concealed his visit to Matthew Harvey? I flatter myself that I am more curious than afeared. I would like to see the case determined, even should I live not more than a second after the ultimate revelation. I will admit to being cold, however. The fire is expiring along with the candle, and I am starting to shiver.

This shivering will end if I climb beneath the blankets and go to sleep. Perhaps *everything* will end in that case, and what matter of it? This commission of the Captain's will not avert my doom; it is merely the acceleration of it. At best, the Sherriff's men will come and take me back into the Castle, and Harvey will be put to thinking up some new entertainment. Lucy Spink will be married to a muddy man in Thirsk; the estate will be enclosed, with not a scrap of waste ground remaining, and sheep meadows running away into infinity.

———

I believe I slept just now, if only for a moment – or perhaps for half an hour, for the candle is long gone, and the fire almost black. I believe I dreamed. I seemed to glimpse a porter pot on some shadowy corner cabinet much like the one in this room. A pair of special scissors were propped up in it, and I heard spoken, in a hollow sort of voice, a phrase I associate with the advertisements of the shade painters: 'Executed particularly neat', it said, several times, as there came to me an image of spilled and flowing Indian ink, which threatened every minute to take on the character of flowing blood.

My dream then returned me to the York Castle, where I was standing by the Day Room window – except that it was night-time and quite black beyond – with under-gaoler Hill close by me. He was pointing his grubby finger at a paragraph inserted into the *York Courant* by a certain eminent gentleman, whose name was somehow not disclosed, but whom it was possible to meet in the Cathedral.

I was then *in* the Cathedral, appointed to meet a gentleman in the choir stall. I discovered him there at prayer. I tapped him on the periwig and a great nose rose up beneath it.

But I am fully awake now, and I hear the creaking of the stairs. My host approaches, and so I leave off my wri

----

[**Mr Erskine's interpolation**: With this half word, the entry for Friday November 23rd concludes.]

Letter from Mr Villiers to Mr Erskine.

4 Bride Lane,
London.

My first letter left off with the departure of Mr Rigge in company with that primus inter pares of the Black Diamonds, Mr Gowers. I will spare you, Mr Erskine, my imaginings as to what depredations our peculiar-looking friend planned to inflict upon the willing myrmidon he seemed to have acquired. My projections were of the blackest, and I believed that if Rigge had merely to put up with a reading from the Johnson book, then he would have got off lightly. But I was not that young man's protector, and I took myself off home to bed.

In my case, however, that nightly action is as likely to be the start of a hectic proceeding as the end of it, for I labour under insomnia, and I am never less likely to sleep than after an evening spent under the rhetorical assaults of Gowers. On that particular evening, I recall abandoning the idea of sleep as the Watch cried midnight. I quit my lodgement and walked along to a certain coffee shop off Chancery Lane, where a well banked-up fire and good chocolate (there is no liquor) attracts the older and more decrepit sorts of draymen or porters. It also attracts many of London's foreigners and provincials, especially the Welsh, whose voices I find pleasingly soporific.

But a repeated, very anomalous, crash of laughter from the corner table drove me out, and I resolved to exhaust myself. I would go for a ramble, and I would 'walk in the way of the Lord', by which I mean I would go by Gowers' place. He lives among writing men, and it does me good to see their houses dark, signifying a let up in the book wars. I was also curious to discover whether he did intend any impropriety with young Rigge. I knew it was more likely, however, that I would glimpse them through the chink in the shutters sharing a bottle of Gowers' mediocre claret, that nonpareil pontificating, the other giving his gracious, enigmatical nod from time to time.

I wandered towards that elusive court, north of Fleet Street, where Gowers lives. Even after repeated visits, I sometimes think I will never again locate his habitation, and that Gowers will prove never to have existed, a mere emanation of my worst nightmares. But I came upon the place at, I suppose, half after one. It was in complete darkness, as were all its neighbours. Evidently, Gowers had left off speechifying for the night. Yet, as I approached, I did make out voices, and they came not from the drawing room in which Gowers usually held court, but from the upper storey, and the speakers were clearly audible, the shutters being open, the window glass cracked and the night otherwise silent.

I was all-too familiar with the sound of Gowers, and one of the two voices was certainly his, but this was not his usual conversational – that is to say, hectoring – tone. He spoke in

*an under-voice entirely new to me, a sort of malignant hiss.
The other voice, more refined, and calmer (yet straining for
that calmness), must be young Rigge's. It was Gowers that I
heard first:*

'Why, sir, should I allow you to quit the house?'

*After a brief delay, Rigge replied, 'The more pertinent
question, surely, is "Why would you not?"'*

*Gowers' reply was obtuse. In fact, it was no reply at all: 'I
would wish you, sir, a little less busy about my affairs.'*

*Rigge again: 'I merely wondered when you were last in
York.' Rigge then made some additional remark I could not
catch, but it was obviously highly provoking to Gowers, who
roared out, 'Why would I murder him, dammit?'*

'Well . . .'

*'None of your "wells", sirrah, come out with it directly or I
will loose this ball.'*

*'It might be that a gentleman in his line of work, a close
observer of—'*

'Of what, confound you?'

'Of the physiognomy of—'

*'There are too many "ofs" in all this. Speak plainly or by
God I will murder you.'*

'There might have been an argument about aesthetics.'

*'You continue opaque. I spend my life in aesthetic
argument. Do you think I wouldn't have slaughtered that
ignorant rabble in Cuthbert's Ale House long since if I took
aesthetics too much to heart?'*

A long pause, in which, Mr Erskine, I made a definite resolve to quit the weekly convocations of the Black Diamonds.

'It might be,' Rigge said at length, 'that Matthew Harvey made too accurate a depiction of your . . . '

At which the hiss of Gowers became a veritable hissing scream: 'My what, sir? Say it, damn you!' There came a small sound, and yet momentous: it was the clicking of a pistol.

'Say it!' screamed Gowers, at which Rigge sadly pronounced: 'Your nose.'

I am quite certain, Mr Erskine, that if it had been within Gowers' power to cock his pistol again, then he would have done so, but the point of decision had been arrived at, and could not be further arrived at.

I heard the cry of the Watch: 'Two of the clock and all well.'

'Get out, damn you!' Gowers roared, from the upper floor. 'Get out directly, before your impertinence brings what it deserves.'

Mr Erskine's memorandum to Mr Taylor, concerning the following three days.

We take up with Mr Rigge's diary on the Tuesday, when he arrived back in York.

It seems he had found a lodgement in London for what remained of the night of Friday 23rd, and for Saturday 24th. He boarded the York stage on the next day, the Sunday. His entries for those dates contain the description of his confrontation with Gowers, as already presented to us from the perspective of Villiers. The two accounts do not differ markedly, and so I do not give Rigge's. He then embarked on a good deal of speculation as to what Gowers' behaviour might signify in relation to the murder of Harvey. His thoughts on the matter are effectually summarised in his entry for Tuesday.

Diary of Fletcher Rigge, Tuesday November 27th.

The coachman on the way back was not the fellow I had on the way up. He was equally interesting, if less likeable. For instance, he approved all the enclosures that enjoined our route. I had asked, 'What about the people turned off the land?' and he replied that his father had been turned off the land, and was very glad of it, since he'd entered the coaching trade. An enclosure had been the making of him. 'Forced him to get on with things . . . Sauntering after cows is a recipe for idleness.'

At our two lay-ups, this fellow 'got on with it' all right, and took the first of the hot water for his bath. The guard didn't mind a bit. In fact, these two got on famously, and passed the time by testing each other's knowledge on a variety of subjects, for example 'Who wrote *Robinson Crusoe*?' I never quite ascertained whether I was invited to join in or not. I knew all the answers (if I may be excused the conceitedness of saying so), therefore it was probably as well that I kept silence. But now that I recollect, I came up short with the following. 'Which book of the Bible makes no mention of God?' The answer is Ezra, and the driver knew it. As they amused themselves with this game, I pondered for the hundredth time my deeper mysteries.

Gowers had come upstairs with his pistol in his hand. He was enraged, but why? Because I had suggested he had lately been in York, and that he had disguised the fact. Why should that offend him? Because he apprehended an accusation of lying? Yes, but that is not sufficient reason. What did he think I was accusing him of lying *about*? I assume he knew Harvey had been killed, either because he did the deed himself, or because he read of it in the *Courant*, which he saw in London.

And so we come to his intention towards me: to kill or frighten? Evidently, he had not originally wanted to frighten me *out of the house*, for he had made a prisoner of me. But then he had released me – fairly *screaming* me out of the house – in such a way that all further converse was impossible. Perhaps he had meant to kill me, and had relented, although I did not say anything to make him relent. Rather the opposite, for I had uttered that dangerous word starting with 'n'. Perhaps

179

he stayed his hand because he was in his own house, and so would be left with a corpse to dispose of. The pistol report would surely be heard by someone in the vicinity, and indeed when I was ejected from the house with bag in hand, I saw a muffled-up figure walking rapidly away. Gowers could not have known about this late-night pedestrian, but I wondered whether it might have been one of the other Diamonds coming to pay a call, but deterred by the shouting. (It might also have weighed with Gowers that his fellow Diamonds knew I was laying over at his place.)

My provisional conclusion is as follows. Gowers did not kill Matthew Harvey. Harvey was killed by a knife, and Gowers came at me with a gun, when a blade would have made more sense – that is to say, less noise. Gowers apprehended an accusation of murder. He believed that I, his accuser, might bring him to the gallows, which must have been particularly provoking, since he had first thought me a besotted admirer of his writing. It is not unlikely, given his pugnacity and vanity, that he really did have a row – albeit not fatal – with Matthew Harvey, himself a dogmatic and charmless individual. But I believe that he took up the pistol and came at me in a blind rage, rather than with the intention to kill.

I remain of the opinion that Jeremiah Smith, a proven murderer, was the culprit, and the discovery I made on climbing down – frozen half to death – from the stagecoach at York reinforced this opinion . . .

In the stable yard of the Black Swan, the London stage is given quite a reception: grooms, chambermaids, barkeepers and cooks line up to bow the new arrivals, and a sort of channel is created by these smiling genuflectors, directing travellers into the dining room of the inn, from which the smells of frying bacon and steak are always issuing when the main coaches pull in. Having breakfasted at Stamford on a shred of burnt toast and a dish of tea, I was unable to resist such clever manipulation, and ten minutes after arrival, I was drinking a glass of port wine by the saloon fire, and anticipating the arrival of veal soup and a sirloin of beef.

As on the last occasion when I had supped at the Swan, I took down a copy of the *Courant* from the mantelpiece. It was yesterday's edition, and my eye was drawn to the column marked 'WANTED', where I read the following:

'Mrs Kendall of the Red House, Clifton, is in immediate want of a TUTOR to her son, who is in preparation for Oxford. A young man of good temper and patience is required. He must have an undeniable character from his last place. An excellent rate of pay is offered. Application by letters.'

This, I thought, must be the very same Mrs Kendall who owned the pug dog. The address gave her away. Evidently she had a son as well as two girls.

I lament the need to make an insincere application for the post, but I will certainly be writing to the lady. It would seem perverse not to, given that I have been stuck for any plausible reason for calling on her; given also my chief imperative, which is to bring this business to a close quickly, with as little harm done as possible. It happens that I do have a character, from Skelton (written, doubtless, to ease his conscience), and my term at the University will probably count for more than it ought.

At that moment, the soup and meat arrived together, and I fell to with an appetite, and in reasonable spirits. Things were indeed moving forward apace. I do not say I was happy, exactly. My London jaunt had naturally been a good deal more expensive than I had envisaged. Having spent three pounds of the Captain's five, I was thinking of applying to him for a further advance, but I can never bring that gentleman to mind without feeling a great unease.

The *Courant* still lay on the table before me. As I made to turn over the page, my eye fell on the following:

'A most shocking accident came to light on Sunday evening. Melissa King, a young woman of no settled home, was found smashed to atoms in a yard to the rear of a house in Pound Lane. She had been lodging on the upper storey of the house for some days previously and it is presumed that suicide was the cause of her sad demise.'

My spirits fled immediately. There would be no inquest for poor Melissa King, that victim of the city and – surely – of Jeremiah Smith. She had been described by the watchman of a week ago as sole witness to the killing of the theatre manager, Mr Cork. I ought to have taken a greater trouble to find out her identity, and warn her; and so I finished my expensive dinner with little relish, and a great heaviness of heart.

Fletcher Rigge, in continuation.

When I regained my lodging, I found waiting for me a letter from an attorney. It was not from my father's man, the dutiful and depressing Mr Pullman, but from a Mr Erskine of Precentor's Court. He wishes to see me as soon as conveniently possible, on a matter concerning my father's estate. Yes, he writes 'your father's estate' rather than Corrigan's, and so my turmoil increases. Might there be some possibility of a restitution of the lands, and therefore some escape from the Captain, and the snare of the Seven Shades? And might Lucy Spink have known of this, hence her promise to tell me how to regain the lands?

I refuse to believe that can be the case; yet I walked immediately to Precentor's Court (which is just by the

Minster), where I spoke to the gentleman's clerk, a bluff fellow called Mr Bright. He seemed to know a good deal about me, which might have bothered me, except that he seemed well intentioned. I have arranged an appointment with Mr Erskine for Friday.

Meanwhile, my writing for today is not yet done.

Letter from Fletcher Rigge to Mrs Kendall.

Over Buckley's Violin Workshop,
Oglethorpe,
York.
Tuesday November 27th

Dear Madam,

I beg leave to apply for the post of Tutor to your son, as advertised in the York Courant. I attended Rugby School and King's College at Cambridge. At present I get my living from literature, and I will be able to furnish a character from Mr Skelton, bookseller, that will, I believe, not prejudice you against

Your most obedient humble servant,

Fletcher Rigge.

Mrs Kendall's reply to Fletcher Rigge.

The Red House,
Clifton Green,
York.
Wednesday November 28th

Sir,

Thank you for yours. If you will be pleased to call on me tomorrow at four o'clock, we will see if we can come to a mutually satisfactory arrangement.

Your humble servant,

Mrs Louisa Kendall

Mr Bright's note concerning the above correspondence, with particular reference to the arrangements at Mr Rigge's lodgings.

I had delivered in person the letter to Mr Rigge from Mr Erskine. I did so on the Tuesday morning, probably as Mr Rigge was dining in the Black Swan. It is needful – for reasons that will become clear – that I should describe how this delivery was effected.

Mr Rigge lives at Ogleforth, a quaint old street behind the Minster. His lodge is over the premises of a violin maker, one Buckley. The lodge is accessible from the yard to the rear of the building. Having obtained no reply when I rapped on this rear door, I tried the handle. Finding the door unlocked, I stepped into a small vestibule, where I found the foot of a narrow staircase immediately before me and a curtained door to my left. This last is the entrance to the living quarters of Mr and Mrs Buckley. I know this because Mrs Buckley came through that aperture – and the curtain – at the moment I entered the vestibule. She had evidently heard me coming in. She asked my business – and that quite pointedly. I said I had a letter for Mr Rigge, at which her manner softened. She indicated the staircase, which evidently led up to Mr Rigge's lodgement. She offered to take the letter up for me, but I said I would do it myself, at which she told me to, 'Leave the letter on the table, dear.'

At the top of the staircase, I discovered the door of Rigge's chambers, which I assumed was locked, and a pedestal table alongside it, on which stood an unlighted candle in a holder. I placed the letter under the candle holder.

I have subsequently discovered that Mrs Buckley would collect any letters for Mr Rigge while picking up her own from the post-office. If Mr Rigge were out, she would place the letters under the candle holder, and with the candle lit if it were dark. Rigge would leave letters for posting – and any postage money owing to Mrs Buckley – in the same place.

Of greater signification, however, is the arrangement about that external door. It was customarily kept unlocked. Indeed, there has never been a working lock upon it. I happened to draw the attention of Mrs Buckley as I opened that door, but if that lady were asleep, or if the caller entered stealthily, then it would be possible to approach Rigge's rooms without detection. It 'would be' possible and, as we shall see, it *was* possible.

Diary of Esther, Wednesday November 28th.

The Captain has been at his desk and writing again. I do not like to see him writing. Some letters of his were the start of all our trouble in London, and the reason we had to come here. But I believe we will be returning to London before long in any case.

The Captain is about one of his campaigns. Or, rather, two, and they have not long to run. Firstly, there is the matter of the shades. Then there are the coal heavers, who are connected to the Captain both personally and business-wise – and I am now quite certain the business in question goes beyond the delivering of coal to the four corners of the city. (I always suspected he went into coal to be at close-quarters with the coal heavers, and now I am sure of it. He evidently finds them fascinating, not least for the occasional trouble they cause him.)

It does not suit the Captain to be writing. He is not used to it. He is a clever man, but his tongue projects when he is about it. He is used to lounging, talking amusingly, and occasionally reading the literature – as I suppose we must call it – passed between him and Stephen. Looking over the Captain's shoulder the other day at the book he was reading, I made out a description of some lovemaking contortion we had not yet attempted or, in my case, ever dreamed of. The Captain turned around, and took my hand. 'Would you like to try it, my dear?' and so we trooped up to the bedchamber.

We adopted the posture, twice breaking off to refer back to the book, and eventually the Captain commenced to drive, but he soon burst out laughing, and he could not [**Mr Bright's interpolation:** in the original, the following word was crossed out and re-tried several times with new spellings.] vitiate. But he achieved that goal a little later, while manualising himself noisily in the bath, with a great sloshing of water over the side, so that drips came through the floorboards, and onto my head as I tried to kindle the fire in the drawing room. He was no doubt picturing himself in some connection with that particular coal heaver – the one he and Stephen particularly favour, who drives the cart, and never looks me in the face when he is brought into the house. They take him upstairs, and undress him (although he is half undressed at his work anyway). They then wash him thoroughly, as though he might be a precious stone they have found in the river mud. They take all the candles in the house into that room, in order to inspect their treasure, which of course they do more than inspect.

Was ever a wife – even a common-law one – subject to such humiliations? But then I consider: the Captain rescued me from the depravities of Covent Garden; he has never struck me, and he has often made me laugh, although not much of late. I am seldom in the humour for mirth these days, and it is more profitable for me to show myself unhappy before him, in which case there come forth numerous tender condolences: another brandy poured; an offer of partridge for dinner, money for lace or ribbon. I believe that I am stirring only his conscience and his guilt, as suggested by this plain fact: the more heedless he has been of me, the more valuable the gift he offers. It is alarming that he now talks of giving me pearls, either on a brooch, or – when he is in liquor – on a necklace. If either trinket should ever come my way, what will I do with it? Nothing but lock it in the writing box on which my present paper rests, together with my trinkets and this diary, which is hardly *worth* locking away, since the Captain never shows the slightest curiosity about it. Indeed, on those occasions when we do share a bed, I will often sit up next to him, writing away, with blotter and ink pot to hand, like some clerk in an office!

The Captain says a diamond is 'on the cards', for the coal trade is prospering. It appears that he knew all the workshops would be going over to the steam engines. In this weather he also profits greatly from sales to ordinary houses. He wishes to start finding his own coal, which he says is 'lying about everywhere'. There are men who will prospect the coal – by walking into a meadow and digging a hole. The Captain would send them out all over the country, becoming a sort of agent for these men. If they found coal, he would buy the land. But he could do all this from London, and so again I think we are about to remove, once the undertaking he has in hand with Mr Rigge is concluded.

I asked him whether he would tell the farmer about the coal before offering to buy the land, and he only laughed in that rather shy way that I used to find so captivating. He tells me that the letters he is writing are to do with this new enterprise in coal. But yesterday, when he left off writing in order to make himself a pot of coffee, I glanced down at a fragment of a letter, half hidden beneath the blotter. All I could make out before he returned were the words 'taken indecent liberties' and I wonder how that can be connected to coal? How could anybody have taken more indecent liberties than he himself? Well, I believe I know what the phrase signifies, and the question is whether my silence in the matter makes me complicit. I am unquestionably a person of immoral principles, and yet my conscience accuses me.

Another letter, sealed and ready for despatch, lay on the Captain's table, beneath the pistol he has taken to using as a paper weight. It was addressed to Mr Rigge, at his lodgings in Ogleforth. I cannot begin to guess at the contents, but I doubt they will make happy reading for Mr Fletcher Rigge.

Diary of Fletcher Rigge, Thursday November 29th.

Yesterday was a day of total idleness. I ought to have revisited the Registry to try again for a sight of the will, but I was exhausted and spent most of the day abed, tormented by thoughts of Miss Spink and her 'termination in gladness'. I took out from beneath the bed my father's copy of the deed by which the estate was transferred to

Corrigan. This expanse of vellum is nearly the same size as the threadbare counterpane that I laid it over, and the close writing upon it is all one sentence, since punctuation might throw off the meaning. I pictured myself sitting on one side of the great fireplace in the Hall at Aden Park (a glass of port wine in my hand), with Miss Spink on the opposite chair, and this abhorred charter writhing and smoking in the flames between us. But while the letter from Mr Erskine, attorney, offers some dim prospect of this becoming reality, the Captain's business must be my immediate concern.

So it was that in the late afternoon today I went by hackney – the roads being icy – to the Red House at Clifton Green, home to the Kendalls and, as I assumed, their pug dog.

The Red House is new, probably built in the past year as part of the general ambush of that innocent Green by mercantile money. It is well named, and there seemed an angry redness in the brickwork, as seen against the cold, violet sky, while the stone of the portico was white almost to dazzling.

As the hackney rumbled away over the dirty snow, I observed that the sky was darkening, at which moment a lamplighter opportunely appeared. He set down his oil can, and touched his hat. After we had exchanged some pleasantries on the subject of the terrible weather, I pushed open the gate of the Red House, at which he said, 'I'd watch out for the infantry, sir, if I was you.'

'The infantry?' I said.

'The young ladies, I mean,' and I realised that he had actually said 'infant-*ry*,' which must be a cant word I had never heard before, and is presumably reserved for the most raucous children. 'Proper varmints, they are,' the lamplighter continued. 'Game as any man I know, that pair.'

'I suppose I ought to have come with sweetmeats,' I suggested, 'or some other means of pacifying them.'

'A pistol might do it,' said the lamplighter.

'I'm here to apply for the post of tutor,' I said.

The lamplighter nodded to himself for a while. The fellow intrigued me. I divined that he might be about to impart some useful intelligence. 'An excellent rate of pay is offered,' I said, hoping to prompt some observation.

'It would have to be,' he said. 'I don't want to talk out of turn,' he continued (a sure sign that he was about to do just that), 'but all I can say is that I come by here twice a day, and there are generally screams coming from the house. That or the mad barking of a dog.'

There were no screams or barks just then, as he had to admit. 'Perhaps the young ladies are taking their tea . . . '

'It's hard to scream with a mouthful of cake,' I conceded.

'They don't find it very hard, I believe, but the meals are taken at the back room, which is—'

He broke off, for the loud yapping of a dog had commenced. I saw the creature through the window of the ground floor front room. It was leaping madly about on the back of a red sofa placed hard against the window. The dog was a pug: whitish with a black mask, the very animal, surely, that had been depicted by Matthew Harvey. It had seen us at the gate, and so we were the cause of the racket.

'Do you like dogs?' asked the lamplighter. 'I believe you'll come to prefer the barking over the screaming in time, sir, should you end up a regular visitor here. It's a wonder their poor mother hasn't gone all to pieces.'

'What about the father?'

'Aloft,' said the lamplighter, and I thought at first that he was indicating the lamp he had just lit; but then I saw he was indicating a higher place. 'Built up a big iron foundry in Leeds. Worried himself to death over it.'

'But the wife seems pretty well circumstanced,' I said, indicating the house.

'On account of being left a fortune by the husband, sir, yes. Even so, I feel sorry for the lady, having those two tearaway girls; and the butler's a queer cove.'

'Trustworthy?'

'I'd say not. Takes advantage of there being no master in the house.'

'Perhaps I could give a hint to the mistress.'

'That would be a kindness.'

'What's his particular . . . proclivity?'

'What's that, sir?'

'What's his line in villainy, I mean?'

'I believe . . . having away the silver. Small articles – salt spoons, thimbles and the like.'

We watched the dog, still leaping at the window.

'Not a right sort of dog, if you ask me,' the lamplighter observed. 'I recall the days, sir, when this was all ploughed fields and meadows. I'd come here as a boy with my own dog. Mack, he was called – a terrier, and a regular good 'un. When the fields were covered by stubble after the harvest – that's when you could see the hares. The hawks would take 'em of course, or my Mack. Do you have experience of the countryside, sir?'

I nodded.

'Have you ever seen a buzzard take a leveret in a field of stubble, sir?'

At this I *half* nodded, feeling somehow ashamed for being unable to recollect such an event. 'You'd not forget if you *had* seen it, sir,' and I realised I had found myself in this uncomfortable position before: a pretended countryman confronted by the genuine article.

'I daresay you preferred it when it was fields,' I said, but to my surprise the lamplighter shook his head.

'Very little work about in those days, whereas I've got a living off these new houses, one way or another, these past five years.'

'Was the land enclosed?' I asked. 'Because I know the work falls off when that happens.'

The lamplighter shook his head. 'It was all farmed in the old way. We had a cottage and cow, and use of the common land. Mack liked it of course, running free all day – no sheep in the fields, you see – but it wasn't enough for a man, sir, not nearly enough.'

The lamplighter's words, echoing those of the driver of the coach from London, gave me pause, or they would have done had not the figure of a young girl appeared at the window. With a cry of rage and a single swipe, she removed the agitated dog from the chair back, and dropped the swagged curtain, thereby disappearing from view.

Fletcher Rigge, in continuation.

I approached the door of the Red House, crossing a garden in which some glum sort of excavation had been taking place. There was nothing green in the garden, only piles of stones, bricks and sand, lightly decorated with snow. Perhaps an ornamental pond was being put in. I was debating town against country in my mind, but then another – less philosophical – thought crept in. I stopped by the hole, and took out my wallet. I transferred two pound notes into my waistcoat pocket. Three remained in the wallet. I advanced to the door, and pounded the knocker, which resounded hollowly. There came high-pitched shouting from within.

A stone-faced servant opened the door; he discovered me fumbling with my wallet, disclosing the three banknotes back into it. One swooped to the snowy ground. I affected not to see it, but the servant could not take the chance. He was obliged to indicate – with the greatest reluctance, and no words but merely a down-pointed finger – the dropped cash. I said I was obliged to him, and returned it – rather negligently – into the pocket book, which I re-inserted into my top-coat pocket. This was all done under the close stare of the manservant.

He showed me into a hall of white marble. It was cold, in spite of the fire that burned in a highly polished iron grate of a fashionable style. The very flames themselves looked new. I gave my name to the manservant, and stated my business, upon which he took my coat and hat into a side room. He returned to the hall, and ascended the stairs, having said barely a word.

Towards the rear of the hallway stood a girl. She seemed tiny; or perhaps it was an illusion, the hall being so tall, the coldly sparkling chandelier dangling a good six feet above her head. She wore a plaid dress, and there were many ribbons in her ringleted hair. She was pretty enough; but then she spoke.

'Who are you?' she demanded, in a cracked, rather grating voice. I bowed and replied that my name was Mr Rigge, and I had come about the position of tutor to her brother. She did not deny that she had a brother, but did not confirm it either.

She eyed me for a while. Another girl was sobbing not very far off, but from behind a door.

'*Parlez-vous français?*' the first girl demanded.

'*Un peu.*'

'That won't do. When mama asks you, you must say, "*Je parle français très bien.*"'

Hardly grammatical, but I was not here to teach French, rather Latin and Greek. I was looking anxiously at the stairs, hoping some adult would soon arrive.

'What is the capital of Spain?' the girl was demanding.

'Young lady, I—'

'Quickly now.'

'Madrid,' I said.

'Have you been there?'

'No.'

'Are you a debtor of the first, second, or third class?'

At this, I fairly gasped. Could she possibly know that I had been in the Castle? I was too stunned to answer.

'We are playing at debtors,' the girl said. 'Sometimes we play coroners' reports, but today it's debtors. My sister is a debtor of the first class. She is in prison in the nursery. I won't let her out till she's paid me a shilling.' She held up a key, saying, 'Do you know Latin and Greek and all the ancient writers?'

'Well now,' I said, wondering how much longer I would be left alone with this miniature termagant, 'I'm tolerably familiar with the principal ones.'

'Sounds to me as if you need a tutor yourself. Can you play the harp?'

'No.'

'Well, that's honest, at least. Mother is a member of the York Musical Society. She wanted a musical young gentleman. But I said she must take what she gets.'

Finally, there came a tread on the staircase, and a tired-looking yet elegant woman came into view. She wore her hair à la Brutus. She was unquestionably the person whose likeness had been painted by Harvey, and the girl before me was surely one of the two depicted with her. Of the brother, there was still no sign.

I bowed to the woman, who introduced herself graciously enough, but in a rather sad, sighing tone, as Mrs Kendall. She quickly apprehended the bizarre game her daughter had been playing, which was evidently a familiar one. 'Give me the key, Mercy dear,' she said, and the little girl handed it over, saying, 'She will say she's been injured. It's nothing to do with me.'

With the key in her hand, Mrs Kendall approached a door to the rear of the hallway. As she did so, her daughter said, 'Mother is very beautiful, is she not?'

The mother opened the door, and another girl – littler than the first, but also demonic – flew out. She was intent on belabouring her sister with her fists, but the mother and the wooden-faced servant, who had returned, kept them apart, although a few blows still found their mark.

'What do you think of my sister?' the first girl asked, not much troubled by this danger to her person. 'I think she's horrid. She's a sort of barnacle,' she added, as her would-be assailant re-doubled her attempts. 'I don't see what she contributes to the world.'

'I will knock you down, Mercy Kendall!' said the second girl, who seemed to be called Anne.

I assumed that – for all her tired appearance – Mrs Kendall would put an end to this riot any minute. But she was in a conflab by the stairs with the wooden-faced servant, who now sported a top-coat and a beaver hat. He and his mistress were muttering about the need to fetch a certain Miss Avery. Still no mention of any young man. Mrs Kendall, mouthing an apology, indicated that I should enter a third room off the hallway. The girls, but not Mrs Kendall, accompanied me into the room, which turned out to be the drawing room, in which the dog was kept, and now the animal's frenzy added to the confusion. 'Oh, do be quiet, Swizzle,' commanded Mercy. So here, indeed, was the famous Swizzle. Mercy did not seem to care for the animal, which was perhaps the particular property of Anne, who scooped it into her arms.

'Have you ever seen those little packets the apothecaries sell?' Mercy was saying, apparently to me. '"Bug destroyer", it says on the side. Well, I would like to buy *pug* destroyer. Can you guess why?'

'I hate you, and Swizzle hates you as well,' said Anne, fondling the dog. She turned to me: 'You see what I have to put up with! She very near killed me when we were playing debtors.'

'Nonsense, you fell over.' Mercy appealed to me: 'She's always falling over. She fell over last week when she was sliding on the Green. There was a prize for who could slide the longest. Being so greedy to win it, she took a tumble on the ice, and split her silly silk frock that she had been expressly told not to wear. All the houses roundabout had let their people out onto the Green, so a great multitude saw. And *what* did they see?' she added, laughing.

'You shan't say!' said Anne.

'Lucky for you I don't know the polite expression for it,' said Mercy, who turned again to me: 'Exposed herself to all our friends. They hardly knew where to look . . . And did you know she means to sell her hair? That horrible old peruke maker in Walmgate. Someone told her that a young girl's crop can fetch thirty pounds. She goes out with mother and she slopes off and stands before the window, and one day she will go in.'

'I will do, yes,' said Anne. 'I do mean to. Because then I will have the money to get away from you. But first I will pay a man to come and kill you!'

'Ha!' said Mercy. 'You see her defective logic. Not much point getting away from me if I'm dead. What man, anyhow?'

'A man with a gun,' supplied Anne. 'A poor man from the militia. They all have guns and they don't get enough pay, and they'd welcome a little extra for doing a quick murder.'

At this, Mercy flew at her sister, but rather than hitting her, as I had anticipated – in which case I knew I must intervene – the two began wrestling for ownership of the dog.

'Give him over! Swizzle's mine,' said Mercy.

'No, he's mine, and he hates you,' was her sister's response.

The agitated creature escaped from the mêlée and bolted through the open door. Greatly to my relief, Mrs Kendall now reappeared. She was followed in turn by the wooden-faced manservant, and a severe-looking female – Miss Avery, no doubt. She must be the governess, I assumed. The girls were delivered into her charge anyhow. She took Mercy firmly by the hand, while picking up Anne, who addressed me over the woman's shoulder: 'Miss Avery won't carry my sister, on account of her weight!'

And so I was left alone in the room with Mrs Kendall,

who observed with a sad smile, 'The girls are not allowed in here.' That, I reasoned, would explain its impeccable condition, although my eye did flash towards a dent in a chair rail, as being the one discernible defect. Noticing my glance, Mrs Kendall qualified her earlier statement: '. . . At least, not for any length of time.' Otherwise she made no allusion to the riotous behaviour of her daughters, but merely smoothed her skirt, and mustered – with some effort – a brave smile. I supposed her to believe that the behaviour of those girls went beyond explanation or apology.

It was a wide, very clean room, heated by another new fireplace. I sat on a great bench with lion's claw feet; Mrs Kendall sat on another. A row of ceramics and vases surmounted a tabletop of lapis lazuli. It was in part a print room, with engravings of architectural or other subjects on the walls. The ceiling had painted compartments showing woods and meadows, perhaps the very ones destroyed by the building of these houses. All was brightly coloured: turquoise, raspberry pinks, yellows. Yet the effect was melancholic, and made more so by the complicated effects – from beyond the window – of a sun going down in a sky full of snow.

A maid brought in tea, and Mrs Kendall began explaining the terms of employment for any tutor. She did not seem to require that I actually produced the character from Skelton. I mentioned Cambridge; I left

the York Castle out of matters. I believe she divined that
I was a gentleman, about which she was quite wrong, for
I sat in her drawing room under entirely false pretences.
I had no intention of seeking employment, but only of
discovering what might have occurred when these three
females visited Matthew Harvey. But I seemed in grave
danger of being taken on. Therefore, when Mrs Kendall
enquired about the wages per diem that I would consider
acceptable, I was about to pitch high, hoping to deflect
her; but she cut me off.

'Would two pounds a day seem reasonable?'

I nodded my thanks at this generous offer. The lady
was obviously as well off as she appeared. I was caught in
a trap, and there seemed no immediate way out, unless
I could ascertain that which I was beginning to suspect:
that there was no young man to teach.

I asked whether he might be shown into us.

Mrs Kendall said, 'Oh, Alexander's in the country for a
few days.'

I couldn't blame him for that.

'He's reading Greek pretty solidly,' she added.

I believe I muttered something about Homer and
Euripides, but Mrs Kendall was already rising to her feet.
She appeared to think our business concluded. A letter
would be drafted setting out the terms of engagement.
It would be presented to me if I cared to return at nine
o'clock on Monday forenoon, when I might meet my

pupil, and begin his instruction. Meanwhile, a picture was composing in my mind as to what might have transpired when the three had visited Harvey, and it was not a pretty one.

As I took my leave, I felt sympathy for this put-upon lady, tragically encumbered – for all her wealth – with daughters who gave every appearance of being violently inclined. Child murder was common enough. Murder *by* children was much rarer, but I recalled the words of Captain Harvey: those special scissors would go into a man's flesh as easily as a knife into butter. If one of the girls – Mercy seemed the likeliest candidate – had struck out at the shade painter, Mrs Kendall must have been witness to the assault. In that case, it was equally certain that she would 'cover up' for the girl, for when a child did commit murder, a hanging was the invariable result.

In the hallway, I was returned into the charge of the silent manservant. He handed me my coat and hat. He seemed to want rid of me pretty fast. But, as he opened the door, revealing the lighted lamp beyond the bleak, excavated garden, I turned to him and said, 'It's likely that you and I will be seeing a good deal more of each other.'

He betrayed limited enthusiasm at the prospect.

'I am to be taken on as tutor to the young gentleman,' I said.

He was hardly listening. The fellow was actually beginning to close the door on me.

'I hope,' I said, 'that I will prove honest in my dealings with Mrs Kendall.'

'I'm sure she hopes the same,' the fellow said. He had me down as a prattling bore, no doubt.

I removed my wallet from my coat. I opened it to see only two pound notes where before there had been three. I looked up at the fellow. There was now, perhaps, a slight crack in his wooden face.

'The difficulty for a tutor,' I said, 'is knowing which transgressions to report to the mistress.'

'What are you getting at?'

'An honest answer to an honest question buys my silence,' I said, feeling somehow like a man in a play.

'I don't follow your meaning,' he said. His next statement, however, proved that he did. 'But I hope I can be relied on to give a straight answer to a straight question.'

'Which one of those two does the dog belong to?'

He started at the question; but he answered it. 'Both; joint shares.'

'But which prefers it?'

'Miss Anne kicks it a little less than Mercy. But the general rule is that when one of 'em's playing with it, the other one wants to get in on the act. Then, for days on end, they'll pay it no mind at all, and be quite happy to see it starve – which I wish it damn well would.'

He was waiting for me to leave, but I wasn't done with him yet.

'I've an interest in silhouette paintings,' I said, at which the fellow looked blank. '*Shade* paintings, I mean.'

'An interest in stealing them, would that be?'

He had me down as a fellow thief, keen to prey on a vulnerable widow. I would encourage this thought. 'Would there be any in this house?'

'There would be several.'

'Any showing the two girls and the dog? There's a particular vogue for the animal paintings.'

'I believe there was one such, yes.'

'*Was?* Where is it?'

'I can't recall,' he said. 'I believe it has been moved.'

I could think of no further questions, and so had no reason for lingering in the doorway. As I walked back into the town, the image in my mind was of Matthew Harvey remarking in passing that the dog seemed to love Anne particularly, or that Anne's dress was especially pretty, and of Mercy reaching for the special scissors, having taken issue with these pronouncements.

Mr Erskine's memorandum concerning his correspondence with Mr Hardcastle, of the York Theatre Royal.

On that early evening of Thursday November 29th, Mr Rigge walked from Clifton Green to the Theatre Royal.

Given below is the first of two letters sent to me by Mr Hardcastle of that establishment. It describes his meeting of that evening with Rigge. The encounter was written up by Rigge himself in his diary, but Mr Hardcastle's version is fuller, and so I interpose it here, before we resume with Rigge's long diary entry for the day in question.

(Mr Hardcastle's second letter – effectually a continuation of the first – will be given later, in its proper chronological place.)

Letter from Mr Hardcastle, Cashier at the York Theatre Royal, to Mr Erskine.

The Theatre Royal,
St Leonard's Place,
York.

I believe that Mr Rigge returned to the theatre early in the evening of the day with which we have to do – that is, Thursday November 29th. He would have found it 'dark', no production taking place, but he was informed by our night watchman, Mr Heppell, that some of the Company had gone along to Mancini's coffee shop on Stonegate, for 'a bit of a jolly'. Well, the Company was much in need of it, Mr Erskine, after the recent occurrences, and although not a drinking man, I was among their number.

A great deal of snow fell during that evening, and when Mr Rigge stepped into the coffee shop he was quite covered. His face was white as the snow on his shoulders. He looked a man much preoccupied, and I observed that when one of the wardrobe girls passed him a glass of wine, he thanked her graciously, but tossed it off as soon as her back was turned. He was continuously scanning the room. He would have found us a merry group in spite of all that has been going on. There were many more jugs of wine than pots of coffee in Mancini's that night, I can assure you, Mr Erskine. The place had been hung with laurels, and other greenery, all in anticipation of Christmas, and the light of the many candles was re-doubled in the big mirrors.

Rigge's eyes met mine. He gave a low bow, even though I had been rather sharp with him during our previous encounter. (I had ejected him from the theatre, in circumstances of which I believe you are aware.) He came over and we fell to talking. He apologised in case he had seemed too pressing on that previous occasion. He then asked how I come to be involved in the theatre, and the answer I gave does have some bearing on the matter in hand, Mr Erskine: namely the scandal of Jeremiah Smith.

I was once an actor in a small way. As I told Mr Rigge, 'I trained under Foote', which is a reference to a theatrical academy – a nursery for the London stage, run by a Mr Foote – but of course it comes out as 'I trained underfoot'. Mr Rigge gave every appearance of enjoying the joke, once I had explained it to him. After Foote's school, I joined a Company that toured the London inns. I was at my best, believe it or not, Mr Erskine, in parts of humour, but I was never taken up by any of the theatres and so I retreated behind the curtain, so to speak, stage managing for a while, before settling down in the box office.

I was never actorly in the commonly understood fashion. I am not especially outgoing, and I will never be found talking out of turn, as Mr Rigge discovered at our first meeting. But when he once again brought up the name of Smith, I was inclined to engage with him. I was, I own, curious about his curiosity over Smith, whose reputed depravity was the talk of the theatre, if not yet the town. He was supposed, among the Company, to be the murderer of our Mr Cork, and his sudden disappearance seemed strongly suggestive in that connection.

But it appeared we might have underestimated Smith's iniquity . . .

Mr Rigge told me – with some embarrassment, I thought – that he had been employed as a kind of agent by a certain Captain Harvey, son of Matthew Harvey, to look into the circumstances of the latter's violent end.

Now I had heard of Matthew Harvey's murder. Who in York has not? I had also known a little of this artistic gentleman, who was often to be seen in a certain side box of the theatre. I told Rigge as much, and he asked me about him. I said Harvey appeared to be a solitary gentleman, who watched the productions very carefully, usually with an upraised pair of viewing glasses. I used to wonder what he made of our painted backcloths, which are of a somewhat variable standard, between the two of us, Mr Erskine.

Harvey did not take liquor into his box; did not shout abuse at the actors, pitch fruit and vegetables at them, or stand to cheer them. He was not the common sort of theatre-goer, then, except in one respect. Not to mince matters, *he liked the bawdier sort of plays. I saw him at least three times during the run of A Provok'd Wife, which did indeed provoke the wives of York (because their husbands enjoyed it too much). In letters to the theatre – and, I believe, the Lord Mayor himself – they termed it rude and vulgar, and so it had to come off, as you might recall.*

On a few occasions only, Mr Harvey was not solitary. He was sometimes seen in the lobby talking to our late manager, Mr Cork, whom I believe he knew of old.

After I had related all this to Mr Rigge, he told me plainly enough that he believed Smith had murdered Harvey as well as poor Mr Cork. Now in repeating that Smith murdered Cork, I am only reflecting the generality of opinion in the theatre. I have no more proof than any other man, but I do know a little more of Smith's character than most, and I told Mr Rigge the whole . . .

It was well known in the Company that Smith was conducting a liaison with Mrs Cork. It was not much remarked on; this was not that lady's first amour. She was never in the Company herself, but as a young woman she had trodden the boards to good effect, becoming tolerably well off. She played tomboy roles, which of course are not taken by the tomboyish females. Quite the opposite: the prettier young ladies have a chance to show off their legs in those parts. The only thing unusual about this latest affair of hers was the discrepancy between her age and that of young Smith: a matter of twenty-five years or so. Mr Cork usually found out about his wife's affairs, just as she generally came to know of his, but a blind eye would be turned on both sides.

All of this explanation clearly gave Mr Rigge pause. He told me he had believed Smith might have killed Harvey in order to prevent the disclosure of his amour to Mr Cork, but if the secret was already generally known, that theory didn't quite fit. Even as he asked the question, however, I could see him refining the matter. Might it be, he suggested, that the painter had made some deprecating remark about Mrs Cork, to the effect that she was too free with her favours, and a tribulation to her husband, thereby provoking Smith?

I told him that was entirely possible; that Smith was liable to fly off about anything. He was not only young and vain, he was also self-opinionated to a superabundant degree; and, I believe, dangerous. He was naturally a good actor, who might have become a local favourite, but he was a poor ensemble player. It was not just that he would play always for his own hand. Half of them do that. No, Smith's faults were of a different order. He had twice blackened the eyes of his fellow players in arguments at rehearsals. Of late he decided that the wrong man – that is, not himself – had been given the leading role in our production of The Rivals, *which at the time of my talk with Rigge was only just announced to be played. Smith had indignantly stated that he would be unable to supply the part he had been offered, that of the servant, Fag. He believed Mr Cork had directed that he should never have any leading roles, in hopes of driving him out of*

213

the Company. He later struck at the preferred player – an amiable and handsome young chap called Wesley Emmett – with a poker at the Cock Tavern.

But this was by no means the only outrage . . .

I reminded Mr Rigge that when the audience takes against a piece, objects will be thrown at the stage. He nodded. He had seen my colleague, Mr Dawson, collecting up some of these missiles. Usually, the actors remain phlegmatic under this assault; it is understood that the audience acts as a kind of chorus to any piece, entitled to give an opinion, and disapproval is usually expressed by a rain of oranges, rotten apples, perhaps walnuts, rather than anything actually lethal. Now on one occasion, I saw Smith struck by a potato, and it was not so rotten. It had been pitched down from the circle by a well-known York ruffian, a gentleman of the militia. I happened to be in the auditorium, lamenting the premature end of what had seemed a promising production of Measure for Measure. *The place became still more riotous as Smith climbed the side boxes like a monkey, swung across into the circle, and fairly dragged the ruffian out through the back doors. His victim was found later on St Leonard's Place, very badly bloodied, and a surgeon had to be called for his eye. Smith had been severely reprimanded by Mr Cork over this, and so they were at odds over many things.*

Mr Rigge then asked whether I thought Smith might still be in town. Indeed, he was periodically scanning the room as though he expected any minute to glimpse Smith's reflection in one of the mirrors. I pointed out that the esprit de corps in the Company did not extend to our protecting such of our players who turn murderer. I made a joke of it: 'The murders we commit are not real, Mr Rigge, our swords are made of wood,' and he was good enough to smile at that.

I said I was pretty certain that Smith had fled the county, and very likely the country. He had talked in the past of making a tour of foreign theatres. He had certainly not returned to his lodge – situated on that short and curiously named street, Whip-Ma-Whop-Ma-Gate – since early in the evening of Cork's murder. Mr Rigge politely requested that I inform him should there be any indication of Smith's return to York. He then asked where he might discover Mrs Cork . . . or was she secluded in mourning? Not a bit of it, I told him; she had disappeared as well.

He bowed a thank you and made towards the door. I saw him pick up a glass of port wine on the way, and he drank it off in one. He was good enough to put a coin down with the glass, but he seemed impelled by some sudden agitation as he removed his tricorn-beaver hat from the hook by the door.

I was left to wonder at the drama that had come to surround the theatre. My principal anxiety was that the business over Smith would cause us to lose our patents. We are His Majesty's Servants, after all, Mr Erskine.

As one of the bandsmen struck up with his fiddle, and another glass of wine was put into my hand by Mr Hague, our prompter, I resolved that the Company must continue *no matter what, even if we became strollers once again, scavenging after audiences at village inns. The dancing had now commenced at Mancini's, and I did not envy Rigge as he stepped out into the fast-increasing snow.*

I believe, from our earlier correspondence, that you know where he was going.

Diary of Fletcher Rigge, entry for Thursday November 29th (resumed).

It was with regret that I quit the festivities at Mancini's in favour of Pound Lane, that place of no good repute. Miseries must await me there, although not – it was to be hoped – as many as had engulfed poor Melissa King.

The streets became meaner, concentrating the darkness as I headed east through the snow. As I turned into Stonebow, the ghostly effusions of the Castle Mill became visible over the rooftops, billowing upwards in defiance of the falling snow.

Pound Lane is off Hungate. It is dominated, as I was reminded when I turned into it, by a manufactory – a coach or wagon maker's – and the business evidently kept late hours, for the red radiance of its forge blazed forth across its yard and out into the street. The house directly opposite had turned its back in disgust at this intrusion of brute commerce, a moral statement somewhat undermined by the peeling plaster and rotten beams it presented to the street. As I approached this scrofulous wall, a shadow was projected upon it – a shadow at once gigantic yet signifying smallness. A boy in a belted smock and jockey cap had interposed himself between the forge and the wall. He belonged to the wagon maker's. He was therefore a martyr to the barbarism of the town, but he was pleased enough at the size of his shadow.

By way of giving this prodigious shade something to do, the boy lifted his hat, then hung it on the side of his head. 'Cold's cruel, en't it?' he observed.

'Good evening to you,' I said.

'Good evening to *you*.'

'What are you about?' I enquired.

'What are *you*?'

'I asked first,' I said, feeling that our ages were somehow becoming transposed.

'Taking a breather,' he said. 'Seeing what's passing.'

'I'm looking for a lodging house,' I said, thus of course inviting the youth to give a knowing grin. He duly obliged, while indicating the blistered plaster of the house alongside the one with its back turned. 'You'll like it in there. That's a grand house, that is.'

'Much frequented, is it?'

'Eh?'

'A busy sort of place?'

He re-set his hat on his head. He then eyed me for a while. 'Famous, it is. But subject to attacks.'

'A murder was done there,' I said, 'on Sunday.'

He nodded.

'You don't know anything about it, I suppose?'

'I was by the forge, having a warm. There was a good deal of shouting in the lane that night.'

'From there?' I asked, indicating the lodging house.

The boy nodded. 'And from other places . . . People bawling out to know what was amiss.'

'Did you see any strange shadows on that night?'

'This lane is full of strange shadows – on account of all the strange people.'

Evidently the boy had not been a material witness to whatever had occurred on Sunday last, which might be just as well for him. I left him to his 'breather', and walked along to the lodging house. The door stood open; and there was a passageway to the side. I chose the passageway, and found myself in a dark and prison-like yard. A back door of the lodge was pushed open, and a woman appeared in the aperture. She wore a dusty coat over what might have been a nightgown, and a bonnet that might have been a nightcap. This, I learnt in due course, was Mrs Faye Harper, the keeper of the lodge. She eyed me with well-merited scepticism as I explained that I was curious about the death of Melissa King. She

asked if I was sent by the magistrates; I said I had not
been. I had in reserve the following lie: that I represented
some citizens who were minded, in view of the late
frequency of murders, to set up an association, and a
fund, for prosecutions. But my first recourse was to hand
over a sovereign – and that turned out to be all that was
required.

Mrs Harper admitted me to the house. Taking hold
of a candle, she led me up some shattered stairs. On the
first landing, two thin dresses hung from a clothes line.
We continued up to the second floor, which suffered
from a shortage of floorboards. Mrs Harper showed me
into a sparsely furnished room coloured a dirty blue. The
fireplace had somehow the aspect of a gravestone rammed
into the wall. There was no window in the casement: only
cold dark, with the snow falling through it. From here,
Miss King had fallen or been pushed.

'Cosy, en't it?' said Mrs Harper, and so it was that I
divined the lady's characteristic tone: she was the most
severely sarcastic of women.

We returned to the ground floor, and a very cold room,
where there was little enough in the way of candlelight (a
single pungent tallow on the table between us), but actual
holes in the walls were pierced by moonlight.

I asked, 'Mrs Harper, did you think it was self-murder
when Melissa King fell out of the window up there?'

'I shouldn't think so, not with her being such a

bright-eyed damsel with all the world at her feet, fairly wilting under proposals of marriage from the young gentlemen of this city; wilting, I say, in spite of being in fine health, never going near a drop of mercury, and being quite unacquainted with Mr Barker the dentist, who is also the York abortionist (I throw that in for nothing for you, Mr Rigge), not to mention being a subscriber at the Assembly, and a regular at the "at homes" of Lord and Lady Muck, who have the mansion next door to this one – you might have seen them stepping into their carriage as you came by.

'She was probably just leaning against the casement, and looking out at the grounds we have laid out at the back. The fountain out there, you know, and the great lawns; the peacocks wandering through. Why else might she have been at the window? I really can't think. Perhaps the room was a trifle warm, what with the sun raying directly in, and the fire being so steeply banked up with coal. I've no doubt at all, Mr Rigge, but that she was sipping a refreshing cordial, and fluttering a silken fan as she gazed down on the beauteous scene.'

After a pause, during which I marvelled at her bitterness, I asked, 'What was she like?'

'Did you not hear me say that she was a bright-eyed damsel?'

'Could you be a little less circuitous?'

'*Circuitous*, indeed,' she said, eyeing me; but, sighing,

she complied. 'She was about thirty, I suppose, a little scarred from the smallpox, but in reasonably good preservation. Of course, she was brought to misfortunes.'

'You mean to say she was . . .'

'On the town. She got her living from the world of amusement. She was a *whore*, for God's sake, but let's have one thing clear, I was not her keeper. I'm no bawd.'

'But does this lodge not consist entirely of women?'

'It does not, no. There is my husband, for a start. *He's* a man . . . after a fashion.'

'What does Mr Harper do for a living?'

'Not a very great deal.'

'Did Miss King have many friends?'

'She had a great many friends and no friends at all. The girl would have her young men in – her culls. They come in by the back door, and Mr Harper and me live at the front. We don't see 'em, and they don't want to be seen. Sometimes a row kicks up. It'll be over the cost, or the cull might be a boozy cove. Or the girl might be boozy.'

'Did Miss King tipple too much?'

'They all do.'

'Was there a row on the night in question?'

'Something like a row, yes. Miss King was shouting out something about "Not a penny less than five guineas."'

'As the price of her favours?'

'I suppose so.'

'Wasn't she pitching rather high at five guineas?'

'I should say so.'

'And how did the . . . cull respond?'

'By pushing her out of the window, Mr Rigge. Unless she jumped.'

'But people don't jump through glass.'

'Perhaps, Mr Rigge, you don't know very much about self-murder.'

'I know a little of it,' I said, eyeing her, but she was not in the least abashed. 'Did you see her fall?'

'*Heard*, Mr Rigge. The breaking glass . . . and a kind of quick *flurry*, like a bag of clothes being thrown down.'

'You were not witness to anything, then?'

'I have now told you the whole, Mr Rigge, which is not very much, as you are beginning to realise. There might be a dozen men a day up to those rooms, and I don't lay eyes on a single one.'

'What about other witnesses?'

'We have three girls in at present. One came in two days ago. Of the other two, one was out in York last Sunday – on the hunt. The other slept through the whole business.'

'You couldn't hear the voice of the cull, during the row?'

'Not distinctly.'

'So he might have been anyone?'

'He might have been *you*, Mr Rigge.'

A silence fell between us. I did not believe the five guineas to have been the price of the girl's favours, but the price of her silence, as stated to Jeremiah Smith. Perhaps she had not only been witness to his killing of Mr Cork, but also knew his identity from some prior occasion.

'Do you know if she frequented the theatre?' I asked.

By this I had meant 'Did she have a taste for watching plays?' I was about to admit the unlikelihood of this – and I was braced for another sarcastic speech – when I realised that the enquiry might not be so far off the mark, given that certain of the side boxes at the Theatre Royal were more or less reserved for the would-be courtesans . . . and indeed Mrs Harper did not blink at the question.

'That's one of the hunting grounds,' she said, 'as you must know very well. Or perhaps you go to the theatre just to watch the plays, Mr Rigge. I've heard it said that *some* young men of the town are inclined that way.'

And so Mrs Harper reverted to the mode of speech to which a life of misfortunes had conditioned her.

Diary of Fletcher Rigge, Friday November 30ᵗʰ.

Much troubled by my visit to Pound Lane, I did not get off to sleep until after three. Consequently I woke late, and in a state of agitation about the two meetings I had in prospect for today, the first with Mr Erskine the attorney, the second with Miss Spink. More shocks were in prospect, I was sure.

After breakfasting, I pressed my best shirt; and I laboured for fully half an hour over my cravat. There is a crack in the mirror where the important crease must occur, which points up the absurdity of my situation very nicely. I then brushed my beaver hat, and polished my boots with the Spanish Blue Black that I had bought specially, and which is expensive. Reviewing the state of my investigations, I was increasingly certain that Smith must have killed Harvey, Mr Cork, and very likely Melissa King. But I was conscious that neither Gowers nor the Kendall girls could be ruled *quite* out of account ... and doubtful that *any* candidate would satisfy the Captain.

I set off at quarter to one. The sky was dove grey – about the colour of my waistcoat. Snow was pending once again.

The door of Mr Erskine's office lies at the end of a pretty little alleyway leading off the pleasingly bowed and buckled houses of Precentor's Court. The alleyway is prefaced by a fancy wrought iron gate and a brass plaque, reading 'Erskine, Attorney'. Beside the actual front door is a still bigger brass plaque repeating the information, should any misgivings have arisen in the mind of any visitor along the way. All the snow had been cleared from the alley, and salt had been thoughtfully laid down to kill the ice. In short, I anticipated a comfortable and well-ordered office.

Comfortable the rooms certainly were, with three good fires blazing in what proved the best sort of little legal labyrinth. I was greeted by Mr Erskine in person, and he led me into a cosy green and red office, where a pot of coffee bubbled on a spirit burner. He poured me out a cup as we took our seats on either side of a fine oaken desk piled with papers colourfully corded and beribboned. I have no doubt that every paper signified an argument, but Mr Erskine himself, mutely bald except for some Romanesque grey wisps, gave a strong hint of twinkling merriment beneath his lawyerly gravitas.

Glancing with amusement at the papers, he said, 'I am up to my eyes, Mr Rigge, in wills. Deeds and wills, but chiefly wills. I blame the weather. This perpetual freeze threatens a clean sweep of our septuagenarians.'

Just then the door opened, and in swept Mr Bright, whom I had already met.

'. . . Our septuagenarians, and our legal clerks,' he said, shaking the snow from his hat into the fire. He did not smile; he seemed a graver – or at least gruffer – gentleman than Mr Erskine. He removed his coat, and threw it over the back of a chair onto which the contents of a bookshelf appeared to have recently collapsed. 'I am worn half to death,' he said.

'Mr Bright,' Mr Erskine explained, 'has just delivered

a very heavy brief to counsel. Mr Davies, barrister-at-law. You might know the gentleman if you have ever attended the Assizes. Or you might have *heard* him, if you were ever walking *past* the Assizes. How *was* our estimable KC?' Mr Erskine asked Mr Bright.

'Well now,' said Bright, 'I delivered the papers to him in person. He looked them over with scepticism, not to say disgust. "Is all this evidence?" he asked. "About half of it," I said. "Fifty pages are Mr Erskine's *opinion* on the matter."'

'And let me guess,' said Mr Erskine, 'he immediately pitched those fifty into the fire?'

'Not in my presence, sir,' Mr Bright replied, 'but I can't answer for his actions once I'd left.'

'An intemperate fellow, Davies,' Erskine mused. He steepled his fingers and watched me for a while.

'You will forgive my peremptory summons,' he said.

I told him there had been nothing peremptory about it.

'When somebody has been left a bequest,' he continued, 'we tell them they are about to hear something to their advantage. That is the customary formula.'

'I have not been left any bequest,' I said. 'I know of no one who has died; apart from my father, and he had nothing to bequeath.'

'Indeed not, having transferred his estate to a certain Corrigan.'

I have learnt better than ever to be in hopes, but my pulses were set racing by his contemptuous pronunciation of the name Corrigan.

'It is all gone,' I said. 'House, park, farms, village.'

'Or so it appears,' said Mr Bright, from somewhere behind me.

My mind was now fairly whirling, and I was weak enough to voice what had become a persistent, secret hope: 'Is there some irregularity with the deed?'

'Oh, I should think that's pretty watertight,' said Erskine, 'if I know old Pullman.'

'Which he does,' put in Mr Bright.

'He is a very fine draughtsman.'

'I have my father's copy of the deed in my lodge,' I said.

'About the size of a flagstone, would it be?' suggested Mr Erskine, re-steepling his fingers.

I nodded. 'Nearer *two* flagstones.'

'Yes, the lease and the re-lease. A freehold is transferred by transferring two leases. If you ask me why, I will tell you.'

'I wouldn't advise it,' Mr Bright put in.

A clock ticked, the fire ticked in the grate.

'We know something of your recent history, Mr Rigge,' said Mr Erskine.

'Perhaps you know me,' I suggested, 'as the young man whose father went to the devil.'

'Not exactly.'

'Then you know me as a late inmate of the Castle.'

'There is no shame in imprisonment for debt,' said Erskine, 'at least not usually. We know from our own practice that about half the debtors in the Castle are guilty of nothing more than having stood surety for some other, who turned out to be incompetent.'

'The creditor is equally guilty of improper trust,' Mr Bright put in.

'We did hear of your incarceration,' Mr Erskine continued. 'We had the news from your late father's attorney, Mr Pullman. He was very distressed about it, and he has been trying to think of a scheme to assist you.'

I thought, but did not say, that Mr Pullman was the sort of man who might spend thirty years pondering any action.

'I am not seeking any outside assistance,' I said, which immediately struck me as pompous.

'Perhaps Mr Rigge would care for a glass of port wine?' suggested Mr Bright.

'A capital idea,' said Erskine and, readily assenting, I thought: this pair know me only too well.

As Mr Bright hunted up bottle and glasses, Mr Erskine said, 'But now you are out, anyway.'

A question was implied.

'I came to an arrangement with my creditor,' I said. 'He is a Mr Burnage. He farms up at Pickering.'

Mr Erskine smiled at me in such a way that a further question was implied.

'Half the amount I owed him was paid over by a third party,' I said. 'That was a man called Captain Robin Harvey. He has a big house in First Water Lane.'

'You're not telling me you've actually walked along that street to see this man?' asked Mr Bright, returning with glasses (a bottle had already been procured). 'I suppose you must have done, since no carriage will go down there.'

'He has asked me to look into the murder of his father, the shade painter, Matthew Harvey. He will pay the balance of my debt if I report satisfactorily.'

'And if you don't?' barked Mr Bright.

'I must return to the Castle,' at which the lawyer and his clerk looked at each other with raised eyebrows, no doubt thinking it a very queer arrangement, which indeed it is.

Mr Erskine said, 'No charge was ever brought, I believe? No arrest was made.'

I shook my head. Trying to make the proceeding sound as innocuous as possible, I said, 'The Captain is curious to know if anything might be done.'

'In other words,' said Erskine, 'whether an arrest and charge might be brought.'

'I suppose so.'

'And have you established grounds for either?'

'Not quite, no.'

'I am not in criminal practice,' said Mr Erskine, 'but it seems to me that if nothing is done within a week, then nothing is ever done.'

I sipped the wine that Mr Bright had handed me. It was the best I'd tasted since Aden Park days.

Mr Erskine, accepting his own wine, said, 'Has it occurred to you that the Captain killed his father, and that he is merely creating a smokescreen by arranging this investigation?'

Mrs Sampson had asked the same. It seemed to be the theory of all clever people. I said as much. Mr Erskine smiled and the subject was dropped. He then turned to the matter of Corrigan, and his speech was as gratifying as the glass of wine before me.

It was indeed the case that Mr Erskine and Mr Bright did not care for Corrigan, or for a certain confederate of his, a ruffian called Cracknell. The intimation was that this pair were little better than common sharpers. There was no absolute proof, but strongly suggestive testimony had come from a certain Mr Handley – a friend of Mr Erskine's who is apparently 'not above an evening of faro' – and others who had gamed with the pair and come off worse. In sum, York rumour said that something wasn't right. The suspicion was that the two colluded, and their collusion was particularly effective when the game being played was loo – the very one at which my father had staked and lost his estate.

'Mr Rigge,' said Erskine, when he had come to the end of his account, 'your father always paid his debts of honour without question.'

'And his other debts, I believe.'

'As you know, there is no legally enforceable contract in all of this. Your father consented to give up his lands from considerations of honour alone. But if chicanery has been involved, such considerations do not apply, would you not say?'

'Mr Erskine, I am indebted to you for even considering this matter. But the transfer is already completed and, as you say, we have no proof.'

'But we have leverage, even if we do not have proof,' Mr Erskine said, as Mr Bright re-filled my glass. 'It lies in Mr Corrigan's insatiable desire for place. His house is in Micklegate; it is new, perhaps you know it.'

I had observed it. I said, 'He has stamped his initials and the date of construction on the rainwater head.'

Mr Erskine nodded. 'In case it should go astray, no doubt.'

It was Mr Bright who spoke up next: 'He has not a wine cellar, so much as a range of vaults beneath. He gave a ball last month for two hundred people. I wasn't invited.'

'But the Duke of Rutland was,' said Mr Erskine, 'and Alderman Henry Baines.'

'Whoever he is,' barked Mr Bright.

'Corrigan aspires to initiate a bank,' said Mr Erskine.

'Like most people in York,' put in Mr Bright.

'Therefore he must command the respect of parties in high positions. If he has forfeited their respect by dishonourable conduct, he must regain it by honourable conduct.'

Mr Bright asked, 'Do you catch our meaning, Mr Rigge?'

'Corrigan might be persuaded to our way of thinking,' said Mr Erskine, smiling. 'After all, no punishment is heavier than infamy.'

'How do we proceed?' I said.

'We get him in,' said Bright, pouring the last of the wine between our three glasses equally.

Fletcher Rigge, in continuation.

I apprehended Miss Spink in the grove of trees that is the notable feature of the southernmost, countrified part of the New Walk. My presence at that spot looked thoroughly accidental, I hope, and Lucy played her part by flinging down the hood of her cape, and calling out, 'Why, Mr Rigge, what on earth are you doing here?' (She protested a little too much, I thought, but it was delightful to watch her do it.) She was with her aunt, whose hood remained up. As I made my bow, that lady smiled at me with a sly charm that I found quite endearing. She was younger than I'd bargained for, yet still not young. I expressed the hope that she was very well, and she smiled and nodded again in a way not incompatible, I suppose, with some degree of deafness.

I fell in with them on the snowy track, and it seemed the aunt would make no trouble about it. Indeed, as we came into the city proper, she started to hang back, as though transfixed by the sights of the river, which were interesting enough, for all the boats – barges, brigs and schooners, and one great, square-sailed Humber keel – were stuck in the ice, held fast like boats in a painting of boats.

'Come on then, Mr Rigge,' said Lucy, 'say something cheerful. You know how I appreciate your high spirits.'

'This freeze,' I said, 'must be costing the river men a fortune.'

'I'm sure of it. Do carry on with your cheerful observations.'

'When it melts, there'll be a flood,' I said, maintaining the dolorous tone she seemed to enjoy.

'Excellent. I'm so glad your trip to London has done nothing to lift your spirits. Was it not fruitful?'

I told her it had been a wild goose errand, which was about right, I was beginning to think. She knew I had gone there on Captain Harvey's business, or perhaps she did not recollect. Either way she did not mention his name. The subject was perhaps distasteful to her, as it was to me. She was looking me up and down as we walked. I hoped she could not tell that I had made a particular effort with my apparel. I was also determined not to remind her of what she'd said about my regaining the estate. She could hardly have forgotten a thing like that, but perhaps she had decided, on reflection, that whatever scheme she'd had in mind was not practicable. That might be like her, I thought, being such a charmingly ardent person. I did wonder whether her thoughts had proceeded along the same lines as those of Mr Erskine, but I was quite decided that it would be ignoble of me to raise the matter.

She said, 'You were closely observed at the Assembly, you know. My mother remarked on your dancing.'

'I will not fish for a compliment by asking to what effect.'

'I think you've just done so. She said you had obviously been very well taught. My father said ... nothing at all about you.'

'I am relieved to hear it.'

'With him that is a good sign. He is generally against young men ... You missed nothing at last week's,' she continued, 'it was so very dull.'

'But your dance card must have been full?'

'I danced two. I suppose you want to know who with?'

'With *whom*.'

'I shan't tell you if you're going to be . . . '

'Supercilious?'

'Exactly.'

'Was it the person from Thirsk? The one you visited?'

'Oh, him,' she said, with a very encouraging lack of enthusiasm. 'In the event we didn't go; couldn't get there.'

(Of *course* – that country town would be quite cut off by the snow, just as Adenwold village would be.)

'He's a handsome enough fellow, I suppose?' I could not resist enquiring.

'A flatterer would say so. And only a flatterer.'

'He is quite plump in the pocket, however.'

'He is generally plump all round. The fact is I can't remember who I danced with on Monday. During a minuet, I was so bored that I fell to counting the columns in the room.'

'There are forty-four. It is amusing to watch the ladies in hooped skirts trying to go through them.'

'I don't like hooped skirts. You can't waltz in them.'

'Do you ever waltz?'

'Only with my sister. Mama says it would be indecent of me to dance a waltz with a man, unless I were engaged to him.'

She stopped dead, and I turned to face her. I believe we were both on the point of commencing a waltz along the New Walk, with no music required. While that would have been too fanciful, it would have been perfectly reasonable for me to say, 'At the next Assembly, I would like to dance a waltz with you, Lucy.' I did not do it, however. From my new angle, facing Miss Spink, I could see the chaperone gazing at the frozen river. Beyond her, the black walls of the York Castle rose high in the cold misty air. That baleful mansion struck me as resembling a great black planet in whose orbit I was trapped. I must make a complete break away before I could make love to Lucy Spink, and I meant to do so or die in the attempt.

'Mr Rigge,' said Lucy, as we resumed our walk, 'your father forfeited his estate in a game of cards?'

We had left the small talk behind.

'That is the unfortunate fact of the matter,' I replied.

'If the estate had been entailed,' she said, 'that could not have happened.'

She must have been interested enough to enquire with some legal person about the matter.

'But it was not entailed,' I said. 'My father could do what he pleased with the lands.'

'There was a pretty big house, I believe.'

'The capital *messuage*.'

'What?'

'That's what it's called, in the deed assigning it to Mr Corrigan.'

'And an elegant park.'

'Most elegant.'

'And two farms and a village.'

'Three farms.'

'The village was called Adenwold.'

'It still is.'

'You yourself then got into debt by undertaking repairs to some of the houses, honouring a promise made by your father. It was very gallant of you.'

'Gallantry doesn't come into it, Miss Spink.'

She gave a glance over to her aunt, who continued to look preoccupied at the water's edge.

'Does she mean to try the ice?' I asked.

'Mr Rigge, she is deaf, not stupid.'

I believed that lady to be very far from stupid, and quite possibly not deaf. Rather, she struck me as highly accommodating – the very soul of discretion.

'Perhaps,' Miss Spink was saying, 'all may yet be set right. As regards the estate, I mean.'

Was it possible that the rumours about Corrigan had reached her ears?

'That is not a serious prospect,' I said, even as I thought of my conference with Mr Erskine and Mr Bright.

Miss Spink said, 'I've heard it suggested . . .' but the rest was lost, for a smoke boat had started up, and commenced smashing through the ice near the Lendal Tower. On being asked to repeat herself, Lucy Spink said, 'I have heard it suggested that your father's opponent plays with downhills.'

'You mean with loaded dice?'

'If that's what it means, then that's what I *mean*. I knew it wasn't anything to his credit. If the estate was taken from you by a fraud, then ...'

'Miss Spink, could I ask from whom you have heard this?'

'It is perhaps better if I don't say, but it is a person who means to assist you if only you will let him.'

'Do I know this person?'

'Mr Rigge, I will not play a game of riddle with you. I believe you will hear from him in due course, or perhaps through his agents.'

I nodded. I believed I already had done, the agents being Messrs Erskine and Bright. As to the identity of my original benefactor, I suspect him to be the small, bald man I had seen with the Spinks at the Assembly.

We had now come to Skeldergate, where a hideous, gigantic mechanical crane marks the end of the sylvan part of the river, and the beginning of the commercial part.

'Fletcher Rigge,' said Lucy, in her mock-formal way, as she turned once again towards me, 'there is no Assembly this coming Monday, but perhaps I will see you at the one on the Monday following.'

I said that I very much hoped so, and she offered her gloved hand to be kissed. I bowed to the aunt and fairly bounded up the steps to the bridge, entertaining further mental images of myself as a landed young gentleman, this time walking hand-in-hand with Lucy through the meadow grounds of Aden Park. But surely the vision is ludicrous. I have not escaped the shadow of the prison, or that of the Captain, and while I do not doubt the amiable intentions of the little bald man, or Mr Erskine and Mr Bright, I do not at all care for the idea of city eminences getting up a kind of subscription fund on my behalf, of the kind by which the New Walk was created. If there is to be a termination in gladness, I must bring it about myself.

On returning to my lodge, I saw that Mrs Buckley had placed two letters beneath the lighted candle. The first of them did nothing to quell my dangerous new optimism; the second of them did the job most effectually, however.

Letter from Mr Erskine to Mr Rigge.

Precentor's Court,
York.

Dear Mr Rigge,

I have prevailed upon Mr Corrigan to attend my offices on Monday next at four o'clock. He has been appraised of the matter we wish to discuss with him. I took the liberty of

informing him that you would be in attendance, for which
please accept the apologies of
    Your humble servant,
    John Erskine.

Letter from Captain Harvey to Fletcher Rigge.

River House,
Near the Coal Staith,
First Water Lane,
York.

My Dear Sir,

    I trust this finds you well. How are you progressing towards apprehending our murderer? I am irresistibly desirous to know what a Cambridge man has made of it all. My enquiry is premature, I admit. I gave you a month, and a month you will have; and yet the desire to hear once again your learned if lugubrious speech is strong upon me. You will oblige me, sir, with a speedy reply stating a time and place it will be convenient to meet and discuss this matter of very pressing concern to

Your most humble and obedient servant,
Richard Harvey
(The Seventh Shade!)

Diary of Esther, Saturday December 1st.

I saw Mr Rigge today.

The Captain and Stephen have taken to sending our nightly joints to the Half Moon on Blake Street for roasting, and I am invariably the carter. In my opinion the Spread Eagle on Micklegate does a better job, and a cheaper one; and that inn is just around the corner from First Water Lane, which is no small consideration when the snow is storming, as it always seems to be in these times. But I believe the Captain likes to have me out of the house while he engages in an unnatural interaction with Stephen, or discusses the affair – the conspiracy, I may say – the two of them have in progress with the coal men.

While he knows I make no moral judgement – my past conduct bars me from any pulpit – the Captain seems to apprehend my distaste both for his way of business and his favourite way of pleasure. It is not really a distaste for the act itself. (If more men amused themselves in that way, many a young girl would be spared a debauch.) It is rather a resentment at the Captain's enjoyment of it, which is greater than his enjoyment with me. My condition is one of simple jealousy, then? I think it is more that I dislike being seen as an embarrassment and an encumbrance.

Anyhow, I am sent on errands and I am as happy to go as they are to be rid of me.

On arriving, I enquired in the kitchen, to learn that the joint was not ready. In fact, it was still pink on the spit. Therefore I wandered into the saloon to partake of its two fires: the one in the grate and the one in the glass. It is almost respectable for a young lady to take a glass of brandy in the parlour of the Half Moon, but perhaps not two. I took two, nonetheless, and was contemplating a third when Mr Fletcher Rigge stepped into the parlour. He removed his beaver hat and his greatcoat and put them on a hook by the fire. (He isn't one to sling his coat over the back of a chair.) The other men in the parlour were observing me as I observed the handsome newcomer. Quite obviously, they believed I was on the town, and that I meant to make this young man my cull, in which supposition they were five years out of date.

Certainly, Mr Rigge cuts an elegant figure, but I wonder about what the Captain would call his 'sportive prowess' after dark. He would be a clumsy lover perhaps, inhibited by notions of gentlemanliness, but he would be susceptible to instruction, I suspect, which many another intelligent fellow is not. He wore a high stock, tied into a very pretty bow, neat from the side as well as from the front, which I believe is the test of style in these matters. He approached the counter to buy a glass of port wine, and that was when he saw me. He made a bow, which was somewhere between absurd and admirable. I thought for a minute he proposed to kiss my hand, yet he was clearly no stranger to the saloon of an inn.

I told him, perfectly absurdly, that I had just 'bolted in' and was about to 'bolt out' again, after I had collected a joint. Of course, he could see the two empty glasses at my elbow, but he affected not to. He asked, smiling kindly, if I would care for a 'tincture' (yes, he employed the term favoured by our mutual acquaintance) while I waited.

We carried our glasses over to the table near the fire. He seemed tongue-tied at first, fiddling with his sleeve links a good deal (which were garnets, I believe), but the port wine unfroze him a little.

'Tell me,' said Mr Rigge, 'what does the Captain call a *large* quantity of liquor?'

'A drench,' I said.

He nodded. He was amused, but not so as you'd know it. I saw a leathern book in the pocket of the coat he'd hung nearby. I asked him about it, and he told me he kept a diary. I said I did likewise, and I could see him wondering about me. I said I would never leave it where it might be found, and he made a polite show of acting on the recommendation, taking the book from the coat and laying it on the table. It was bound in good calfskin, but appeared as well creased as my own diary. His whole life was in it, I suspected, just as mine is in mine.

'On the subject of writing,' I said, 'I believe you may have had a letter from the Captain?'

Mr Rigge nodded. 'He has requested a conflab. I have not yet replied.'

That's right, I thought. When the devil comes calling, put him off. Get him hence.

'What do you make of that gentleman?' I asked. Of course, his answer must be polite, knowing the Captain to be my husband (or something of the kind).

'He paid off my debt, or half of it,' said Mr Rigge. 'That's more than any of the noted York philanthropists would do.'

'Well, philanthropy's not much in his line.'

'He does pretty well from the coal trade, I believe?' Mr Rigge enquired.

'Yes, but that doesn't satisfy him. He must have excitement.'

'I suppose he had that once? In the French wars? Or was he in the York militia?'

I pictured the Captain in his regimentals. Tall, firm and graceful; and with hair.

'He was in the dragoons for about six months,' I said. 'He never left London in that time.'

'He hasn't been continuously in York?'

'No. Born here, left, returned.'

'. . . To First Water Lane.'

'You think it an odd choice, I suppose?'

'It's picturesque in an antiquarian way,' said Mr Rigge, '. . . for those that survive a walk along it. But I suppose it was conveniently near his father's house?'

I made no reply, discretion intervening, and so a silence fell between us. 'Hey-ho,' I heard myself uttering, which silly phrase disgusts me no end . . . and so I said what I was going to say all along: 'The advantage of First Water Lane was that the Captain's father, in common with most people in the town, would *never think* of walking along it.'

'But you said he loved his father.'

'In his fashion,' I said, discretion intervening again.

'The two of you met in London?' Mr Rigge enquired.

'Yes, I was in a very bad taking. The Captain rescued me, after a fashion.'

Mr Rigge knew better than to ask further.

'How did he occupy himself down there?'

'Oh, he had interests in a number of parlours and lodgements. He got his living off the people that came there . . . one way or another.'

'How?'

'He understands people's characters; their strengths and their weaknesses . . .'

I had said as much as I dared, but not as much as I ought, and I do not know whether Mr Rigge took my meaning.

'He takes me to be a great discoverer of hidden information,' Mr Rigge said, at length.

'In which I'm sure he is right, and I daresay you discovered the identity of the sitters? The people painted, I mean?'

'I have, as the Captain will hear . . . And so if that is my strength, I wonder what he takes my weakness to be? Feel free to speculate,' he added, smiling, 'there are quite a number of possibilities.'

'An excess of honour?' I suggested, and this I intended as a warning, although whether it was taken as such, once again I cannot say.

'Tell me,' said Mr Rigge, 'how does he come to be lame?'

'Oh, it was nothing that you might think,' I said, and I'm afraid I laughed. I resolved to tell the tale; it couldn't do much harm. 'There was a dispute,' I said, 'over a duck. It belonged to our neighbour in London. It made the most fearful racket at all hours, and it would go for you as you went along the lane.'

'Are you sure it wasn't a goose?' asked Mr Rigge. 'They're notorious reprobates, but ducks are pretty easy-going, as a rule.'

'I should know what it was. We ate it, after all.'

'You have skipped out the important part,' he said. 'How did it come to be on your plate?'

'The Captain shot it, and then our neighbour shot the Captain in revenge the next time he was going along the lane.'

'A case of foul *play*,' said Mr Rigge, with a pretty, slow smile, and of course he had meant the different spelling. 'Did the Captain not seek satisfaction?'

'Fight a duel, you mean? That is not his way. But he is not to be slighted.'

'What then ... ?'

'The neighbour's house was burned to the ground a month later. I did not enquire too minutely into the cause.'

Mr Rigge nodded. 'They all escaped alive, I hope?'

'Oh yes, all got safely away: wife, children, servants.'

But I felt I had said too much, and I was back to my wretched hey-hoing as Mr Rigge drained his glass.

He was rescued from my inanities when a servant announced that my joint was ready to be collected from the kitchen door. At the same moment, I observed a young man at the door of the saloon; or rather he had pushed open the door, but remained standing in the aperture, looking with scandalised amazement at me and my companion.

Mr Rigge had his back to this affronted stranger, but he turned around in time – I believe – to have a clear sight of him just before he withdrew and disappeared from sight. Well, I have called him a stranger, but I believe he was well known to Mr Rigge.

Diary of Fletcher Rigge, Saturday December 1st.

[**Mr Erskine's prefatory note:** We omit here Mr Rigge's account of his talk with Esther as largely duplicating her own, given above.]

... I quit the tavern – stepping into the falling dark, and swirling snow – having gained some insight into the Captain's mind, but I knew I could not press that rather haunted lady, his mistress, too far. It is up to me to settle with him, and I will bring matters to a head at our meeting.

As I revolved matters, I set off walking, I hardly knew where.

The streets are so narrow in this town, the houses so compressed – I almost believe their antiquity constitutes a nuisance. The labyrinth traps the swirling snow, as it traps the people. It has been doing so for centuries. Somebody described a town – towns in general, I mean – as 'a mad, premature coffin of mind, body and estate', and when, passing a lighted ground floor window in Davygate, I heard the rattling of a dice box, it came to my ears as a veritable death rattle. But it is only the sound of somebody trying to escape the coffin.

Seeking alleviation of my claustrophobia I was minded to head out beyond the Castle, to the Foss River, and the marsh; but turning into the silent square of the Thursday Market, I saw . . . the very last person I would have expected to find in the stone labyrinth. It was Phil Brown of Adenwold, who is the son of Ned Brown, the man I'd helped at ploughing before I almost expired under that frosty hedge.

Phil is about my age. I last saw him a year ago, shortly before my father's suicide. He had just been apprenticed to Lambert Driscoll, the thatcher at Coxwold, but he did not now look countrified. In place of his habitual rough trousers and short jacket were breeches and a jaunty blue coat with lace pocket holes and cuffs; he carried a cane – a gold, or at any rate brass-topped one. His outfit somewhat resembled the rig we had both worn when plundering my father's cast-offs to dress up as soldiers. His bicorn hat wanted only a trim cockade for the effect to be complete. But I banished this mean thought, for my boyhood friend had unquestionably 'improved' himself.

After our enthusiastic greeting, it was established that my father's steward, Mr Knight, was in charge at Adenwold, prior to Corrigan's own man coming in. I enquired after our mutual friend Tom Clough, son of the Adenwold publican. Tom had also 'made good', I discovered. He had learnt cross multiplication on his own time and become a shoemaker; and so he had left the village.

'But are you still there, Phil?' I asked: an imbecilic question, in view of his attire.

He shook his head. 'I'm with the Excise now, in Leeds.'

I congratulated him heartily, but all I could think was that, when he was fourteen, he had believed in witches. He was on his way to Mancini's, where he had an appointment with friends. I was discomfited by our meeting, and so inclined to let him go, but since he had half an hour to spare, it would have been churlish not to suggest we step around the corner, into Coney Street and the Black Swan.

The red-curtained windows gave out a promising glow, as we approached the tavern. Phil thanked me for the repairs to the village houses, and I told him to 'Say no more about it', or words to that effect, and he left off the subject readily enough, so I suspected he considered me a fool for having undertaken them.

He asked how I got my living, and for want of anything better, I said, 'By literature.'

'Ah yes,' he said, 'that is my memory of you. Forever flopped down under a hedge writing or reading.' He reminded me of the time I had nearly died, and I was tempted to mention that I had been neither reading nor writing on that occasion, but merely sleeping.

As we entered the common room of the Swan, I proposed a jug of beer, but Phil Brown insisted on wine, and on paying for it.

We found a table near the fire, into which Phil confidently applied a taper to light his pipe. He smoked leisurely as I expressed my regret that the Adenwold estate would now most likely be enclosed, with many villagers turned off the land as soon as their tenancies had expired, perhaps including Phil's own parents.

But I learnt that they had already left. In anticipation of Corrigan's regime, Mr Knight had offered to buy them out of their tenancy. They'd considered the cash to be manna from heaven, since it would last the rest of their days, which they would pass in a sturdy little cottage by the Green in Oulston. The whole 'top end' of Adenwold village, Phil explained, would be cleared of houses and tenants for the creation of a new meadow. I had re-roofed two of the cottages in this 'top end', for the perpetuation of a style of life Phil Brown obviously thought doomed.

It seemed the Excise had made an economist of him, and I sat, mortified, as he stated the case for enclosures. 'Of late,' he commenced, blowing smoke, 'large farms have been cried down, as depriving the labouring class of employment. A lot has been said about this without due examination into the subject . . . ' The large farmer, he explained, has sufficient capital to cultivate the land properly, and that benefited everyone. If 'clumps' of little houses happened to get in the way of cultivation or sheep grazing they ought to be removed, or perhaps turned over as shelters to those very sheep.

Sheep were the answer to every question, in conjunction with winter planting of that miraculous vegetable, the turnip. There was no argument to be had, and I'm afraid I wound up our conversation as soon as possible, almost pushing the fellow towards the door, and his engagement at Mancini's.

I returned home to find a letter under the candle.

Letter from Mrs Sampson to Fletcher Rigge.

3 Monk Street,
York.

Sir,

If you wish further discussion of the matter we broached after the Assembly, it will be agreeable for me to see you here at my house at about one o'clock on Monday. Please don't

trouble to reply. I will either see you or I will not. If the latter,
perhaps you will make an alternative proposal.

    Your obedient servant,
    Mrs Maria Sampson.

Diary of Fletcher Rigge, Sunday December 2nd.

My meeting with Phil has troubled me. I myself don't care
for Leeds, but who am I to deprive him of it? And what
was the purpose of the village school my father established
if not to open up the world to the pupils?

    I hardly slept last night, images from my past composing
and dissolving like a sort of mental kaleidoscope. Mainly
they concerned summer days on the estate, the hay-making
time when the sun seems reluctant to set. Phil Brown and
Tom Clough featured as their former selves: country lads.
I had considered myself one as well. Of course, I was from
'the big house', but were not the villagers welcome at any
time around our mahogany table, which was presented in a
homely way, with no cloth or napkins?

    I saw us building houses of twigs and straw, consuming
ale and tobacco inside them, or stealing peas from
the cottage of some gardener safe at church. I saw us
inspecting old bookstalls at a fair.

. . . No, for that was only me.

I pictured a hot summer's afternoon of about ten years ago. It was in preparation for Rugby School. My mother and I were sitting on the baulk between two wheat fields, she with a French grammar and a quantity of strawberries on her lap. She was testing my vocabulary, and if I gave a right answer, she lobbed a strawberry towards me. After a long succession of right answers I had given a wrong one, yet she had instinctively thrown a strawberry, which I gobbled up before she could demand its return. For some reason, we had laughed immoderately at that.

Tomorrow, I begin my duties as tutor to Mrs Kendall's son, and I fear my first day there must also be my last. I will then call on Mrs Sampson, who seems impatient either to disclose information about the murder of Harvey, or to commence dissembling about it.

I have still not replied to Captain Harvey. I hope I will sleep tonight. My head has been – is – a good deal disordered.

Diary of Fletcher Rigge, Monday December 3rd.

This morning I set off at half past eight to take up my post as tutor at the Red House at Clifton: the first of three appointments, any one – or all – of which might prove momentous.

Today has been milder than previous days, the snow reduced to dirty mush; but it has also been darker, and the drawing room of the Red House had lost some of its vari-coloured mystery. I was shown into it by the suspect manservant, who had resumed a total woodenness. My arrival had set Swizzle, the pug, barking in some distant room, but the row abated as I sat by a low fire, fretting about many things, but principally curious about whether Mrs Kendall would be able to produce an Oxford-bound son. The house was mainly silent, except for occasional, muted thumps from above, which must betoken the presence of Mercy and Anne.

I watched the brand-new carriage clock on the mantle approach the hour of ten. It was making laborious progress, and it had still not reached its goal when Mrs Kendall entered, followed by a meek-looking young man, whose shirt and waistcoat were of good quality, but worn negligently, and spattered here and there with ink. The impression of studiousness was compounded by a reserved manner, and somewhat disordered and thinning hair. Alexander Kendall gave a rather shy, blushing bow, as if he knew he was not such a remarkable specimen as his siblings. After Mrs Kendall had made the introductions, she urged her son to engage with me directly on the question of his studies. As he began to speak, the clock began to chime, and this caused him to turn a deeper red, as though the clock were somehow chastising him.

He asked with great diffidence if he might lead me upstairs to his study, and as we ascended, the silent house gradually became less silent.

The thumping noise had re-doubled and, as we came to the top landing, it re-doubled again. I shot a questioning look at Alexander, and he said, 'It's Mercy and Anne. They're in the schoolroom.'

'Unsupervised?' I said.

Alexander nodded regretfully. 'Miss Avery is late today.'

He indicated a certain closed door. Since the repeated percussions had gained an ominous rhythmical intensity, and were now accompanied by a loud and triumphant cackling, I suggested we might look in on the young ladies, just to make sure there was nothing amiss.

Alexander paused, deliberating. 'Very well,' he said, and he opened the above-mentioned door.

Mercy and Anne were both skipping at a great rate, being engaged, evidently, in a sort of skipping race. A rocking horse that had rocked right over and had a hole in its head – as though it had been shot by the knacker – was the principal piece of debris in a scene that might have been created by the detonation of a bomb in a toy shop. It was surely more nursery than schoolroom for there was hardly a book to be seen. But the walls were fairly covered with shade paintings.

Having established that the girls were not in any danger of suffering – or causing – any immediate harm, Alexander Kendall drew the door to. It had been impossible to see whether the work painted by Harvey in the Race Week was among those on the walls, and now I must play the part of tutor.

Alexander led me into the next but one room along, his study, into which he had evidently carried all the books in the house. Many of them, I saw, were new volumes, but the authors of course were old, and there were corresponding scenes of recently painted antiquity on the walls.

A trunk lay in the corner of the room, all corded and ready for travel. It held books, Alexander shyly informed me. I suggested that, since he had almost a year in hand before going up to the University, it was rather early to prepare his luggage, and he gently corrected me. He would be off soon on a tour of the European capitals – in which, I supposed, he would be paying particular attention to their libraries. With a modesty that seemed characteristic, he asked me to inspect his books and see if he had overlooked any authors in his bibliomania.

I gave five minutes to the task, thinking all the while how much I would rather be inspecting the other room. At length, I suggested he might think of getting round to some Chaucer, and possibly Swift.

We then discussed – at his behest – Dryden's

translation of *The Aeneid*, with which I am tolerably familiar, and whether the Latin rule that a sentence cannot end in a preposition be extended to English. It was a case of holding my own in the face of a considerable intellect. I had no doubt that young Alexander would prove cleverer than his Oxford tutors, and I told him so. He expressed incredulity at this, in a way that appeared genuine and therefore much to his credit. We seemed to get on well, to the extent that he proposed showing me some of his own Latin verses. 'The muse sometimes visits me when I am asleep,' he said, as though confessing to some indecency. 'I wake up and set down the result.'

Mercy and Anne were now producing a new noise: a competitive shouting with occasional screams. They were not yet in a full-blown state of war, such as I had observed on my first visit, but there were ructions enough to suggest that another check on the room might be called for. Alexander agreed, but it was with reluctance that he put down the sheaf of his own poems he had collected from his desk. We walked along to the door of the playroom-cum-schoolroom, and this time I opened it.

'*You* again,' said Mercy, eyeing me without enthusiasm. She sat on the floor; she was throwing a tennis ball against the opposite wall, where sat Anne, who wore a man's tricorn hat decorated with red ribbons.

Mercy returned her attention to her sister. 'You are to be a sort of bagman,' she commanded.

'How can a young girl be a bagman?' enquired Anne.

'You see, they are writing a sort of play,' Alexander explained in an under-voice. 'They have rather loaded imaginations.'

He seemed half admiring of the girls, half afraid of them.

'I don't even have a bag,' Anne was complaining. 'All I have is this hat.'

'No,' said Mercy, 'the hat's mine,' and she rose and made a grab for it. They began to squabble, but there was nothing much in it by their standards. As their brother began a gentle remonstrance, I was scrutinising the shade paintings. Some showed the two girls, and there was one of the family entire, including the late Mr Kendall. The four were shown at a table set for tea. Mr Kendall was an unexpectedly small, bespectacled gentleman. He looked somewhat dejected at the head of the table. In the painting, young Alexander himself also looked quiet and studious, whereas the girls appeared animated. As for Mrs Kendall she looked reserved but dignified. It struck me that all the strength of this family reposed in its females.

'I have an interest in shade paintings,' I said, the familiar feeling coming over me: regret at dissembling combined with an overmastering curiosity.

'Oh yes?' said Alexander. 'We're devotees of the art. The ladies of the family are, anyhow.'

'I was acquainted a little with a shade painter of this town,' I said. 'Matthew Harvey.'

Mercy was observing me with great interest. She walked up to me, and beckoned me down to her level; and so I stooped.

'He was murdered,' she whispered – rather loudly. 'We are not to speak of it in front of her,' she added, pointing to her sister. 'Oh well, it is too late now!'

'Murdered,' said Anne, 'who was?'

'The man in Coney Street who painted our shades,' said Mercy. 'Mama said you were on no account to be told of it, just because you are so nervous and silly, and you would have a nightmare about it.'

I was braced for an explosion, but Anne remained calm. 'I *will* have a nightmare about it,' she said decidedly, but her tone suggested a pleasurable anticipation rather than dread.

'We all read of it in the *Courant*,' said Mercy. 'All except her. It was a terrible shame, but so fascinating, don't you think?'

I was at a loss for an answer, but the idea of these girls as murderesses was quite banished from my mind. I resolved there and then to write a letter of resignation to Mrs Kendall. (My letter will be profusely apologetic. I will mention a sudden book-writing commission that must take up all my time. I will throw in some free advice for the young man, alongside praise of his evident intellect and imagination. I will suggest that he get his weekly exercises by heart. I will counsel against lingering in the college buttery – which will be hypocritical of me, since it was in the buttery at King's that I nurtured my taste for port wine. I will warn against being caught playing marbles on the steps of the Bodleian Library, for – and this is a true statement, therefore a rare thing in my dealings with Mrs Kendall – I knew a fellow who was rusticated for doing that.)

As I left the Red House, under the eye of the wooden-faced butler, I resolved that my letter would also hint at that gentleman's proclivities. It was the very least I could do for Mrs Kendall.

Fletcher Rigge, in continuation.

The dullness of the day persisted as I made my way along Lord Mayor's Walk towards Mrs Sampson's house. The wagons and carts splashed through the dirty snow, flinging a good deal of it up at my coat. This sort of winter's day lacked all glamour, and everyone was in a hurry to be elsewhere, preferably by a warm hearth.

I felt a degree of satisfaction, nonetheless, at having

crossed the Kendalls off my notional list, for surely
Mercy's account of having learnt of the murder only upon
looking into the *Courant* had been completely credible . . .
and so there were three of the seven possible murderers
eliminated for the price of one. Samuel Gowers in London
might also be crossed off – at least for the time being.
I must now satisfy myself as to the innocence of Mrs
Sampson. As I walked, I recollected with misgivings
her agitation in the carriage coming away from the
Assembly – brought on at the mention of Harvey's
murder – but I expected to receive a countervailing
impression once arrived at her house. I expected to
reacquaint myself with a competent and business-like lady,
in charge of a well-regulated home. It was, therefore, an
unwelcome surprise to discover that number three was the
'avoided house' of the street.

The term requires explanation.

One of the reasons I do not care for the York streets
is that all the houses, like all the people, seem to
be in perpetual jostling competition. But there will
occasionally be found, especially those outwith the
walls, a house that has given up the ghost. In First
Water Lane, *all* the houses have given up, but there is
something harmonious about such a gang of reprobates.
I own to finding a kind of fascination about that
street, with the river making its surly progress at the
bottom, and the church-like aspect of some of the

houses – including Captain Harvey's – with their oak timbers and steepling roofs.

On Monk Street, the houses are newish, and with some of the bleakness of those new ones (including Mrs Kendall's) at Clifton, but without any pretty Green to alleviate an overall bleakness. The houses on either side stare at each other in a kind of stand-off, but one, as I say, seems to avert its gaze in shame: number three. An avoided house may not have cracked windows, but certainly does not have clean ones. It may not face north, but it shuns the light. The door lantern is generally a redundant article. The railings are spiked and mournful, like those enclosing tombs in graveyards.

There being no bell, I clattered the knocker. It resounded hollowly. At length, an elderly and harassed woman answered. Her apron suggested she was also the cook, and the hallway was filled with the smell of some not very appetising meat; or it might have been that cheap tallow candles burned out of sight. In the hallway itself, there was no illumination save the greyness of the day itself, filtering through the dusty fanlight.

As I asked if the mistress was at home, I saw the lady herself, in a plain, pale blue morning gown on the stairs. Even without the cocked hat, she looked trim, precise, calculated, and that calculation had extended to a rather low décolletage. Her face appeared more deeply lined than before, but it was *correctly* lined, giving the lineaments of a beauty not entirely faded, a beauty with – it seemed possible to make a fairly exact calculation – five or six years left to run. Her dark hair was perhaps a little thinner than it ought to have been. Can this be symptomatic of nervous strain? She approached me as I approached her; I almost made the error of climbing the stairs to meet her halfway. As I have mentioned before, we two seemed mysteriously impelled towards each other.

[**Mr Bright's interpolation**: the foregoing sentence, and several of the following, had been scored out in Mr Rigge's diary.]

Of Mr Sampson, that slightly comical, complacent gentleman, there was no sign, and I somehow knew that he was about some ineffectual business, in some down-at-heel chambers in the town.

'Mr Rigge,' said Mrs Sampson, apparently offhand, 'follow me.'

The house was chill, and under-furnished.

'You must excuse this place,' she said. 'I don't go in very much for housewifery.'

We passed one room that was wainscoted, another with plain walls. This last contained several sketches, cheaply framed and haphazardly hung. All the subjects were female. On the mantelpiece were two black-bordered cards: very likely mourning cards, commiserating with a loss. Of course, Mrs Sampson noticed me noticing them.

'My mother died in October,' she said, her tone perhaps a little less abrupt than usual.

We ended up in what might have been a dining room – there was a big, uncovered table in it – or it might have been a sitting room, for two small, dusty sofas were pulled up close to the fireplace. At any rate, we sat. The walls were covered with a yellow and brown marbled wallpaper that was peeling here and there, and was surely too finicking to have been the lady's personal choice. In the ceiling were heavy plaster cofferings and mouldings in the form of endless bands of grimy foliage. I'm afraid I glanced up at these with anxiety as we took our seats (one sofa apiece), lest they suddenly give up the ghost and collapse onto our heads.

The dilapidated servant brought tea. When she had left, I turned to Mrs Sampson.

[**Mr Bright's interpolation:** this next sentence had been struck out.]

She said, 'Well now, have you found out who killed the painter?'

He had been demoted from 'Mr Harvey'. Or perhaps she had forgotten the name, but I doubted that Mrs Sampson forgot very much.

'Not positively,' I said. 'But everything – most things – point to an actor called Jeremiah Smith.'

'Ah,' she said, 'now he has been a busy young man. Did he not also kill the theatre manager, Mr Cork?'

'Very likely.'

'He has fled York, they say. I should look for him in London: auditioning for Drury Lane.'

She had picked up the gossip of the town, but she did not seem to know of the connection between Smith and Matthew Harvey, and this I endeavoured to explain.

'It appears you have got your man,' she said. 'But would you like to examine me, just in case?'

She sat back on the sofa, and in my moment of hesitation, she offered to supply 'a full account' of what was transacted between her and Matthew Harvey.

She explained that she had not seen Mr Harvey's advertisement in the *Courant*, but had heard of it from a friend. She had then spotted Mr Harvey coming out of the Minster on the Thursday prior to the Race Week. She knew his identity, and she made a verbal arrangement to see him for a sitting at two o'clock on the following Thursday, all of which was commensurate with her character as I understood it: she kept her ears pricked for the latest information; she walked abroad in the town a good deal.

I asked, 'Had you been in the Minster yourself?'

'I had not,' she said, with some indignation, for of course she was a great rationalist. 'I wanted a painting of myself.'

'Why?'

'What an extraordinary question. To have a memento of

my appearance before the last vestiges of youth disappear.'

'And to give to Mr Sampson?'

'Of course, yes. It was his birthday last August. He is sixty-five – and he is always very kind to me.'

Neither of these last two remarks was exactly a compliment, I thought. Mrs Sampson then explained that she had read of the murder of Harvey a week later.

'You had no discussion with him as he painted you?' I asked.

'A little. He said he had been ill. He thought he might have a cancer.'

'Where?'

'It would have been rather forward to enquire, don't you think? But perhaps you have a better understanding of the etiquette concerning tumours.'

Not much sympathy here for Harvey and his possible cancer.

'Anything else?'

'He said the week before, he had gone down to Skeldergate to paint the river, but he found the water very low and stagnant. I suggested that a system of locks would keep the water always at a good level.'

'What did he say to that?'

'Nothing. It was not a sufficiently aesthetic point.'

'He evidently wasn't much to your liking.'

'I can't say that he was, no. A rather pious man, self-satisfied. I'm curious about his son, this . . . Captain who has employed you. He is not seen about in the town very much.'

'He keeps to his house. He is badly lame.'

'That is his own fault, I daresay. I mean, he will have come by the injury in some drunken escapade, no doubt?'

I explained about the duck, at which Mrs Sampson laughed, snorting on her tea in a way that bordered on indelicacy – and that I liked.

She said, 'He has a rather beautiful mistress, I am told.'

'Yes.'

I gave this trenchant affirmation partly to restore some dignity to the Captain (I felt a little guilty at having told the belittling story of the duck), and partly because it was true ... but chiefly because something about Mrs Sampson invited frankness and intimacy.

She said, 'Do you care to know what I have found out about you?'

'Not especially,' I said.

'That is a feeble attempt at nonchalance, Mr Rigge.'

And indeed it was.

'The first thing people say is that you are excessively principled, but gentlemanly in your conduct and tolerably handsome with it.'

'I would rather they were *not* the first things people said.'

'Are you sure? What would you prefer?'

'That I was a considerate landlord.'

'But for that you need land, and yours were lost in a card game.'

This was said so dismissively that I almost mentioned the possibility of their restitution.

'And they say you have a particular friend.'

'Who?'

'Who says it or who is the friend?'

'Both.'

'Assembly people.'

'You and Mr Sampson are regulars at the Assembly?'

'What? Oh, we sometimes happen to meet up there.' She sat back, lounging rather, and smiled at me. 'I am a fashionably negligent sort of wife, wouldn't you say?'

No reply was possible, as Mrs Sampson well knew.

'Now,' she continued, 'I am told that a Miss Spink has set her cap at you. Personally, I can't see why, assuming that the normal, trite considerations apply. You have been in the Castle. You were, and presumably still are, in debt. You have no expectations, and she is the daughter of a rich, if vulgar, man.'

'What else were you told?'

'That you despise the literary profession, but write continually. They say you don't care for the town as it is, but oppose all improvements to it. I suppose you're against the building of those locks, for example?'

'They'll wreck the landscape up at Bishopthorpe,' I said.

269

'But I'd rather locks on the river than the destruction of the City Walls.'

'That is not seriously proposed.'

'The Magistrates have applied to Parliament for permission to pull them down. They're considered nuisances; too narrow for the stages, which are rebuilt bigger every year, even though the dimensions of the horses remain fairly consistent, I believe.'

'We seem to be conducting a meeting of the City Corporation. Very well. What do you think of conducting rain from house roofs by leaden pipes?'

'I'm against it; against them.'

She laughed. 'But they keep the streets clear of puddles!'

'I like puddles, Mrs Sampson.'

'Probably because you can see your face in them.'

'The owners habitually stamp their initials on the pipes, as if they owned the rain itself.'

'You are against all aspects of modernity.'

'Most of them, yes.'

'. . . And you venerate everything antiquated . . . in which case, you ought to approve of me, Mr Rigge.'

I smiled at her, quite defeated.

After an interval of tea-sipping silence, I asked, 'Where is the shade painting by Harvey? The one he painted of you?'

'Upstairs, Mr Rigge. Propped on the mantle in my

bedchamber. Would you care to come up and see it?'

Whether this extraordinary invitation was meant seriously, I could not say, for Mrs Sampson's smile was perfectly ambiguous. The servant re-entered to remove the tea things, and Mrs Sampson rose from her sofa, and walked over to the window. She looked out at the houses opposite, and the lowering sky. The servant asked whether she would be at home for dinner, and Mrs Sampson made a half turn in order to reply that she would not be; that she and Mr Sampson would be dining with friends. As the servant departed, Mrs Sampson added, for my benefit, 'He to his friends and I to mine.'

I rose from the sofa to take my leave. As I did so, I studied the elegant profile of Mrs Sampson, as clearly delineated against the fading light of day.

Fletcher Rigge, in continuation.

On my way to Mr Erskine's I called in at the post-office, and scribbled out a note to Captain Harvey, proposing we convene on Wednesday afternoon at half past one. Pleading my reluctance to risk another walk down First Water Lane, I requested this should be at his late father's house in Coney Street. Taking a leaf out of Mrs Sampson's book, I stipulated that he need not trouble to reply if the suggestion be agreeable to him.

It was quarter to four as I walked along the pathway to Mr Erskine's office. I had anticipated a fifteen-minute briefing from Mr Erskine, preparatory to the arrival of Corrigan. But I found that gentleman – if that be the word – already talking with the lawyer and his clerk, Mr Bright. There was another in the room, and I will come to him in a minute.

Corrigan was saying, 'If the weather is the same up there, the snow will be falling into the servants' wing, which I believe is now actually roofless. I have been wondering what snow will do for dry rot, which is apparently infesting the entire house.'

My blood was immediately up, for he was speaking of my boyhood home. I was distressed to learn of its condition, and still more so at the equanimity of Corrigan's tone. His voice lacked character, like his soft grey face.

He glanced up at me with an utter lack of concern, saying, 'Before long it will be impossible to bring the place into order.'

'We will have to knock the house down and build a new one,' said the other man, who sat on a chair to the side of Corrigan's, but also somewhat behind. The fellow's voice *did* have a character, being hoarse, with a trace of cockney. His face had a character too: criminal, and with a three days' growth of beard. He looked vaguely familiar. Perhaps I had seen him in the undercroft of the Assembly Rooms.

As Mr Erskine made the introductions, this ruffian was too busy taking snuff to sketch a bow. His name was Mr Cracknell, and so here were two C's. I will not spell out what I thought that letter might stand for beside the surnames in each case. It struck me that Cracknell might be destined for Adenwold as Mr Corrigan's steward, once my father's man had handed over the reins.

Mr Erskine, who had been standing by the fire, took his seat at his heavy-laden desk. He bade me sit next to him. His clerk, Mr Bright, had modestly located himself in a corner chair. Mr Erskine, presiding, did seem to command the room, by virtue – it seemed to me – of an overriding integrity.

The fellow Cracknell said, with a sour smile, 'I'm never in the company of a lawyer, but I fancy myself in the dock.'

Mr Corrigan directed a questioning look towards his friend, but if this was by way of a reproof, it was an extremely mild one.

'To business, then,' said Mr Erskine, with a greater austerity in his tone than I had heard from him before. 'Have you come to any resolution, Mr Corrigan, concerning the matter of the lands?'

'I might more speedily arrive at one, sir,' said Corrigan, with a fatigued air, 'if you would be so good as to make a pronouncement before the aggrieved young gentleman, here.' He waved a plump, surprisingly small hand in my direction. 'It must be understood that my presence here does not betoken any—'

Mr Erskine cut him off. 'It is without prejudice; that is understood.'

Mr Cracknell closed his snuff box with a loud crack. It obviously had a very strong spring. He flashed a fast, unpleasant smile at me.

'You mean, I *hope*,' said Corrigan, 'that the legality of my title is not in doubt.'

'We are not here to discuss the legality,' said Mr Erskine, and Corrigan turned and smiled rather sadly at his companion, for he had not quite received his desired answer. 'Honour,' Erskine continued, 'was the sole foundation of the transaction.'

Cracknell now crossed his legs so rapidly that I started. He smiled at me again.

'Young Mr Rigge's father honoured the debt he had incurred at a game of loo,' said Corrigan, 'but just in case anybody here present might think that the honour was all on one side, I would like to mention that I repeatedly warned him against increasing the stakes, but I'm afraid his habitual rejoinder was "I dare you to another trial." I would have dishonoured both Mr Rigge and myself if I had refused. When, finally, he could no longer stake ready cash, I agreed to accept his promissory notes. The upshot was that I found myself in possession of an uneconomical estate, a collapsing house, a hotch-potch of tenancies and a hamlet from which half the populace has lately fled in search of better prospects.'

I rose to my feet. 'I will not hear my father traduced in that way by a common sharper.'

I bowed to Mr Erskine and made for the door. Mr Bright was coming after me, with the intention of blocking my departure, and I fear that I squared up to that gentleman.

'Kindly sit down, Mr Rigge,' said Mr Erskine, fixing me with a deep stare.

I said, 'We continue the negotiation if Mr Corrigan will apologise.'

Mr Erskine shot an exasperated look towards Mr Bright, who said, 'Look here, Rigge—' but he was cut off by Corrigan, who said, in his habitual, sighing tone, 'It is not a matter of negotiation, but if it will help us all to be on our way more speedily, I will consent to apologise. Young Mr Rigge's father ran his estate in the old-fashioned way; on patrician lines, and I'm quite sure that some logic – albeit foreign to me – obtained.'

Mr Erskine looked at me, requiring my answer. I nodded, no doubt preposterously, and regained my seat. Cracknell snapped the lid of his snuff box again. He removed a handkerchief from his pocket, but then did nothing with it.

'Please continue, Mr Corrigan,' said Erskine.

'I find,' he said, 'that for my pains in indulging Mr Rigge's father at the gaming table, I am whispered against, by some ill-informed people of this town. It appears I am the wicked disinheritor of a noble young gentleman. I am sure that young Mr Rigge here was always very much in his father's thoughts, but no mention was made of him when he staked his estate. Nonetheless, a rather baffling accusation is implicitly levelled: that of immorality.'

'It is, perhaps, a word of rather loose signification,' said Mr Erskine, steepling his fingers.

Cracknell, now rocking back on his chair, said, 'Physicians are the most learned, lawyers the most amusing; and then comes the clergy.'

'I have talked over this with my friends, Mr Erskine,' said Corrigan. 'They are all gentlemen, and the consensus among them is that I am not obliged in any way on the matter.'

'Then why are we all here, sir?' asked Mr Bright from the corner.

'You are here because it is your place of work, sir,' said Corrigan, without bothering to turn around, 'and I am here because you wrote asking me to come. But now that I *am* here, I might as well turn this meeting to some account.'

'He hates a wasted journey,' Cracknell interjected.

I fairly held my breath, as Corrigan said, 'Let us imagine the estate split in two. On the one side the house and the park; on the other, the village and farms ... and I throw in the common – for what that's worth, being subject to so many covenants and rights of way that will sooner or later have to be paid off.'

Mr Erskine asked, 'To what purpose are we envisaging this sub-division?'

'Young Mr Rigge can have one half,' said Corrigan with the upmost casualness, 'I'll keep the other.'

It was just as Mr Erskine had suggested. Corrigan was endeavouring to repair his damaged reputation – perhaps only because its loss would cost him dear financially and might scupper the projected bank. Even so, I was amazed.

'Who gets which half?' I said, and it was a job to keep a steady tone.

'Up to you,' said Corrigan, with a shrug.

'Toss for it, if you like,' grinned Cracknell.

'It'll cost a small fortune to bring the house into order,' said Corrigan, 'and the rents from the lands amount to little more than small change ...'

'It's between the devil and the deep sea,' said Cracknell, and I began to wonder whether his mischief might not be in a lighter vein than I had thought.

All eyes were on me. The re-acquisition of either part of the estate would free me from the clutches of Captain

Harvey, since money could be borrowed against the freeholds. I loved the house and park. I pictured the double avenue of oaks, its regularity offset by the random disposition of the cattle beneath. Yes, the house was in a poor state of repair, but Corrigan might have overstated the dereliction. The house was the jewel in the crown, but my obligation was to the tenants – to spare them an enclosure. A small voice in my head whispered, '. . . whether they want to be spared it or not', but this would not deflect me. Nor would the question of where I myself might live. I would take a cottage in Adenwold, or build a new one.

'I accept the restitution of the tenanted lands,' I said, which I immediately considered a churlish reply, 'restitution' probably being the wrong word in law. Mr Corrigan sighed again, apparently accustomed to my incivilities, but too weary to correct me. Cracknell was playing with a coin and grinning.

'Then it is a done thing,' said Mr Erskine. 'Mr Pullman will draw up the new deed, or I will see to it myself.'

If I had been churlish, then it seemed Mr Erskine was similarly inclined, for he neither thanked Corrigan for his magnanimity, nor hinted that I should do so. It could only be that he genuinely considered Corrigan and Cracknell to have been cheating in the original game. I took my cue from the lawyer, and there was no shaking of hands as the conference was wound up. I thanked only Mr Erskine and Mr Bright as I took my leave, in the wake of Corrigan and Cracknell, who still played with the coin – a shining new penny piece, I saw – which he expertly tossed and caught overhanded as he took his leave. Mr Erskine had seen him do it. 'A very dextrous gentleman,' he observed, as he handed me my hat.

Mr Erskine's memorandum concerning the immediate aftermath of the meeting described above.

I am no psychologist, but there was something in young Rigge's expression as he left my chambers that I did not care for. I was still more discomfited by the manner of the man Cracknell who, I was increasingly sure, had the operative role in his mysterious partnership with Corrigan.

In young Rigge, I detected a dangerous romantic fatalism of the sort that seems to have afflicted his late father. If I read him aright, he was preoccupied once again with that accursed 'honour', which comes so close to vanity in young men of a certain kind. In Cracknell, I detected simple malice. A quick word with Mr Bright confirmed that we were thinking alike.

The two of us hastily collected up our hats and coats, and we stepped outside, where we beheld Rigge, Corrigan and Cracknell in discussion at the head of the alleyway that leads to my chambers. Advancing towards them, I heard, from Cracknell, the fatal words, 'Very well, sir, double or quit it shall be.'

Who made the first suggestion of another trial, I don't know, and have never discovered, but I believe it to have been Rigge. I believe, also, that this proposition had been in the air ever since Corrigan had first mooted the sub-division of the estate. Rigge, in short, was a gamester like his father – but not in the literal sense, and I saw him shaking his head when Cracknell said, 'We will play hazard. Who will be the caster?'

Rigge said, 'I do not know the rules of any dice game.'

Corrigan, who had been smiling abstractedly, now spoke up. 'Then one throw. A single toss of a single dice.'

His own man disavowed this proposal. 'But we have no dice, cup or table.'

'We could go to an inn,' said Corrigan.

At this, Mr Bright and I attempted to intervene, but Rigge waved us away. I attempted to command him with a raised voice, but there was nothing to be done. He was determined to go to hell at the fastest possible pace. Or perhaps not quite the very fastest, for when Cracknell said, 'A single toss of a coin then,' and held up the shining penny he had been toying with, Rigge said, 'Might we use a neutral coin?'

'Why, sir,' said Corrigan, 'all coins are neutral.'

Rigge turned to Mr Bright. 'Sir,' he said. 'May I trouble you for the loan of a penny?'

With a look of the greatest misgiving, my friend fished in his breeches for what turned out to be a halfpenny, which he handed to Rigge with a look of embarrassment.

'Might I see that, sir?' asked Cracknell, and Rigge passed it over to him. (Of course it would have been dishonourable not to, since he had stipulated against Cracknell's penny.)

I have re-played that scene many times in my mind – that brief instant, less than two seconds, in which Cracknell took the coin, and turned it to look at the reverse. It is possible that he gave the briefest shrug as he performed the action, and certainly he gave a cough. Whether there was any subtle chicanery – it was inconceivable . . . almost. He passed the coin back to Rigge, saying, 'Very well, sir. Fly the mag.' (I have since discovered that 'mag' is a cant term for a halfpenny piece.)

'Who calls?' enquired Rigge.

'You, sir,' said Corrigan.

'No, sir,' said Rigge. 'The honour is yours.'

'Heads,' said Corrigan.

Fletcher Rigge tossed the coin.

It came up tails.

His entire estate was forfeit for the second time, and he could have no grounds of complaint; or at least, none that any third party could have thought reasonable – which outcome I believe he had not only foreseen, but also perversely desired. His own diary account of the incident is sketchy and not quite coherent, perhaps owing to the circumstance described below.

Mr Derek Hill, Under-gaoler, examined by Mr Bright concerning his sighting of Fletcher Rigge during the evening of the day following.

Now on the Tuesday night you speak of, Mr Bright, December 4th, I saw him in the Tiger Inn. It's on Jubbergate, and pretty ancient. It's sometimes called the Leopard, since that's what the creature on the sign is taken by some to be. The artist was hedging his bets, I reckon, for he made the beast both spotted and striped.

Now you might wonder why they'll serve a turnkey in there.

[**Mr Bright's interpolation:** I told him I wasn't in the least concerned and would he kindly press on to the question of Mr Rigge.]

You must know the place, Mr Bright, even if you've never looked in. It's notable for its chimney, which rises up peculiarly – in a spiral, pretty near, almost like a twist of smoke itself.

Anyhow, I'd dropped in for an alleviator, a quick one, as you might say. I was standing at the parlour bar, which gives a clear view through to the little back room, which is like a sort of ship's cabin – old wood, and a rolling floor that makes you think you've had a pint of wine instead of a pint of ale. Well, there was our Mr Rigge, and he *had* drunk a pint of wine, or maybe more. He sat alone by the fire, looking all wrong for the location. With his pale face, and his habitual washed and pressed cambric, he was like 'a vision in bright raiment', as they say in the ghost stories.

I cut through the bar, and stood directly before him. But I must needs tap him on the shoulder before he noticed . . . I am not so presuming as to say his friend, but his old acquaintance. Lost, he was, sunk in a dream. I'd say he was glooming rather than fuddled by drink. It was *The Anatomy of Melancholy* all over again, only without the book.

'How are you, sir?' I said, and he gradually returned to the land of the living, so to say.

Instead of answering my question – for he had a dread of boring on about his affairs – he asked me for my own news. But I pressed my enquiry, and he replied, 'Every cloud is vanishing from the horizon,' and it was very evident to me that the opposite was the case. He asked if I could take a glass with him, but I forbore to do it, sir, since I knew his secret desire was to be left alone.

The writing book of his was on the table before him, along with some drawings or paintings – shade paintings – and two letters, Mr Bright, on goodish paper. It was none of my business of course but having got a glimpse of one of them, I'd have said from the writing that it was from a young woman.

I went back into the parlour, where Bill Walker – that's the landlord – told me that Rigge had been in the same back room spot, and glooming in just the same way the night before as well, but he reckoned he'd only had the paintings before him then, and not the letters.

Well, I passed a convivial enough evening in the parlour. Come ten o'clock or so, I peeped again into the back room, and Rigge was still there, more or less immobile, with the papers before him. I called out, 'A good night to you, Mr Rigge,' and I believe he hardly heard me. I had the impression of a man without a friend, and the back room of the Tiger is a hard place to be alone, sir, on a stormy night, on account of the way the wind roars in that twisted chimney.

Mr Bright's postscript to the above.

Given below are the letters referred to by Hill. Both had been delivered to Rigge's lodge during that same Tuesday, but by separate posts.

Letter from Lucy Spink to Fletcher Rigge.

North Bank Villa,
Wellington Row,
York.

Sir,

I know that I am acting wrong in writing to you. Our relations are not on the footing for a correspondence, but I believe you know me to have a passion violent enough to break through customary decorums. It has been reported to me (and I suppose you will not deny it) that you were seen talking in a tavern — a place, I am reliably informed, of no good repute — to a young woman of a character obviously dubious, and I am led to understand that the earnestness of your discourse showed that you were no stranger to her.

I have been aware that your recent misfortunes had left you peculiarly situated that you must enter an association with individuals less respectable than they might be. I chose not to question you about this connection, but made allowances, believing it to be temporary, and not incompatible with what I always took to be your own principled nature. I see now that I was quite wrong; that you have gone too far down this evil road, forfeiting your own good character, as you have forfeited the esteem of one who valued your friendship above all others.

It is too painful for me to continue with this, sir. I began by saying we were not on a footing for a correspondence, and I must tell you that we never now can be, and so please not to squander away your time with some attempted explanation, for I assure you that your letter will be refused.

Yours, & c.

Letter from Mr Carl Spink to Fletcher Rigge.

North Bank Villa,
Wellington Row,
York.

Sir,

You will be surprised to receive a communication from one who isn't known to you, but my daughter could hardly write to you herself.

I have known for some time that you have been making overtures towards her, in the way of courtship. I must ask you to suspend your designs.

I am aware that you have been through a time of trial and pecuniary difficulties – all very unfortunate, I am sure – and that you have chosen to rectify matters by entering into an association with a man of whom (for I have taken the liberty of enquiring) I hear no good reports, to say the very least. You know who I mean, sir, and I have evidence of your having participated in his odious libertinism.

I will speak plainly, sir: you have been observed by a reliable witness in close company with his common-law wife, who is little better than a harlot. It would appear unnecessary to add that I by no means approve of you as a husband to my daughter, who has been made aware of all related here and has been inexpressibly distressed to learn of your base conduct. Your suit, sir, can receive no encouragement, and should you attempt any further contact with my daughter, it will be the worse for you.

Yours, & c.

Diary of Fletcher Rigge, Wednesday December 5th.

This morning I rose early, my head not too bad after my customary excess of wine, but still in need of clearing.

I walked through the town, a cold grey dawn coming up but all the draymen and shopkeepers determined to get the world turning. I drank a cup of coffee and ate a pastry at Mancini's. I then walked over to the Foss Marsh, where the dawn only disclosed a white mist, but a beautiful one, pointing up the blackness of the river, which in turn emphasised the whiteness of some swans upon it, and making all seem mysterious yet profound, offering a kind of comfort, but no false consolation.

I believed I was content, for I was beginning to relinquish Monday and Tuesday. I resolved to drop a note to Mr Erskine thanking him for his mediation with Corrigan, and explaining my behaviour, at which he had no doubt despaired. He'd had no opportunity to remonstrate with me, since I had walked – nay, stalked – out of Precentor's Court so peremptorily. Instead, he had been remonstrating with Corrigan and Cracknell as I turned the corner into High Petergate, and Corrigan had sounded somewhat contrite ... which signified not in the least. Had there been anything amiss with the coin I had tossed? I had surely received back from Cracknell that same one I had presented to him for inspection. But again, no matter, since the outcome was the one I had invited.

'Double or quit' was always in the offing; I could not have refused the offer, therefore I made it myself. I could never have accepted Corrigan's charity; and how could I be his neighbour in the country, with his house and park (formerly mine) pressing on the compensatory lands I had been granted? He will now enclose those lands, but I am almost persuaded by recent conversations that I would have been driven to the same course myself.

I could never have retreated into that Arcadia, still less taken Miss Spink with me. I was to her a fitting character in a novel, but then it became a novel she didn't care for. Her first informant, of course, was Bob Richmond: I saw him in the Half Moon, at the end of my talk with Esther. I am sure he believes he has made a decisive intervention (the thought of which might, I rather hope, come to torment him) but he was only the immediate cause of a sundering bound to occur. All last evening I was rehearsing phrases for a letter of reply to Miss Spink, but they all – from 'the lady you refer to is a very old friend of mine', to 'my whole heart is in this letter', to 'yours most truly' – struck me as lies. Besides, my letter would not have been read, as Miss Spink had informed me.

Her second informant, I assume, was the small bald man. Having tipped her off about the possible restitution of my lands, he had then told her of the impossibility of this occurring owing to my cavalier behaviour in the lawyer's office. At any rate, she had learnt the outcome of my meeting with Corrigan and Cracknell. If my three thousand a year was lost, she must revert to one of the muddy brothers of Thirsk, with their two thousand apiece.

But perhaps I do her injustice. What she had heard, her father had also heard. He would have commanded her not to write, and she had shown spirit in disobeying him, even if her letter was an effectual duplication of his. This suggests to me that the first intelligence – that concerning Esther – counted for more with her than the second, concerning the money. In any event, she is consecrated to the ways of this town, and I have been living under a delusion, of which I am now free.

The totally monochromatic world I surveyed at the marsh was a reminder of the shades, and of the Captain who has laid them before me. That gentleman is not to be evaded. I resolved that, on the contrary, he – and those surrounding shadows – must be taken on, and this whole affair speedily wound up.

Fletcher Rigge, in continuation.

'Tincture?' enquired Captain Harvey, as I stepped into the room in which his father had painted. He was at the long table, which was still loaded with the black inks and paints, and all the means of applying them. He was withdrawing a cork from a bottle – it was from his late father's cellar, no doubt – as I stood near the rear window, watching the snow silently descending into the black river. The Captain believed I was concerned with the poignant capitulation of so many snowflakes, but I was also studying the profile of the murdered man, which hung on the wall nearby. It was almost two o'clock, but the colour of the sky suggested a later hour.

'Come, sir,' he said, 'it is a reasonable Burgundy, and dissipation is better than melancholia. You have been in difficulties, I take it? I hope not connected with the matter of the shades?'

'This week,' I said, 'I had the prospect of more agreeable days; but it was only a temporary remission.'

'That's the fellow!' said the Captain. 'Always in spirits! *Everything* is temporary, you know,' he said with mock severity, as I accepted the proffered glass.

I surveyed the Captain: his twisted smile . . . his twisted leg. He had a new cane, with a silver top. On the other hand, his rusty black coat was inferior to the last one I'd seen on him. I admired the severity of the cutaway, however. His breeches were no cleaner than the last time, but then Captain Harvey was a coal merchant, among other things.

'Now what about the shades, sir?' said the Captain, who was commencing his upright lounging against the mantelpiece.

'I have been collecting my thoughts, sir,' I said, perching on the end of the long table. 'It has been a busy three weeks . . .'

'And a little more,' said Harvey. 'Really you have had no want of time.' As if to verify the fact, he looked at his watch: a rather elegant one, in gold pair cases. As he returned it to his fob pocket, I imagined it ticking through the next thirty years as I languished in the Castle – for the Sheriff's men would be coming after me in ten days' time. 'Two of the shades were already identified for you,' the Captain continued, 'and if you have found the right family, then there's another three at a stroke.'

He took out his pipe, lit it from the fire.

'I was required not merely to identify the sitters,' I said,

'I was also charged with assessing the likelihood of any one of them being a murderer.'

'That applies only in six of the seven cases,' said the Captain, blowing smoke, 'but I will overlook the provocation. I have been called worse things than a murderer.'

I could well believe it.

I commenced to recount my adventures in pursuit of the shades, beginning with my visit to London, and Mr Samuel Gowers. As I spoke, Harvey retrieved paper, a quill and a pot of ink from the long table. He took them over to the chair by the fireplace, where he settled down to make notes of my speech. He also removed a pistol from his coat pocket, and laid it by him on the floorboards, this for no apparent purpose other than to intimidate me.

'You tell a good story,' he said, amiably enough, when I'd finished my accounts of not only Gowers but also the Kendall females, 'and you exonerate all these four?'

'Not quite,' I said. 'But it is unlikely that our murderer is among them.'

'And the pretty lady in the cocked hat?'

I told him her identity. I said I believed her to be a very determined person, not without a streak of bitterness and frustration in her character, but that I could see no reason for her to have killed Matthew Harvey. Here, I gave another instinctive glance towards the image of that gentleman on the wall. The Captain seemed to take ill my paying attention, so to speak, to his late parent, for his smile hardened as he said:

'The lady resides on Monkgate, you say. She must be pretty rich.'

'Monk *Street*,' I said, 'and the house is not well appointed.'

The Captain nodded, frowning rather.

'The youth with the weak chin,' he said.

'He is an actor,' I said, 'connected to the Theatre Royal. You have perhaps heard the name: Jeremiah Smith.'

The Captain poured himself another glass of wine, saying, 'He is the one suspected of killing Mr Cork.'

It was something between a statement and a question. I nodded anyhow, and began recounting what I believed to be the murderous history of Smith, presenting him as the likely killer of Matthew Harvey, Mr Cork, and of the material witness to the latter, Melissa King.

'Then this Smith,' the Captain said, 'has killed not only my father, but my father's best – indeed only – friend . . . According to your account.'

I eyed him across the cold room. I knew that his true villainy was about to be disclosed.

'This Smith,' he said, 'an impoverished young actor, who has disappeared.' He shook his head. 'He is of no earthly use to me.'

'Perhaps you would prefer to bring an innocent person to the scaffold,' I suggested.

'It is not necessarily a matter of bringing anyone to the scaffold,' he said. 'I am not a constable; nor am I a magistrate, gaoler or hangman.'

'Then what are you?' I said, although by now my speculation was all but confirmed.

'By your account,' said the Captain, ignoring my question, 'any one of these people might be our culprit. They all have the noose dangling over their heads. It will take but one visit to a magistrate, with evidence logically marshalled, to lower the rope around any one of their necks, the Kendall children included.'

He stood, with difficulty; he mustered a smile with still more difficulty. 'A true bill is likely to be raised against any one of them. Do you not think they would be only too glad to have the threat averted?'

'Glad to the tune of how much?' I said. 'Two hundred pounds? Or perhaps a lesser sum will be acceptable at first, but amounting to the same or more after regular instalments? There is a word for your sort, sir.'

'And what is it, pray?'

Absurdly enough, I found that I could not remember. The best I could come up with was 'Bloodsucker'.

'Any advance on that?' he said.

'Extortionist,' I said. (The cant word 'Black-mailer' would have hit the nail on the head, but I have only just recollected it.) 'The seventy-five pounds you paid on my behalf—'

'A hundred and fifty,' he cut in, 'including the bail.'

'... Which would seem a good investment set against a return of many hundreds. I suppose, by the way, that you have no intention of discharging the balance of my debt?'

'So far,' he said, 'I have paid a small fortune in order to be insulted.'

'Perhaps I will reveal your design to the Sheriff's men?' I said. 'Or to the magistrates?'

'Some outburst or other from you will be anticipated on all sides,' said the Captain. 'You have not answered my expectations and you will be – you are – naturally aggrieved at your projected return to prison. But I advise you to think carefully. There is a contract between us. It reaches its term within ten days. If you traduce me before then, it will naturally be voided.'

By which time, I thought, Captain Harvey, will have written his letters, enjoining the recipients to absolute silence on pain of exposure as a murderer. Within that time also, he might reap his rewards. Gowers might be good for two or three hundred pounds, Mrs Kendall for a great deal more. Even Mrs Sampson might come up with a hundred or so, I supposed, in spite of her apparently straitened circumstances. Then again, there was nothing against her. Or at least nothing the Captain knew.

The Captain had been restless these past days, Esther had said. He no doubt intended to quit York before very long. He would skulk on the edge of another town, perhaps by another wharf, where he could receive the sea-coal that sustained him. Or he would return to London, where any man can effectually disappear. Therefore, minimal risk attached to his black-mailing scheme. He might, in fact, carry it on perfectly easily from London. Having poured himself another glass of wine, he was pointing languidly towards the door with his cane. Our interview was concluded.

I saw myself out of the house, and began walking fast to the York Registry.

Fletcher Rigge, in continuation.

It was about three o'clock when I took my place among those shuffling antiquarians or pedigree hunters who have occasion to search the wills in that dirty cabin. The number of enquirers was not as great as before, probably on account of the thick soft snow that had been falling the past hour. Then again, some boy choristers, killing time before Evensong, kept coming in and out of the Registry, to try how long snowballs would last when placed on top of the stove. Whenever they opened the door, a whirl of snow would blow in. It was well for them that the officious Myers, Deputy Under-Registrar (as he is absurdly styled), was nowhere to be seen. Nor was the Chief Clerk of before, Wilkinson. A new man stood at the long counter that bars the way to the wills. In common with his predecessors, he looked harassed, but he gave some indications – an occasional smile, for instance – of being more accommodating. Indeed, the two shuffling archaeologists before me were furnished pretty quickly with the documents they sought.

I paid over my guinea and gave the name of Matthew Harvey as being the testator I was interested in.

'Ah!' exclaimed the clerk excitedly. 'The murdered man! The murdered man! I myself received the will from the executor, and gave out the certificate of probate.'

In that case, I suggested – as politely as my agitation would allow – perhaps he might recollect where he had put it.

'Of course! Of course!'

And the excitable fellow carried on saying 'Of course!' many times over – while repeatedly removing and replacing his bent spectacles – as he retreated to the shelves. It occurred to me to wonder who the executor was. Apparently, Harvey had had only two friends: the painter Goodricke and Mr Cork of the Theatre Royal, who had also become a 'murdered man'.

As the clerk commenced his search, the great inadequacy of the arrangements made me despair of ever being able to confirm the suspicion that was now strong upon me. The wills, tied with nothing but common string, are supposedly held alphabetically, but the shelves are utterly chaotic, their contents stalked over by spiders, and covered in dust, which makes the parchments in which they are rolled quite black. As he caught up and discarded one after another, the clerk changed his exclamation, beginning now to mutter, 'The Murdered Man, the Murdered Man! Where can he be?'

Evidently, he was not mouldering away under 'H' . . . and then I had an inspiration.

'Try under "M",' I suggested.

'"M"? Why?'

'You think of him as "The Murdered Man",' I said. Perhaps you filed him away accordingly. It would be an easy mistake to make,' I added, by way of conciliation, 'anyone might have done it.'

The clerk looked doubtful at first. 'I really don't think I would have . . . '

But he recommenced his search in a new place, and I could hardly contain my exultation when he cried, 'Well, would you believe it? Here he is alongside two Murdochs!'

In return for the will, I offered further blandishments together with my guinea: 'Such a very hectic office; it's a wonder you don't go distracted.'

'Well, I obviously *do*,' the fellow said, rather endearingly.

At one of the tables reserved for the searchers, I unrolled the parchment. The string was not yet rotten; indeed, I was a good while about the un-tying. When this was accomplished, I found two paper weights to hold it down, and I began to read.

The testator in this case had also been the drafter – our parsimonious artist had not run to the expense of a lawyer – but the main dispositions were clear enough. After an unusually protracted religious preamble, Harvey had left to his son, Captain Robin Harvey, his gold watch. His house, all his household goods, his furniture and stock in trade, together with the very substantial sum of eight hundred pounds, went to his housekeeper, Susan. As must be the case when a bequest is to a woman, this was to be held on trust for her, the trustee being Mr Goodricke, he of the Royal Academy, who was also the sole executor of the will. (His signature had been appended to the document on July 20th 1798, in other words about a month before Harvey's murder.) The cash sum had originally been five hundred pounds, but that had been scored out and eight hundred inserted.

The principal interest of the document, however, lay beneath this, in the shape of another, more emphatic crossing out, made by what appeared to be black oil paint that had congealed into a veritable lump. I must see beneath this lump, and I thought of the label on a bottle I'd glimpsed in Harvey's work room:

'Turpentine'. That was the stuff used to dissolve oil paint. It was bound to have some spurious purported medical application, and so I knew exactly where I might come by a bottle.

I asked the clerk whether I might leave the will in his care for a moment, before dashing out into the snowy town. Five minutes later, I was among the cosseted customers of M. Garencier, whose representative on earth, Mr Hurst, eyed me suspiciously as he counselled a neurotic lady. 'Take it with rhubarb, rice water and . . . wine,' he said, no doubt improvising freely as he handed over an expensive-looking bottle, 'and come back in two days if the bowels are still costive.'

He turned to me. 'You are dripping snow all over my Turkey carpet,' he observed.

Apologising, I asked, 'I hope you are well, sir? And how is Tom-Tom?'

'Tum-Tum, I think you mean. He is indisposed – a *mal de tête*. Have you acquired your own pug dog yet?'

I told him truthfully that I had been thinking about the breed a good deal and that I had no intention of purchasing any other sort of dog. I then asked whether he might sell me a bottle of turpentine.

He made an expression of distaste. 'I have pine resin,' he said.

'That's pretty much the same, is it?'

'It is more refined. It is for muscle pain, I suppose?'

'It's to remove oil paint,' I said, and Mr Hurst suffered to hear me out as I explained that I needed to remove paint from parchment in order to disclose some writing beneath.

'You are a very mysterious young man indeed,' he pronounced, adding, 'Surely the ink will come away with the paint? Wait a moment.'

And he disappeared into his back room. He returned holding a small scalpel. 'Its proper use is the removal of bunions,' he said, 'but it will also serve to scrape away the paint.'

I fumbled in my pocket for coins; handed over a shilling, and was fumbling for more, when Mr Hurst said, '*Cela suffit.*'

At a quarter to four, I was back in the Registry with the blade in my hand and the will of Harvey before me. As I scraped away, an aborted bequest was disclosed. By it, three hundred pounds was left to a trustee – again, Mr Goodricke – 'to be held on such trusts as I have declared to him'. The bequest, that is to say, was to have been a secret between Harvey and Mr Goodricke, but Harvey had thought better of it.

And so my suspicions would appear to be confirmed.

Mr Erskine's postscript to the above.

I have since spoken to Mr Goodricke, and he was never consulted about any trusteeship, although he assured me he would have been willing to undertake one for an esteemed fellow Royal Academician. What is evident to me is that Matthew Harvey had intended the creation of a half-secret trust, by which a testator makes clear that a legatee is to hold property on the terms of a trust, but those terms are privately communicated and not stated on the face of the will. It is of course a more common – and more secure – way of making a discreet bequest than a fully secret trust, by which no trust at all is disclosed on the face of the will.

Matthew Harvey had obviously thought better of the bequest, and so struck it out in the most emphatic manner, before transferring the earmarked sum to his sister's legacy. But who had been the intended beneficiary? Mr Goodricke could not assist me, nor could Susan Harvey. But Fletcher Rigge believed that he knew.

Letter from Esther to Fletcher Rigge.

River House,
Near the Coal Staith,
First Water Lane,
York.

Sir,

When I recollect our conversation about the Captain I find myself a good deal troubled. I deliberately reserved my remarks, from a loyalty to that gentleman that I begin to find very much misplaced.

For a start, the term 'gentleman' does not apply. 'Extortionist' would be a better appellation. His true business is not the despatch of coal from the lighters on the wharf but the despatch of letters by which the receivers find their reputations menaced. They are accused of crimes they may or may not have committed – it hardly matters to the Captain. This is why you have been charged with the job of finding those poor people who might have been in the general vicinity at the general time of a murder. Ideally there must be the prospect of the gallows for his letters to gain their object.

The matter of the shades is really only a side line to him, for while a charge of murder will serve, better still is a charge of sodomy, which will take away a man's life even more swiftly and surely. So the Captain accuses many of his correspondents of that, supposedly the greatest of all crimes . . . which he commits almost every day, and sometimes – I assure you, Mr Rigge – twice a day. It seems there are not enough gentleman-sodomites for his purposes, and so he must create a few new ones. In London, he would draw men into his various inns – which would strike genteel observers as remarkably akin to bagnios or brothels – where they would be encouraged to take indecent liberties with pretty-faced young men. Here in York, he has a new scheme. The susceptible persons need not trouble to visit the inns, for the pretty young gentlemen come to them, with bags of coal on their shoulders, and the buttons of their forelaps already undone.

By a letter sent a few days later, the Captain feigns indignation at this debauching of his employee. Being a Christian sort of coal merchant (as he presents himself) he must dispense with the services of the coal heavers in question, and so must be compensated. They all – not only the timid gentlemen – comply, especially since the first demand is quite modest. But once they 'bite' they are hooked forever, unless they make away with themselves, or until the Captain tires of the correspondence. And so they must look to the Captain's boredom, which is the only thing that mitigates his evil, and I must tell you, sir, that he is not yet grown bored with the question of those seven shades – even

305

though the question there is only murder – and I hope that you will have the sense to flee this town, which is the earnest recommendation of

Your friend and well-wisher,
Esther.

Mr Bright's postscript to the above:

The above letter was never sent. It was discovered in the pages of Esther's diary, in the circumstances to be disclosed.

Letter from Mr Hardcastle, Box Office Manager of the Theatre Royal, to Fletcher Rigge.

Theatre Royal,
St Leonard's Place,
York.
Wednesday December 5th

Dear Mr Rigge,

You requested that I inform you of any new intelligence concerning the whereabouts of Jeremiah Smith. Well, sir, it is not impossible that our fugitive player has returned to this city. His former place of lodgement, in Whip-Ma-Whop-Ma-Gate, is reputed to have been raided. Somebody – let us say – gained admittance by breaking a rear window and then entered the rooms formerly occupied by Smith, which had not been re-let. If it was indeed Smith who made the incursion, then he stole only from himself. Some clothes, a clock (broken, I am told), two candlesticks and two pound notes were taken, together with a file of articles containing reviews of Smith's performances.

Your obedient servant,
Timothy Hardcastle.

Mr Bright's postscript to the above.

Unlike the letter from Esther, the above certainly was received by Rigge. Mr Hardcastle delivered it by hand, on Wednesday December 5th (while Rigge was at the Registry), to the pedestal table outside his rooms.

Diary of Fletcher Rigge, Thursday December 6th.

At eight o'clock this evening, I lay prostrate on my bed, thinking about what I had found out at the Registry, and reading over this diary. The deed of transfer to Corrigan lay on the floor by the bed. I could look at it now without wistfulness; it was simply a memorandum of a completed transaction. The ragged curtains at my window did a poor job of keeping out the moonlight, and none at all of keeping out the cold. As I looked over that way, the curtain flinched, and the window behind banged in its casement. Somebody had opened the back door, and had commenced climbing the stairs towards my rooms. It was a light tread, which worried me less than if it had been a heavy one, but puzzled me more, at least for an instant.

'Good evening, Mrs Sampson,' I said, opening the door.

'I hope you did not anticipate my arrival,' she said, stepping into the room, and removing her cocked hat. 'That would have been rather presumptuous.' She was noticing, as she spoke, that she had entered directly upon my bedchamber. I apologised for it, ushering her through into the other room, which passes for my sitting room, and assuring her that her arrival had come as a complete, but very pleasant, surprise.

I showed her to my one upholstered chair, which is a small couch. I myself stood by the fireplace.

'I would offer to take your coat,' I said, 'but . . .'

'I'll freeze to death without it,' she supplied.

We both contemplated the tiny fire. I stood in my shirt sleeves with cuffs undone. I wore rough woollen trousers rather than breeches. My father's oldest, but best, green silk slippers were not enough to save me from a feeling of complete mortification, which Mrs Sampson's smile did little to mitigate.

'Mrs Buckley might bring us up some tea,' I suggested.

'Who is she?'

'My landlady.'

'The person I've just successfully avoided meeting, you mean?'

'Or I have some port wine,' I said, 'if you would care for a glass?'

'Yes,' she said. 'I think I would. Thank you.'

Removing the bottle from the corner cabinet, I poured out two glasses, which was as many glasses as I had.

'What is that?' she said, indicating the deed.

Glad of a diversion from the question of where I might sit, I told her what it was, and what it signified, namely the lands I'd lost owing to my father's gaming.

'My husband is also a gamester,' she said.

'And you?' I said.

'Not a bit; except when I married him.'

'You disapprove of his gaming?'

'He cannot afford it, and neither can I. I also disapprove most strongly,' she continued, 'of his sitting *down* so much. He has an inaptitude for exercise.'

Evidently Mr and Mrs Sampson were not in very close alliance. I could not think of many reasons why she should be making this perfectly plain. I had found two candles, but they were only tallows, and she told me not to bother lighting them. 'We can converse by firelight,' she said. 'That would be the country way, and I believe you would rather remove to the countryside, where you came from?'

'I no longer know. I used to think so.'

'You find York too much in the metropolitan school? This little town of ten thousand people?'

'Twenty; and it's not so much the town, but the philosophy it engenders.'

'Explain.'

310

'Universal civicism; belief in the perfectibility of human nature.'

'I think you do rather well in the town. You have a pretty good understanding of it. You can dance; you are quite dandified in the way the town likes. In fact, you have an immoderate fondness for dress. You are like a woman.'

'Nobody could accuse you of making sly hits.'

'For myself, I hate any dandification: caps, bonnets, the whole mischief of trimmings.'

I weighed the wine in the bottle, finding more remaining than I had thought.

'A suicide note was once left,' I said, filling Mrs Sampson's glass. 'It read, "All this buttoning and unbuttoning."'

'By whom?'

'Anonymous.'

'But it must have been a town person,' she said.

'I don't see how that follows.'

'Because it's amusing, and country people are so so dull.'

'You like factories, I suppose?' I asked.

'I find them rather Gothic and handsome. Will you not sit by me, Mr Rigge?'

'You are well disposed towards thick, black smoke, I take it?'

'Mr Rigge,' she said, patting the counterpane so as to indicate the vacant space next to her, 'are you holding off for reasons of chivalry? Is there another lady in the case? Well, of course, there's your particular friend, Miss Spink, the upholsterer's daughter.'

'I believe you murdered Matthew Harvey.'

She did not seem in the least deflected from whatever her purpose might be.

'Yes, well, I know you do. You rudely intimated as much when we first met.'

'I think you are his daughter.'

'Why?'

'Because I have seen his portrait, and you look like him.'

'You are a good physiognomist. I am his daughter, Mr Rigge. But he is not my father.'

Fletcher Rigge, in continuation.

'It is my turn to lament, Mr Rigge,' said Mrs Sampson. But there was no undue sentimentality in what followed, which, for reasons of narrative condensation, I give in my own words.

Mrs Maria Sampson's mother, Jane Ackroyd, was kitchen servant in the big house that overlooks the Thursday Market Square. When barely more than a girl, she was spotted walking along the river by Matthew Harvey, who asked if he might sketch her. He did more than that, however, and Miss Ackroyd fell pregnant, with the result that she was dismissed from the house on Market Square. She took a cheap lodgement in Fishergate and became a cook at an inn – so Mrs Sampson's early girlhood was largely passed on the stone flags of a kitchen floor. Matthew Harvey married a parson's daughter soon after. He did nothing to help Jane Ackroyd, or not much. He would occasionally turn up at the lodge and, under the guise of sketching Jane, he might make some desultory enquiries about her welfare, and perhaps hand over a pound or two, which sums were the more readily forthcoming if Jane performed a certain favour in return. When Maria was aged five, her mother – who had been living as 'a widow' – married a man called Hugh Smillie. After a very short acquaintance with Smillie, Maria wished her mother a 'widow' once again. Smillie, like Carl Spink, was an upholsterer, but in a smaller way of business: 'He made cushions, but not for mother and me. He had a good supply of long needles, and with these he would prick me.'

I asked whether Matthew Harvey was out of touch all this time.

'Sometimes he would send a letter with a guinea beneath the seal. Sometimes he would turn up with his easel. His interest now was in sketching or painting *me*. They were nicely managed, those sketches, but of course he never signed them. I believe he was always working himself up to some impropriety.'

'And was he guilty of any such thing?' I enquired.

'Not quite, no. He sketched me on a swing once, and he was very keenly interested in the placement of my legs, but no.'

After a few years, Mrs Sampson's mother left Hugh Smillie. She removed to the country near York, where she married a certain Mr Barnes. 'He called himself a sacristan, but really he was a gravedigger.' Nonetheless, he wasn't as bad as Smillie, and he made some efforts for the girl, who would still be sent occasional sums by Harvey. 'He got rather Christian late on, so it might be that he apprehended the need to atone.'

Maria Sampson received an education, of sorts: 'Three years at a country school, a veritable factory for turning out governesses. Well, I educated myself while educating my charges. But ought you not to be setting all this down in your diary?'

When she was twenty – which was twenty years *ago* – Maria Barnes married Harry Sampson, an insurer. He was forty-five at the time, 'and quite a gallant fellow, believe it or not'. The marriage has been childless. When Maria's mother really was widowed, some seven years ago, she moved in with them.

Matthew Harvey would no longer have anything to do with Maria's mother, but as for Maria herself – he never quite cast her off completely, and she would visit him as an adult, always under the pretence of sitting for a portrait. Sometimes he would sketch her. In the Race Week of the present year, he had taken her profile, and made a record of doing so, lest anyone should question the reason for her visit. Maria had requested the interview. Her mother was ill, and Mr Sampson's business was failing. Mrs Sampson knew that Matthew Harvey was in poor health; might he make some bequest to either his daughter or his former mistress? He conceded that he had been revolving the idea, but he worried about the scandal. How, for example, would it reflect on his son? Mrs Sampson had suggested that a little extra scandal attaching to Captain Harvey would make no material difference, and anyhow, there were ways of making a bequest secret.

'He really did think of doing it,' I said. 'His will shows the start of a secret bequest, but it is scored out.'

'You've looked at his will?'

'I am charged by Captain Harvey with finding the identity of his murderer, so naturally I have looked at the will, yes. By the way, does the Captain know your true identity?'

'What do *you* think?'

'If he did know,' I replied, 'he'd have tried to turn it to account. So I think he does not. I believe Matthew Harvey told you point blank that there would be no bequest; that he had weighed the matter and decided against. In a sudden rage, you took up the scissors.'

'Mr Rigge, I deny it.'

'Quite so.'

'But you do not believe me?'

'No.'

'Well then,' she said, smiling, 'that leaves us at quite a stand.'

The second letter from Mr Hardcastle, of the Theatre Royal, to Mr Erskine.

I had been anxious lest the rumours touching on the possible return of Jeremiah Smith should deflect the Company from its preparations for the playing of The Rivals. *Fortunately our usual first night frenzy banished all questions of Smith.*

We were even more flurried than usual on that night of Monday December 10th. A great deal was dependent on this production, for the sake of which we had deferred our pantomime. It was a risk willingly taken, for Sheridan's play is much admired within the profession, in spite of its length, and its exacting nature (the comedic nuance being very subtle on occasion). In my London days, I myself once took the role of the Irish baronet, Sir Lucius O'Trigger, one authority commending my 'brave stab' at the impersonation, and finding my accent to be 'only a little "off" in the good Celt's more impassioned moments'. But that is by-the-by.

It is my custom on the opening nights to have everything correctly laid out in the box office, with the fire well banked up (the office being open to the promenade), a good stock of change laid in, and every booked seat clearly marked on the chart. I then hand over to my deputy, young Mr House (who is well named, I venture to suggest). He deals with the early arrivals, while I go backstage to help in any way possible and – I freely own – to savour the bustle of anticipation. I used always to have a conflab with Mr Cork in the scene dock about an hour previous to the play, but of course we are now managerless, no replacement for poor Cork having been appointed, and this may have contributed to the very backward state of things that evening.

Among our tribulations were the following: Mr Dawson could not get the stove in the pit to ignite, and about half the lamps were short of oil, of which new supplies had been laid in (I had made sure of that), only to be mislaid by one of the stage manager's boys, who was just then indisposed with illness. Mr Bradley, who was to have taken the part of the servant, Thomas, was also ill, and so Mr Mason would have to go on, probably with the book, but he was making a concerted attempt to learn the part, while lying flat on his back in the dressing room, being fed cues by Mr Hague who was meanwhile marking up his prompter's copy of the play. Nobody could find our leading female, Mrs Wakefield, who was to play Lydia Languish. I was about to despatch the carpenter's apprentice to her lodge when I recalled that this lady, a very

317

fine – but rather fretful – player, often found solace in the enforced darkness of the painting room, where no candles are allowed (the paint being combustible). I found her up there in tears, but she brightened a little when I ventured that, 'Here is Lydia . . . languishing!' She permitted me to accompany her into the dressing room, and when, giving her into the care of our wardrobe mistress, Mrs Dubois, I said, 'Success attend you, my dear,' she favoured me with a kiss on the cheek and – an even greater reward – a most delightful smile.

I myself took delivery, at the back door, of the cake and wine that is always ordered from Mancini's on any opening night. I carried it through to the Green Room, but not before reserving a couple of bottles of the wine, because Mr Parker (to play Sir Lucius) and Mrs Dyson (Mrs Malaprop) are known to tipple before going on – almost always, I might add, with no ill effects. I discovered Mr Emmett (Sir Jack Absolute) in smiling, phlegmatic form, running over his lines while imbibing nothing more worrisome than coffee, accompanied by a round of anchovy sandwiches.

It was the sight of young Emmett that re-kindled thoughts of the pestilential Smith, who had coveted the role of Jack. It crossed my mind for the first time that if he really were back in town, his vanity might carry him into the theatre, in hopes of seeing Emmett fall short as Jack. He might be tempted to this even though his description had been circulated among the Watch, with orders to send for a constable should he be spotted in the town.

Well, he could not gain admittance without a ticket, the doorkeepers would see to that, but it was not impossible that my young colleague Mr House had already sold Smith a seat, having failed to recognise him. I therefore entered the auditorium, and, from a vantage point on the edge of the orchestra pit (of which the band members were taking occupation), I looked up, and about. Only a couple of dozen were in so far, pretty evenly dispersed between galleries, boxes and pit. I could not see Smith, but I own that I could not take full account of everyone in the auditorium, the lights being particularly dim, owing to the contingency mentioned above.

I continued forward into the lobby, and thence the box office, where I took over the cash desk from young House, who informed me that business was already brisk. As usual, I remained at my post until a few minutes after the raising of the stage curtain, whereupon I closed the smaller curtain of the box office window. (It is bad policy to keep the office open much after the play's commencement; it encourages late arrivals.) As I performed this action, I was perfectly satisfied that I had not served any ticket to Mr Jeremiah Smith. But misgivings once again came over me. He might easily have asked some other fellow to buy a ticket on his behalf. That was quite commonly done, especially by the box and lower gallery candidates, who often send a servant to fetch the tickets while they carouse in the saloon. But there was nothing to be done, now that the play was under way.

Scene Two of Act One was in progress when I regained

319

the scene dock. I have often observed in jest that the playing of a first act ought to be accompanied by a reading of the Riot Act. On this occasion I heard, and occasionally peeped out at, a lively crowd becoming by degrees reverent (yet also greatly amused). I saw Mrs Malaprop, Julia and Sir Anthony Absolute being played with great skill, and after the brief entr'acte – in which not so much as a single orange was thrown – I saw that I might add Mr Emmett's portrayal of Sir Jack to the role of honour. I kept peeping out to look for Smith in pit or gallery (he wouldn't risk the exposure of a box, I was sure) and I drew a blank every time.

I did not return to the box office that evening, but kept to my post in the wings, looking out into the crowd betimes, and giving a word of encouragement to the players as they made their entrances and exits. (As Mr Emmett went by, I whispered that his Jack was 'Absolute perfection', and he was gracious to a degree in acknowledgement.)

I was still at my post by the time of Act Three. From my vantage point, I could see diagonally across the stage and up into the left side of the upper gallery.

In Scene Two of that act, Mr Emmett – as Jack – and Mr Pearce – as his father, Sir Anthony – were raising a great laugh with their exchange in which Jack makes a play of indifference towards the beauty of his projected wife. The greatest surge of laughter came at the following from Jack: 'I own I should rather choose a wife of mine to have the usual number of limbs, and a limited quantity of back; and though one eye may be very agreeable, yet as the prejudice has always run in favour of two, I would not wish to affect a singularity in that article.'

Mr Pearce was about to make his rejoinder when a small missile came arrowing towards Mr Emmett, only to fall short and shatter on the side of the orchestra pit. Shatter is quite the word, for this was no rotten orange. I could not just then tell what it was (I later found out it was a small clock) but the force of the impact checked the players for an instant, and there were cries of 'Shame!' from around the auditorium. The projectile had come from the left side of the upper gallery, and I saw a man turning and retreating from the front of that gallery. He pushed away a couple of men who attempted to remonstrate with and restrain him. All I could make out of the miscreant – in the gloom of that topmost tier – was that he wore a muffler and a low-crowned hat.

As he retreated from view – he was obviously heading towards the exit – I headed down the side-corridor, with the plan of intercepting him in the lobby. I hardly know what I was thinking. That the fellow was Smith? Yes, perhaps, but above all I must take to task anyone who had so insulted our Company and endangered one of the players.

I arrived at the lobby in time to see this low-hatted figure going through the exit door into the promenade. Another man was pursuing him. When I saw that this 'other' was Mr Fletcher Rigge, all became clear to me. He and I had alike concluded that Smith would not be able to keep from the

321

theatre on the opening night of a play in which he was to have been involved.

I called after Mr Rigge, but he either did not hear me or affected not to. I followed the two along the promenade. Rigge was now calling after Mr Emmett's would-be assailant, 'You, sir. I would like a word!' But the fellow strode rapidly on, going out from under the final arch of the promenade, and so gaining the Theatre Green.

One pathway traverses that Green diagonally, another hugs close to the side-wall of the theatre, which is propped up by brick buttresses. The first man took this path, therefore so did Rigge. He hallooed again, and the first man finally stopped and turned about. In order to speak, he must loosen his muffler, and it was then that I saw he had not much chin, but – as though in compensation – an extremely forward-directed nose. It was Smith, of course, in his caped coat and with new side curls to his hair that I had not remarked before.

Rigge was now closing on Smith, who said, with extreme vehemence, 'Who the devil are you, sir, and what do you want?'

'Only a word,' repeated Rigge.

'You wanted a word before,' said Smith, indicating the theatre, which towered blackly above them, 'inside that . . . slum.'

I dived into the recess made by the first two buttresses, as Smith and Rigge closed with each other in the next one along.

322

The snow-covered Green was deserted; the carpenter's horse, under its usual blanket, stood silent in the middle of it, and only the faintest reverberations could be heard from within the theatre as the performance continued. It struck me, Mr Erskine, that here was a case of Rivals within and rivals without – and I could hear most of the latter's parlay.

'This whole damned town would like a word with me,' said Smith, sounding greatly aggrieved.

'I daresay,' said Rigge.

'It seems I am to be perpetually harried, and I won't stand for it. Sir, I believe I will take out your eye.'

At which, I presume, he had produced a blade, but Rigge's voice held firm: 'You killed Mr Cork.'

'So rumour has it. That ... abomination had for years misused not only a supposed theatre company, but also a lady of the utmost refinement – a delicate treasure, sir, with which he was no longer to be trusted. I called him out on the matter. Naturally, he refused to engage.'

'Therefore you killed him.'

It amazed me that Rigge should be so provocative. Mindful of the fate of his father, I was beginning to think the son must also be bent on self-destruction. But Smith seemed almost flattered at the accusation, and there was a note of damnable pride in his voice, as he said, 'In the end he came over quite handsomely, quite handsomely indeed. And you, I suppose, are some species of mercenary? A thief-taker? A spy? Do you mean to say that some wretch has put up a bounty for

323

him? Some theatrical person, perhaps? I don't see that at all. Even his supposed fellows in there – that damned rabble – will be giving thanks at his removal.'

'I have a letter of commission, sir,' said Rigge, and I heard the rustling of paper. He must have been producing the letter you have mentioned to me, Mr Erskine, the one from Captain Harvey requesting a conference about the murder of Matthew Harvey.

'As you can see,' said Rigge, after a moment, in which Smith must have perused the note, 'the murder in question is a different one. This gentleman, Captain Harvey, will very likely come after you as the killer of his father.'

'It appears,' said Smith, 'that my infamy increases by the day. Matthew Harvey . . . who paints everyone in the likeness of a blackamore.'

'You will not deny that you obtained such a likeness of yourself.'

'I went to him for a trifle, a keepsake. I did not bargain on receiving moral instruction. That gentleman has – had, it appears – a sorely misplaced loyalty. I might have killed him for it, but as it happens, I did not. Let this . . . Captain go to the magistrate, I say; let him try to swear my life away. He shall not succeed. There can be no witness to anything that took place between me and Harvey. We were quite alone all the time. Come to that, there is no witness against me in the matter of Cork, either.'

'Not any longer,' said Rigge. 'You have seen to that.'

324

There came the sound of a short and desperate scuffle. I was about to step out from my own bay, and into theirs, when the sound subsided as quickly as it had begun. I apprehended from this that Smith had Rigge pinned against the wall – and at the point of that same blade he had produced before.

'You are a little bloodied, sir,' said Smith, slightly short-winded. 'But that is only the start. Now say on, while you can.'

'Perhaps,' said Rigge, while recovering his own breath, 'Harvey will support his case by deposing to your involvement in another murder. That of Melissa King.'

'You lie, sir. He can have nothing on me for that. But perhaps you are the one. Perhaps you are the one who will swear against me.'

'Why would I be telling you all this if that were the case? I have as great a dislike of Captain Harvey as you yourself, and he will hound you, however you use me. You would do us both a service if you went after him directly.'

Silence for a space. Even the blanketed horse seemed engrossed in the outcome.

'If you mean to finish me, sir,' Rigge resumed, 'then you'd better do it now. The theatre lets out in a minute,' and just then there came a muffled, but very palpable roar of approval from the auditorium.

'That is only the end of Act Four,' said Smith, and indeed it was. Nobody came out of the theatre; silence settled once again over the Green.

'What they were cheering about I've no notion,' said Smith, in a somewhat quieter tone than hitherto. 'They are watching an effectual satire on the piece. Nobody troubled himself for a single instant to comprehend the meaning with which each scene is pregnant. And it was a particularly poor delineation of Jack Absolute, would you not say?'

'Sir,' said Rigge, 'you have a knife at my throat. I am therefore inclined to be at one with your assessment of the playing.'

'This is above a joke,' said Smith. 'Kill this Captain, you say? Where is he to be found?'

'First Water Lane, as on the letter.'

'Is it a large household?'

'He is attended by a manservant and . . . there might be some coal heavers about the place.'

'What?'

'He keeps a wharf. It would be better to draw him away from the house a little way. He's lamed in the leg, so—'

'Lamed, you say? That's good.'

'But he'll come if you drop a note saying you wish to pay over some money to avoid an embarrassing connection with a murder. Perhaps say you are an agent for a certain lady whose portrait was painted by his father in the Race Week. He will not be surprised at such a statement.'

'It seems he is a fellow of unlimited spite. Does he go armed?'

At this, Mr Erskine, Rigge hesitated; then came the answer, 'Never.'

A further pause, then Smith said, 'I don't know why I don't kill you as well. I don't know why I don't kill everybody in this damned town.'

'You make a perfectly reasonable point,' said Rigge.

Finding the ensuing silence to be quite unbearable, I stepped from my place while at the same time giving an innocent-sounding cough, so as to suggest (you will recall, Mr Erskine, that I was once a player myself) a man passing by on his nightly stroll. The stratagem worked, for Smith marched off without a further word, and Rigge – apparently nursing a wound to his arm – struck out in another direction, ignoring my appeals for him to return, but pausing briefly in the centre of the Green in order to turn and sketch a bow of thanks.

It had been quite a pretty performance of his, I think, albeit reckless to a degree.

Christopher Ryder, lunatic, examined by Mr Erskine.

Christopher, or Chris, Ryder is a young man who has spent about half of his thirty or so years in that dreary mansion, the York Lunatic Asylum, and he will have been on the end of a short chain fixed into the wall if the usual 'remedy' was applied. If not thoroughly deranged before his incarceration, the poor fellow certainly is now. He is not dangerous, however, and to the best of my knowledge no complaint has been made at his being allowed to roam about in the middle of the town, living on the charity and the occasional meal taken in the Poor House. I dare say that his habitual cry of 'How's your poor feet?' must have occasioned some irritation, since he endeavours to keep it up throughout the night, but there is something almost mannerly in the solicitation. He certainly does not require any answer, and most passers-by treat the question as strictly rhetorical, while giving young Ryder a wide berth.

(How, incidentally, to account for that cry of his? It occurs to me that his own feet must have been persistently cold while he was imprisoned, for the inmates of the asylum are permitted nothing but a long nightshirt or smock, and have no shoes upon their feet. Hence, perhaps, the poor fellow's preoccupation with those extremities.)

Mr Bright had volunteered to question Ryder, but as a trustee of the new and (I contend) more humane asylum on the edge of the town, I thought the task should fall to me. Young Ryder's case intrigues me, and I hope in time he may be enfolded into the care of that place whose charitable mission is conveyed in its name: The Retreat.

For the time being, Ryder does not like to be indoors, even in spite of the cold. (He is now the proud possessor of two sturdy boots. I do not say a pair, exactly, since they are somewhat diverse, but each one is sturdy enough.) I believe that where any ordinary person sees four walls, Ryder perceives a cell. He has no objection to being under a *roof*, as we will see, and he has nightly resort to some sack-lined hollow or dry ditch on the Hilly Fields out towards Bishopthorpe. But solid walls ... these he cannot abide, which explains why he would not consent to come into my chambers, requiring that I interview him in the middle of Precentor's Court, to the amazement of my neighbours.

I am not a literary man, and I have set down our converse in the manner of the Assize court transcriptions – that is to say, giving the dialogue only. It will be seen that Ryder's speech has the virtue of brevity, but few others. It might be as well, therefore, if I state the known facts at the outset.

On the night of Wednesday December 12th, Christopher Ryder was sheltering from the snow under the brick arch of the Ouse Bridge. Here he observed a fight between two men, the sight of which disturbed him to the extent that he was still bemoaning the scene some two days later. In this, he was overheard by some of the keepers of the workhouse, who believed his lamentations might throw light on the events we have been describing. I believe those gentlemen to have been correct, and that Ryder witnessed the very culmination of our tale.

Q: How did you come to be under the bridge, Chris?

A: There is a lamp there, and no snow. The water reflects on the stones above in a pretty way.

Q: You saw two men.

A: First one, then two.

Q: Can you describe them for me?

A: Gentlemen.

Q: Can I press you for any further detail?

A: The first one had a cane. He was lame.

Q: Did you make your usual enquiry?

A: How do you mean?

Q: Did you ask after his feet, Chris?

A: Yes. The people find it very reviving when I say that.

Q: How did he respond?

A: He did not take kindly.

Q: Meaning?

A: He made to strike me with his cane. He said, 'You may take that as a warning. Now be gone.'

Q: But you did not go?

A: Only a little way.

Q: What was the gentleman about?

A: I believe, waiting.

Q: For what?

A: The other gentleman.

Q: How long did he wait?

A: Not long. Only while the bell was ringing.

Q: The bell of the nearby church, St Michael's?

A: It is the church on the dog's street.

Q: It was striking the hour of midnight, perhaps?

A: Yes, and that was his doom out of Heaven.

Q: The hour was still chiming when the other man arrived?

A: Yes, sir.

Q: What did the other man look like?

A: A pretty sort of gentleman, I suppose.

Q: Why only 'suppose'?

A: His coat was high.

Q: He wore a muffler, perhaps?

A: Yes, muffled up.

Q: Younger or older than the first?

A: Younger.

Q: Would you say they were meeting for the first time?

A: First, and last.

Q: What was said between them?

A: 'How do you do, sir. You would have commerce with me?' *That* was said.

Q: By the man with the cane?

A: Yes, sir.

Q: And the other replied?

A: 'You wish to be paid. Well, sir, you will get your due this night.' I cannot remember any more.

Q: But they continued to talk?

A: A little. But I could not well understand.

Q: It was too quiet for you to hear?

A: Too *loud*.

Q: It was then they began to fight?

A: Pretty near.

Q: Can you describe the fight, Chris?

A: I can recollect something about it.

[**Mr Erskine's interpolation:** The poor fellow would not speak for some time after, but I pressed him.]

A: One had a pistol. He shot a ball out of it. The other had a knife. He pretty near took off the other one's head. I called out, 'Stop! You gentlemen must not interrupt the quiet of the town!' I said God would make all their afflictions turn to good, if they would but hold their noise.

Q: But it was too late?

A: I saw the red puddle. I said, 'We must have a surgeon to this.' But their doom had come.

Q: They were both dead.

A: Pretty near.

Q: And what did you do then, Chris?

A: Then I ran over the bridge and down.

Q: Down?

A: Into the pudding holes.

Mr Bright's memorandum, explaining how he came into possession of Mr Rigge's diary.

On Friday December 14th, of the year just past, I was walking along Micklegate from my lodge on Trinity Lane. It was six o'clock in the morning, and I was on my way to the Black Swan, from where I proposed taking the coach to Malton, to visit my sister. As I stepped on to Ouse Bridge, I saw the London coach (which had let out from that same Black Swan only a few minutes before) approaching from the opposite side – that is, from Low Ousegate. The driver was obviously a hard-goer, and the roof passengers, I noticed, had their hands clamped down on their hats, such was the coachman's rate of progress. He was closing in upon a dray – pulled by a donkey – that carried planks of wood. A four-wheeled phaeton, also moving pretty briskly, was approaching from the opposite direction.

The roadway on the bridge is narrow, but then so was the dray, and this, I believe, was a temptation to the driver. 'Ought to just shave by!' I recall him shouting at his passengers, in a sportive way, as he whipped on his horses. He was proposing to go between the two other vehicles – and at the maximum velocity.

The coach *did* shave by, although not without sustaining a long scrape along its door panel, nearly upending the drayman and incurring furious shouts of protest from the driver of the phaeton. And I hope I will not be thought self-pitying if I mention that I myself was the worst affected by this idiocy, for not only did I sustain a bruise to my arm as a result of a – very necessary – leap towards the balustrade of the bridge, but I was also struck upon the head by a heavy cloak bag that slipped from its mooring on the roof of the coach. Once I had recovered myself, and assured several passers-by that I had taken no serious harm, the coach was halfway up Micklegate, and almost out of sight.

Since I was going to the Swan anyway, I carried the bag with me – in spite of its considerable weight – and gave it in to the ostler in the yard, explaining how I had come by it, which tale obviously amused him considerably. I said, 'Presumably, we can discover the owner of the bag from the passenger list?'

'Yes,' he said, 'or from looking inside.'

He unbuckled the bag, and commenced to ferret about inside it, revealing a couple of fine cambric shirts, two good waistcoats and a pasteboard file that held some letters – evidently addressed to Mr Fletcher Rigge, whom of course I knew. There was also a quantity of shade paintings, and I recollected that Rigge – the fellow Mr Erskine and I had endeavoured to assist in the matter of his estate – had been somehow involved with the son of the murdered shade painter. I prevailed on the ostler to consult his register, whereon he confirmed that Mr Rigge was aboard the London coach that would just then be approaching Tadcaster or thereabouts, no doubt at ferocious speed.

Over the course of the next week I made enquiries, discovering that Rigge had quit his lodge – having paid his rent up to date – and that the Sheriff's men were looking for him with a view to returning him to the Castle.

I called in at the Black Swan again to enquire of that same ostler what had become of the bag. Had it been reunited with its owner? No; Mr Rigge had not applied for its return (no doubt because he did not want to disclose his new address). I was by now thoroughly curious about Mr Rigge, and so I asked the ostler whether it might be given over to me, or some officer of the law, if a warrant were to be obtained? 'I tell you what, friend,' said the ostler, 'it's yours for a shilling.'

An irregular proposal, to say the least, but since the questions surrounding the behaviour of this Mr Rigge were becoming rather pressing, I handed over the cash. I brought the bag back to Precentor's Court, where Mr Erskine and I examined it together.

Some three days later, I thought to visit the posting-office on Lendal, to ask whether any letters had been uncollected by Mr Rigge. There were none. There was, however, a parcel for one of Mr Rigge's correspondents (as disclosed by the contents of the bag), Mrs Sampson, which had lain uncollected for five days. This had come from London, but with the sender's address withheld. A warrant was obtained and the parcel opened. It was Rigge's diary, presumably sent to that lady *by* Mr Rigge, so that she might destroy its incriminating testimony against herself, and *see* that it was destroyed. It had remained uncollected because – as Mr Erskine and I discovered – Mrs Sampson had quit her home on Monk Street. Her husband had no idea where she had gone, but believed – or affected to believe – that she would 'no doubt be back any day'. It was not the first time she had taken herself off, he said.

Mr Erskine's postscript to the above.

In Rigge's diary, Mr Bright and I read all about Captain Harvey. We did so in the knowledge that his house in First Water Lane had burnt to the ground on the day after his body was discovered, alongside that of Smith, beneath the arch of Ouse Bridge.

What connection might lie between these two events was – and is – unknown, but it is rumoured in that part of town that one or more of the coal heavers was to blame. Certainly there are fewer of those fellows at the wharf than before, and Mr Bright and I surmise that they had either become disaffected at the uses Captain Harvey had put them to, or they had simply not been paid.

The engine was called out to deal with the fire, but the horse – like so many York citizens – flatly refused to go down First Water Lane. In its case, naturally, the inhibition must have been caused by sight of the flames rather than apprehension of an attack.

The fire was certainly fuelled by the great stocks of coal on the wharf and in Harvey's basement. Nobody connected with the house has come forward, and no human remains were discovered in the ashes, but the diary of Esther, together with her unsent warning to Mr Rigge, was found preserved in a portable writing desk that had survived the fire, being brass-bound, and otherwise of good-quality hard wood that had merely charred rather than being burnt through. Of the fate of Esther herself, and of the manservant, Stephen, we have to date no news.

Mr Erskine's closing memorandum to Mr Taylor.

Mr Bright having explained how we came to begin our tale, it now falls to me to conclude it.

The mystery of who commissioned the unknown burglar to steal the shades remains outstanding. It is possible he was never 'commissioned' at all; that he was merely a common thief acting on his own account.

I had meant to adduce here a second, self-lacerating

letter from young Bob Richmond of Skelton's shop, in which he admits to having fallen prey to 'an odious jealousy', which caused him to tell Miss Spink, and her father, that he had seen Rigge in company with Esther. But there seems little to be served by presenting this, and the young man's conduct is now a matter between him and his Maker.

I conclude, my dear Taylor, with another, more significant letter, which must serve as our *finale*. It arrived at my chambers a week ago, from Mr Villiers, the *belle-lettrist*, and 'Black Diamond', of London.

Letter from Mr Villiers to Mr Erskine.

4 Bride Lane,
London.
January 7th 1799

Mindful of our recent correspondence, I thought the following vignette may be of interest.

Three days ago, I was walking along the Strand with Mr Bird. It was a fine morning (the first for many weeks); the street was a colourful bustle, and the ordinary traffic of the river had the look of a regatta rather than a slow, floating funeral, as is usually the case in winter. We were both in tolerably good spirits. Mr Bird had recently learnt that he was to be paid twelve pounds by way of advance for a forthcoming book of poems. This was only two pounds more than he got for his last production, Birdsong, but I told him to consider all those brilliant young men who have never received a penny for their lyrics. (Naturally, he couldn't think of any.)

I have no new volume under way, but it is enough for me that the Black Diamonds will soon be no more, the rudeness of Gowers having finally proved intolerable to most of the members. I knew that Noble had continued to attend the weekly meetings at Cuthbert's Ale House, but only in hopes that Gowers would write favourably of his literary debut – a slender volume entitled simply Thoughts – in The Critical Examiner. Last week, a short review by Gowers did appear in that august journal, but given that it damned the work with faint praise under the heading, 'The Modest Thoughts of a Modest Man', I anticipate that our strange-looking colleague will soon be sitting at the head of an empty table.

Mr Bird and I turned off the Strand into a little court where lurks Pennington's bookshop. With a nod to old Pennington – a perfectly delightful fellow, if you can forgive his absurd and outsized wig – who was shelving by the door, we walked through to the back room, where the poetry is kept. Mr Bird likes to look at – and sometimes even purchase – old volumes of poetry no longer in print, and it is perhaps best *if I do not say why. I myself had stepped through to the next little room, dedicated to 'Miscellaneous' works, where my own productions are sometimes to be found, in which case I remove them from the shelf, and put them in a conspicuous position on the central display table, while doing the opposite with any works whose prominence seems unmerited.*

I was just commencing some adjustments when I heard a vaguely familiar voice, rather subdued, followed by Pennington's louder speech: 'Good afternoon to you, Fletcher, and I will see you bright and early tomorrow.'

I hastened back to the front of the shop, only to see the etiolated (and I suppose elegant) figure of your – perhaps by now I should say our – Mr Rigge turning the corner of the court, and disappearing along the Strand.

Naturally, I began quizzing Pennington about him, and Mr Bird – likewise intrigued – stood by me as I did so. It appeared that Rigge had walked into Pennington's shop in the middle of December, enquiring about the availability of work. He had experience of the book trade, he said, and could supply a character from a well-known shop in York. It happened that Pennington was in need of an assistant, and so he gave Rigge his start.

He proved to be a conscientious employee, although 'rather better with the books than the bookkeeping', meaning he was bad at the money side of things, although there was no question of any dishonesty. Another fault was that he would sit glooming for long periods when he thought himself unobserved. By night, and sometimes at quiet moments in the shop, Rigge would be writing on his own account, and Mr Pennington had discovered only two days before that he had sold the manuscript of a novel to the firm of Constable, whose office is at Russell Square.

'How much for?' Mr Bird enquired, with some trepidation.

'Brace yourself,' said old Pennington. 'Two hundred and fifty pounds!'

I gave a whistle.

'It must be a terrible book indeed,' said Mr Bird.

'Why?' I asked my competitive friend.

'. . . Merit being in inverse proportion to money,' he said.

'Oh, of course,' Pennington chimed in, 'I've no doubt it's meretricious to a degree.'

Bird was somewhat consoled by this speculation, but I believe he was cast down again when Pennington added, 'Even Rigge himself says so.'

'What is the subject?' I asked.

'I haven't read it,' said Pennington, 'and I believe I would never have heard of it at all, if it had been down to Rigge. I picked up the news quite by accident when gossiping at Cuthbert's with a couple of writing men. Apparently it concerns the iniquities of the town when set against the country life. He's gone off to Russell Square now for a conference about it.'

With our correspondence in mind, Mr Erskine, I asked if the tale had anything to do with shade paintings. Pennington

341

replied that, from the outline of the work he'd been given, he thought not.

'And what do you suppose he will do with the money?' I enquired.

'Well, he's given me notice to quit,' said Pennington, mildly enough, 'and I believe some of it went to discharge a debt that had been owing up in York. As for the rest . . . I understand he is projecting a removal to the countryside. I believe he hopes to purchase a small farm. He has certainly been setting about my books on agriculture and husbandry with a vengeance.'

'And so he will leave off writing?' ventured Bird.

'I believe that is his intention.'

'I'm glad to hear it,' said Bird.

But old Pennington wasn't quite done, I could tell.

'Say on, sir,' I encouraged him.

'A young woman called for him yesterday. Well, perhaps not so young, but still an attractive enough lady, with a very fetching cocked hat.' (It must have been fetching indeed, I thought, for old man Pennington to have remarked it.) 'Rigge had departed for the day, but she left a card, and I handed it to him this morning.'

'A lover?' I suggested.

'Hard to say,' said Pennington, 'but for a clear hour, he sat at his desk with the card in his hands, turning it over and over, and lost, sir, quite lost in contemplation.'